I0532602

In the Bones

RENÉE MILLER

Copyright © 2013 Renée Miller

1

ALL RIGHTS RESERVED. This book contains material protected
under International and Federal Copyright Laws and Treaties. Any
unauthorized reprint or use of this material is prohibited. No part of
this book may be reproduced or transmitted in any form or by any
means, electronic or mechanical, including photocopying, recording,
or by any information storage and retrieval system without express
written permission from the author / publisher.

ISBN: 978-0-9878112-2-6

For my dad.
No longer by my side, but always in my corner.

CHAPTER 1

...to give you a reason to stay in Albertsville. When you find the clues, you'll know why.

His grandfather's letter made no sense. If he wanted him in Albertsville, why the years of silence? Now it was too late.

A siren blared outside while the lawyer prattled on about signatures and legalities. Ryan rose from the stiff backed chair, and strolled to the window opposite a large shelf of books.

Beyond the window, traffic crawled through the midday rush. A man in a black leather jacket darted between cars making his way across the busy intersection; tie flapping into his face as the brisk October wind whirled around him. Watching the movement on the street did little to organize his thoughts. The will posed many questions, but offered no answers.

"I'm not sure what I should do." Ryan turned to the man behind the oak desk.

His grandfather's attorney, Jeffery—a man who spoke with a suspicious British accent—smiled. His bald head shone under the glare from the pot lights that ran along the ceiling "You should do what you feel is right."

"What I think is right? But I don't know anything about these people. Not one birthday card my whole life. Just like

1

that they leave me everything? It doesn't make sense."

Jeffery sighed. "The Cassidys are an old family. Even if it didn't amount to much, everything has always been passed to the oldest living descendant. Your grandparents simply followed tradition by offering you what they had."

Ryan held up the letter. "And this?"

"I'm sorry. I don't know. Melvin, your grandfather, asked that it remain sealed."

"Did you know them?"

"Obviously." Jeffery tugged at the sleeves of his blue suit.

"I mean, did you know them well? Why would they travel more than two thousand kilometers to come to you? Don't they have lawyers up there?"

"Actually I only met your grandparents once, when they came to sign the documents. Everything else was done by email and over the phone. Really, I can't comment on why he chose my office to represent his estate. I'm going to assume that our reputation preceded us."

"I suppose, but it's kind of strange. So if I don't go to Albertsville and live in the house, as they ask me to do, then what?"

"Then the estate and the money will go to the town of Albertsville."

"Is that legal?"

"If your grandparents willed it so, then it is."

Ryan considered the letter in his hands. Judging by his words, Melvin Cassidy would never have turned his estate over to Albertsville. It made more sense for him to donate it to charity than to give it to a town he obviously loathed. "What if I don't stay for the entire year? This is some shithole in the sticks, for crying out loud. What if work requires me to leave for a few days?"

Jeffery rolled his eyes, smacking his lips in disdain.

Ryan resisted the urge to slap him. *I'm thirty-four years old, not five.* The lawyer treated him like a wayward kindergartener from the moment he stepped into his wood-paneled tomb.

"To inherit everything, as I explained, you must go to

Albertsville and live in the house for one year. If you should move, or leave the house empty, you receive nothing. Travel is not forbidden as long as your absence is temporary." Jeffery folded his hands on the desk.

"And is anyone in charge of making sure I stay?"

"As you can clearly see in the papers, Audrey Perry is their executor."

"Where is she?"

Jeffery raised a bushy eyebrow. "I'm not sure I follow. She's in Albertsville, of course."

"I mean as executor, doesn't she need to be here for the reading of the will?"

"No. She will meet you when you arrive at the Cassidy farm. Audrey will track everything you spend in regard to the house, and keep records. In the event that you do not fulfill the requirements, you'll not be compensated for any costs that aren't related to the house." He glanced at his watch and cleared his throat. "I wish you luck in making your decision."

Jeffery gathered the papers on his desk, the ones Ryan signed until his hand cramped, and stuffed them into a manila folder. He could take a hint.

Ryan shoved the sheaf of papers into their envelope and paused to rub the key to his new old house. He slipped it into his pocket with his grandfather's letter and followed Jeffery out of the office.

Traveling didn't appeal to Ryan. Northern Ontario, Jeffery said. Past Timmins. That told him almost nothing. Just that he'd have to move to an outpost in the middle of nowhere.

Jeffery turned right, disappearing through a door at the end of a hallway. It swung closed behind him.

"Bye?" Ryan passed the door to the end of the hall. He crossed the reception area, where an elderly woman examined her nails by a ringing phone, and he pushed through the main door into the bustle outside. The money could buy him enough time to finish his book, but he wasn't about to put his life on hold to stay in some redneck heaven or to claim a broken down farm. No amount of money was worth going to the town that his mother refused to talk about.

The coffee tasted like lukewarm nasty. Ryan pushed it away and fiddled with the envelope. With the value of the land, the house, and the savings his grandparents put into bonds and investment accounts, he could write for the next ten years without worrying about bills or food. The sudden windfall didn't make him happy, not with the strings attached to it.

Who was his dad? What was he like? *Was he a dreamer like me?* Ryan's mother had no time to dream. Too busy raising a son on her own and trying to forget events that forced her to run away.

"More coffee?"

Startled by the waitress's soft voice Ryan blinked. "Uh, no thanks. I'm good."

She shrugged, bunching the collar of her oversized golf shirt and effectively swallowing her neck in the process. "I'm going off shift, so you can call Patty if you need anything."

"Okay."

Ryan followed her backside as she disappeared down the narrow aisle. The sway of her hips encased in tight black pants would have appealed to him an hour earlier. Instead, his mind gauged the distance between her rounded bottom and the barstools on the left side of the coffee shop. How often had she bumped them on the way by?

Back to the envelope, he lifted the flap and pulled the letter out. He didn't like the condition on his inheritance. Why bother going all the way from Alberta to Ontario, leaving everything behind if the money wouldn't be his for a full year?

Rubbing his eyes, he turned to the window. People bustled past, already bundled in coats and scarves although they'd barely reached the end of October.

What would his mother have advised? She would have been suspicious. *I don't like it, Ryan.* But she'd have given him sound advice without telling him what to do. *I can't make your decision for you, baby.* Ryan rapped his knuckles on the table. What did he have to lose by going to Albertsville? Nothing. He lived alone, worked freelance, could break his lease….

The words in the letter floated before him. *Monster*. What kind of monster lived in Albertsville?

If he didn't go, he would get nothing. His life would remain as it stood; freelancing for local papers, living in a shitty apartment, and dreaming of finishing the book he'd always vowed to write.

He would only gain by going and checking it out. But he also faced dealing with this monster, whatever it was. He chewed the inside of his cheek as he considered the risks. The monster had to be metaphorical, something or someone Melvin Cassidy considered dangerous. Would it try to get rid of him? Ryan chastised his brain for getting carried away.

He pulled a Toonie from his pocket and toyed with the hated coin that the government replaced their two-dollar bill with, rolling it over his fingers.

He sighed and held the coin on his thumb. *Heads I go, tails I stay*. Tossing the coin in the air, Ryan let chance make his decision.

The Toonie fell to the table.

Heads.

He picked up the letter.

RENÉE MILLER

CHAPTER 2

"So he's coming?"

The chair creaked as Fred leaned toward Carroll's desk to butt his cigarette in a large crystal ashtray. Carroll wanted a solution, but Fred didn't have one for him. Worrying about Cassidy before they had reason to made little sense, but Carroll didn't work that way.

Fred shrugged. "We knew he would. Right? He's a damn Cassidy ain't he? Melvin and Rachel had a heap of money, plus all that land. Shit, only you got more land than they do around here. Anyone with half a brain would want to claim it."

The Cassidys had never followed the status quo. Mel fought hard to keep what he had. He certainly wouldn't hand it over just because he died. It mattered even less to him now that Carroll was the Reeve. His grandson, being an outsider with no clue how Albertsville worked, certainly wouldn't give a shit either. The kid had no reason to be scared, nothing to lose. The rest of them knew what they risked, and gave Carroll whatever kept them on his good side.

Fred had cemented his place as Carroll's right hand and so far it paid off. That might change with Ryan Cassidy's arrival. They could lose everything they'd built.

Carroll paced across the pale beige carpet, dragging a hand

over his face.

Fred placed his hands on the wide desk. *Here comes the tantrum.*

"I want to know where the hell that asshole kept his money. I knew about the land. I could have taken that easily, and I would have if I'd known about the money. They were supposed to use *my* bank. This is my town, and that's my money. Christ why am I constantly surrounded by incompetence? The idiots I pay to notice these things should have been on top of this. I specifically said I wanted to know what went in and out of their account. What happened to tracking where they went, their mail? Does no one listen to me anymore? No one knew they'd left town until I figured it out. Fuck, Freddie, they even had a lawyer out there that they paid with money I can't control." Carroll fingered his tie.

Fred shifted but said nothing.

Hands stuffed into his pants pockets Carroll resumed pacing. "I didn't want their bastard grandson here. He could really cause a shit show if he starts snooping around. You make sure you tell Calvin and Farley that they're to shoot anyone, and I mean *anyone* they see near the mill. No questions. Just shoot them on sight."

"Bit extreme, don't you think?"

"I don't even know what they told him in that will. Sure, we got what Melvin hid at the house, but what did he give to that kid? We can't afford not to be extreme here."

Twirling a blue fountain pen in his hand, Fred avoided Carroll's glare. Carroll Albert wasn't used to losing even a fraction of his control. Although, he still looked good despite the stress of the past weeks. When they'd been kids, the girls trailed after Carroll. Hell, so did their mothers. At fifty-two, he looked even better than he did in high school. Fred hated playing the less attractive sidekick initially, but he'd grown used to it when he realized his position was more alluring than mere good looks.

Even with a third eye or a hideous scar, Fred would bet that Carroll reel anyone into his web. Power affected people in strange ways. So did money. Look at Donald Trump. Ugly as shit and still the bastard married supermodels. Carroll had more money than anyone in Albertsville could imagine, but he shared his wealth and, more importantly, his power with those loyal to him. Tossing the pen, Fred reached for the ashtray and followed Carroll's path as he strode to the large bookshelf that ran along the opposite wall near the door, and turned. Expensive white teeth bit a full lower lip.

Carroll caught Fred's gaze and winked, putting a finger to his head.

Fred returned the sly grin. God, look at that smile. He could sell snow to an Eskimo.

Carroll passed the desk to the outer wall and paused at the French doors that opened onto a large deck. Winter was closing in. The temperature already hovered at the freezing mark for a couple of weeks and they'd barely started November. Fred had to scrape the frost from his windshield that morning, which didn't bode well for the remaining months. It would only get colder.

He'd wasted hours in the reeve's office. Now the late afternoon sun faded into the trees outside the window, casting a grey hue over Carroll's sharp features. Didn't he realize that as the chief of police, Fred had things to do elsewhere? No, that wouldn't occur to the great and powerful Carroll Albert.

"I want the roads out of town watched. Up by Merle's and Farley's place especially; those sheds are a bit obvious. I don't want anyone driving by and getting curious. Hear?"

Fred nodded. Great, more work.

"You didn't find anything we can use? Nothing that would make me feel more confident that this boy might fit in?" Carroll ran a finger over the frosty pane as though checking for dust.

"No, he's clean as a whistle."

"Impossible. No one's spotless. Not when I'm through with them they aren't."

Fred smiled. Leaning back in the leather chair, he cradled his fingers behind his head and waited. Carroll thought best in silence. Interruptions broke his train of thought and that irritated him.

"He likes women?"

Fred nodded. "Appears to. He lived with one for a couple years. I talked to his landlord. Said she was a hot little thing, but she got a job in Vancouver. He didn't go with her because his mom was sick at the time."

"A mama's boy. Figures. What about the Chambers girl? She'd turn his head I bet."

He's not a pedophile. "Yeah, but she's what—sixteen? I'm sure he's not stupid enough to be tempted when he's coming into town as the new guy. Melvin and Rachel probably warned him anyway."

"They weren't that fucking smart. But now that you mention it, they might have told him to keep his eye on me. I can see Mel doing that if he thought the boy would be in danger coming here. But they didn't plan on dying, and that's where they made mistakes. Mel figured he'd get me. They didn't know we were onto them."

"You think Cassidy has no idea what he's walking into?"

"Does it make sense that they'd warn their long lost kin about us, and then leave the damn estate to him stipulating he *had* to live here? Audrey said he had to stay the year or Albertsville gets the money. I can't see Rachel going along with that. Not if her precious grandbaby was in danger."

"Okay, so they probably didn't tell him everything. What do we do then? Can't we just give the little prick the money and tell him to get lost?" Fred asked.

"No."

"But he'd take it and run. Even if we can't give it to him, we can let him piss around here for the year, and then we're free of him." Fred didn't see the point in making work for themselves where it wasn't necessary.

"Bastards did this to piss me off. Nothing more. I bet they had the will drawn up after Chad died. Nothing to do with what Mel dug up on me at all. The kid probably has no idea what's going on here, but I can't have him nosing around for a year. What if he drives out for a tour of the mine, sees what's in the fields? I need something to make him toe the line if he stays long enough to stumble across these things."

"I don't have much at the moment. Got himself some fancy writing degree and then had a cushy job as a reporter for some newspaper. I don't doubt there's some skeleton in his closet. Writers are a weird bunch. Problem is, he's got it buried too deep for me to find it. Maybe he's baked all the time."

"I need something more than a pothead or some oddball artsy fartsy type. I bet in the city they're all smoking grass. That won't scare him, especially if he learns what else is happening around here."

A soft tap at the door and Julia, Carroll's wife, stuck her head in. Now there was a woman Fred would love to snuggle up to every night. Fuck the snuggling. He'd just like to nail her once or twice.

Fifteen years his junior, Carroll's second wife was nothing less than gorgeous; built like a brick shithouse. Not like his wife, Roberta. The old heifer sagged everywhere. He'd told her to do something with her hair so the stupid bitch bought a bleach kit and fried it to a yellow-orange mess. The only thing the woman had going for her was that she kept her mouth shut and did as she was told. Too bad he couldn't get rid of her the way Carroll got rid of his first wife, and find someone like Julia.

Julia inched forward, stopping just inside the door. Fred drank in the sight of her body, lingering on her ample chest. Her black pantsuit hugged every delicious inch. Fred shifted, his pants tightening at the way her breasts pressed against the low neckline of her top. Her pants showed the contours of her endless legs. She'd pulled her honey-colored hair into one of those twisty things women liked to do so men could rip them back out.

"Sorry to interrupt, but you wanted to know when the new guy arrived," Julia said.

"He's here already?" Carroll lunged from the window.

She backed against the doorframe. "No, he's not in town yet. Calvin called just a minute ago. He said to let you know that he stopped to get directions at Smitty's. He'll be here in under an hour."

Fred smiled. So his suggestion to post a lookout hadn't turned out as silly as Carroll originally believed.

"Fred, we have a guest to greet. Call Farley and Millicent, tell them to meet us at the Cassidy farm."

Fred touched his pocket, checking for his cell phone. "Bringing out the big guns are we?"

"No guns needed. Yet."

Shifting into park, Ryan surveyed the scenery, breathless at the beauty. From the cramped seat, he felt insignificant gaping at massive trees. He had no clue what any of them were but damn, they were impressive. Blue Spruce, Pine and Douglas Firs dominated this area, but according to Google, the town's mill produced many other woods too. Whatever they were the trees grew huge and lush, and displayed more shades of green than he could count.

He'd left earlier than planned, his curiosity getting the better of him. Well, that and the final admission that Calgary held nothing anymore. His mother passed two years ago and his stepfather—who Ryan had loved as though they'd been blood—couldn't manage life without her. They found him in the garage a month after her death, holding her picture in the front seat of his idling car.

Everyone told him that change was good. It might just be, but it also terrified him. He found out about the will on the seventh of October. Within a week, he'd gone from a predictable, less than satisfying existence, to a shaky and uncertain future.

He cancelled his lease the day he met with the lawyer. Although Ryan didn't recall anything about a five-year lease, he paid the crook that was his landlord the *penalty* for leaving his crappy building. By the fifteenth, he sold off whatever he could. Living in an empty apartment made for an interesting two weeks. Now, as November loomed, Ryan arrived at his future.

A tiny blue sign; "Albertsville, Population 400" stood in front of his car, almost blending into the trees. Ryan's thoughts scattered in too many directions.

Glancing at the passenger seat, Ryan picked up his grandfather's letter. Why would they want him to live in a town they believed to be dangerous? Revenge? No, his mother never described them as that type. She didn't have a bad word to say about them. If they were sane and not suffering from some form of dementia—something he hadn't decided yet—then his grandparents wanted him to go to Albertsville... as a savior.

He unfolded the worn paper.

Ryan,

I know that we've been absent throughout your life, and we deeply regret that. I have no excuse that can justify our silence. We've missed the important details of your life but I'm confident that with a mother like yours, you are an intelligent and fair man. I am sorry that we didn't know you. More than you can ever know.

Your mother did what she had to do and we understood her decision. She tried to protect us, but we never expected her to leave forever.

This letter will come as a shock to you I'm sure. No matter what the circumstances of our deaths, the estate has always been yours. Recently I decided to amend it to include the stipulation that you live at the farm. Your grandmother knows none of this. She'd kill me again for asking this of you just to claim what is rightfully yours, but I need to give you a reason to stay in Albertsville. When you find the clues, you'll know why.

Don't be fooled by appearances. Hidden beneath the layers of small-town hospitality, slow grins, and good old boy attitudes, is a dark and ugly monster. This monster lives in the fields, the industry, and the foundations of the local politics. As they say, one lie leads to another, and this town is drowning under the weight of lies piled upon more lies. A single crime has made us all guilty. I know I seem to be talking in circles, but you'll figure it out. It won't take long.

At the helm controlling this monster is a man who holds more power over these people than I can ever describe. You have a chance to stop him, to reveal the secrets and lies that are destroying these people, and to save them from themselves. I know you feel you owe nothing to this town.

You're probably right. What have they done for you? But you have something they desperately need; the absence of guilt.

Do it for your mother, for what they did to her. She left with her soul shattered and her heart broken. This town did that to her. Do it for your father, my son. They murdered him, although they'll tell you it was an accident.

I am hoping that after a living in Albertsville for a year you'll want to make a difference. If not, then you'll have earned your inheritance and then some. I can give you only a couple of clues, but they'll put you on the right track. The mill is just a prop. The secrets are on display for anyone who takes the time to look for them. You just have to keep your eyes peeled and your nose clean. And don't fall into bed with Carroll Albert.

Ryan folded the letter and tossed it on the passenger seat. He turned the key and then shifted out of park before pulling off the shoulder. When the first house came into view—a weathered log cabin covered with a sloped roof—the light shifted. Shadows fell over the brown fields and a sense of foreboding settled into his guts. Suddenly the trees weren't so beautiful.

CHAPTER 3

Nestled against a backdrop of densely wooded hills, and lit with a rare autumn sun, a paved main street signaled Ryan's arrival in Albertsville. The blue sky and late afternoon light created the illusion of warmth outside, despite the heavy coats and hats on pedestrians traveling the street. Grass grew in patches between the small buildings lining the narrow road. A sidewalk ran along the right side; the left had curb and more grass.

Ryan recalled having seen something similar on a summer when workers repaved his street. The crews finished short, stopping about ten feet before the street forked out into two more streets. Unless the city paid, they wouldn't finish. The city balked about the overextended budget and delayed completion until the following summer. The ruts and cracks in the weather-beaten concrete hinted that Albertsville would continue to have one sidewalk for a while.

On the side with walkway honors, Albert's Grocery sat amid tall pine trees and a small embankment of grass decorated with carefully plotted gardens. Within that store—according to the signs plastered to the side of the building—were the post office and... a bank? Ryan's mother had told him about these things being here before she left years ago, but surely they'd moved ahead. It was as if the place was trapped in time. Perhaps Albertsville's residents were all weird and backward like the characters in Deliverance. Ryan shuddered.

Next to the grocery store, in a tiny brick building that resembled a house more than a storefront, a bright green sign announced "Frosty's Ice Cream Dreams." Across the street, a tall grey stone building—threatening to topple at any moment—boasted an equally wretched sign, "Sal's Bar and Grill."

Ryan slowed to gawk at the strange picture, his tired eyes now wide despite driving more than two thousand kilometers with only a brief stop to sleep.

Development must have halted twenty years ago. The buildings still aged, crumbling and tarnishing here and there, but no exterior repairs had been done. At the end of the main road, Ryan stopped before a Town Hall standing out like a neon sign after the simplicity and overall shabbiness of the buildings before it. He gave a low whistle. Tall white columns flanked a vast set of steps that climbed toward ornate wooden doors. The enormous building sprawled across the corner lot, nestled against a small hill dotted with trees and terracotta planters. It reeked of money. How much of the town's funds had gone into that?

Stepping on the gas, Ryan left the main street and drove down a narrow dirt road. Battered signposts announced Mill Road and Douglas Lane. According to the map included with his grandfather's letter, the farmhouse lay just past these; a mile from town and secluded on its own stretch of land. The Cassidys had farmed for years, dairy primarily, though Jeffery had mentioned that now the barns and outbuildings were useless.

A crooked mailbox on the side of the road marked Ryan's new home for the next three hundred and sixty five days. He slowed and turned into the long driveway, pausing to stare for a moment at "Cassidy," written in brilliant white against the red metal box.

The car lurched over the rutted driveway. Ryan ignored the jostling, his attention riveted on the landscape. He drew a breath and held it.

The curving lane leading to the house wound through a covering of tall pines, reducing the blue sky above to infrequent glimpses. Enveloped in the green cocoon, Ryan released his breath. While not unpleasant to look at, it felt stifling. He navigated his car up the driveway, turning into a wide bend before the house came into view.

The Cassidy farm, passed down through four generations, reminded Ryan of the old sprawling messes he used to create out of Lego as a boy. The main section, sided in blue vinyl, rose up three stories, where the steeple roof climbed to the sky above. Adjacent to the main house, a single level covered in grey stucco jutted out and extended toward the back. Huge windows covered the southern side of the lower addition, the panes dressed in lacy curtains. A Victorian-style veranda swept along the front.

When he rounded the last bend, the house drifted from his mind. Three vehicles waited in the roundabout driveway. Two large trucks with wheels much taller than Ryan's little car parked on either side of a squat black Hummer. Next to the vehicles stood Ryan's Welcome Wagon.

A tall man dressed in a black suit and leather overcoat stood straight, his chin jutting and his eyes fixed on the approaching car. A woman wrung her hands into her red scarf and glanced up at the man in the suit. Another man stood beside her, not quite as regal as the first. His wide middle strained against the buttons of his police uniform. The last man, smaller and scruffy-looking compared to the others, stood apart from his companions, dressed in dirty blue jeans and a plaid jacket. He scowled at Ryan's car.

Ryan pulled up on the right side, careful not to block them in, and put the car into park. He gathered the papers from the passenger seat, his grandfather's words loud in his mind. Would he meet the monster this afternoon?

The figure in the blue shit-box rifled around the passenger seat. Carroll shifted his feet. Mr. Cassidy should be eager to meet the elite of his new town, not pissing around. Good thing he had Fred bring the computers back yesterday. Carroll was almost blindsided by Melvin's careful attention to details that would make his life difficult. Not only did the bastard include a list of his property but he also wrote out a list of files on the computer and laptop that he didn't know Melvin had. Carroll had informed residents more than a year ago that Albertsville couldn't get Internet, being too far out of the way for such things. How did Melvin of all people figure out the lie?

Carroll found the evidence, though, and it hadn't been in any computer files. A plain white folder stuffed into the back of the grandfather clock, which was not included on Melvin's list of property. Fucking Farley had bent the damn mechanism inside the clock while getting it out, but Carroll didn't stress over that. This kid wouldn't guess the clock had worked fine before Farley got his grubby hands on it. The files on the computer held nothing of significance. It annoyed Carroll that he'd wasted his time going through them.

The door opened and a tall, lanky figure emerged from the car. Carroll's chest tightened and he pressed his lips to stop the profanity that leapt to the tip of his tongue. A ghost from his younger years stretched and smiled at him. Hate curled up and made itself comfortable in Carroll's belly. Except for the tousled mane of sandy brown hair, Ryan Cassidy was the spitting image of his father and grandfather. The same sparkle that Carroll so hated in the elder Cassidys reflected in Ryan's blue gaze, mocking him.

"Hello," Ryan strode toward them.

His easy gait, so like Chad's, sent Carroll's stomach churning. The only man he'd ever envied had been Ryan's father. Everything came to Chad naturally, everyone liked him, and he didn't lift so much as a finger for their approval. Carroll had to work his ass off to get even a fraction of the respect they'd simply given to Chad. Christ, he never understood it. He had money, looks, and a first rate education. What did Chad have? Nothing. That damn shit-eating grin and those fucking eyes. He'd enjoyed every minute of Chad Cassidy's death.

"You must be Ryan." Carroll extended his arm, a smile planted on his face.

Loose fingers gripped Carroll's a little too firmly. "Well, you're ahead of me already. You are?"

Carroll bit off his instinctive reply. For now, Cassidy needed to believe he posed no threat. Carroll struggled to resume the role of the kind and generous reeve. "I'm sorry. I'm Carroll Albert. Reeve. This here is Millicent Douglas."

Ryan offered his hand to the woman standing to Carroll's right. She blushed as Ryan smiled.

Damn fool woman.

Millicent covered his fingers with hers. "Ryan—I can call you Ryan right? Oh, you are the image of your father."

"Thanks, I think." Ryan pulled away.

The boy flinched at the mention of his father. Not so anyone else would have seen it, but Carroll made a point to pay attention to details like that. What did he know?

Clearing his throat, Fred drew Ryan's gaze. "I'm Fred Smith, chief of Albertsville's police department."

Fred pushed his fists into his pockets. Carroll glared, but Fred ignored him. Instead, he leaned over and nudged Farley Swift. The manager of the mill stared up at the boy as though he had three eyes or something.

"That there is Farley Swift, he runs the mill," Carroll supplied.

"Nice to meet you, Farley," Ryan said

Farley stared for a moment and then shoved his perpetually dirty paw out, to shake the boy's hand once. "Yeah," he mumbled.

Carroll turned to the barn and overgrown cornfield to hide his smile. Farley hated the Cassidys. His father had taught him to do so after Randall Cassidy bought the farm from Farley's great-great-grandfather. The old man's gambling debts nearly buried the family. True, Randall couldn't be blamed for the way Farley's family managed their money, but Carroll understood his resentment. In a town like Albertsville, people supported each other, helped their fellow neighbor out when they'd fallen on hard times. Randall didn't do that. He stumbled across a weakness and pounced. To see the land just going to fodder, the barns and the fields lying useless and covered in weeds must drive poor Farley nuts. Writer boy wouldn't get much from Farley, no matter how friendly he tried to be.

"So, thanks for meeting me. I'm surprised to see you all here. I wasn't supposed to arrive until Monday." Ryan raised an eyebrow at Carroll.

"Well, of course your attorney called so that we could put the house in order for your arrival."

Ryan tilted his head, his eyes narrowing a fraction.

Carroll's skin warmed, and chastised himself for allowing even that small tell.

"Funny, I don't recall letting Jeffery know when I'd arrive."

Damn. *Cocky little bastard.*

Millicent stepped forward. "What matters is that you're here and we're happy to finally meet you. Melvin talked about you all the time."

Ryan frowned. "Melvin didn't know me."

"Oh but he wanted to." Millicent reached over, threading her arm through Ryan's. She smiled and guided him up the steps to the front door.

He took out his key and turned to the small group gathered behind him. "I'm sorry if I seem rude, but I'd rather go in alone."

"Oh, don't be sorry," Millicent soothed. "It's understandable you'd want to do this alone. You must be so curious about them."

"No, it's not that. It's just that I'm beat. I want to go inside, turn on the heat and go to bed."

Carroll smiled. "Of course, you do. Not a problem. We just wanted to make sure you'd arrived and that you knew where to come if you have any questions."

"Thanks, it's nice to meet you all." Ryan turned to the door, slipped the key in and turned the knob. He didn't turn for so much as a wave, but walked inside and shut them out.

Nice to meet them? Liar. But Ryan had good instincts. He

had to give him that. If Carroll were in his shoes, he wouldn't trust any of them either. But then he knew things that Ryan Cassidy didn't.

The Welcome Wagon stood for a moment, staring at the house. Ryan watched them through a small window next to the door. Dusk approached, lending tall shadows to the small group in the driveway.

Carroll Albert barked something at the woman. She reddened, scurrying down the steps and to the man's side. Despite her association to Albert—which made Ryan's skin crawl—she didn't unnerve him as the men did. But it was obvious she allowed herself to be controlled by Albert. Ryan couldn't stand people without a backbone.

They went to their vehicles, climbed in and turned out of the driveway. He waited until they disappeared from view before opening the door again. He hadn't unloaded his bags, and he didn't intend to go to bed at all. Christ, it was barely dinnertime.

A thin layer of dust covered the many surfaces inside the house. Ryan would lay a bet that the Welcome Wagon had inspected things long before he arrived. The detailed list his grandfather left didn't seem so insane anymore.

Down the long hallway, Ryan found a living room, a den, and two small closets. At the end of the hall was the kitchen. Through a double set of French doors next to a small nook by the entrance, he stepped into a large, high-ceilinged living room.

The dark hardwood floors that ran throughout the lower level of the house shone in the places not covered by area rugs. He cringed at the fussy patterns. To make things even more crowded, his grandmother had layered them.

Large windows flanked by thick mocha-colored drapes stretched floor to ceiling, filtering the dull evening light into the room. Ryan fingered the velvety fabric while gazing at the orange-pink sky outside.

The setting sun dusted the empty fields beyond the house in an eerie glow. He imagined the farmhouse as it had been twenty years ago, when the fields had grown more than weeds and wildflowers, and the tractor sitting in the middle hadn't rusted into place but rambled over the fields, tilling the ground and readying it for harvest.

He pictured cattle grazing further back, out of sight from the big window, but close enough to hear them softly baying while they munched on the rich green grass of the back section of fields. Before leaving the city he'd read a little about farming to salvage something from the old place. Jeffery warned that the barns and their equipment would be in as poor a shape as the fields and likely unusable. With little do-it-yourself ability and no skills when it came to livestock and agriculture, he'd given up on the idea of farming. Hell, he didn't even know how to go about getting cattle, much less how to milk them.

Ryan circled the couch, a fluffy affair framed in wood carved with an ornate floral pattern that mimicked the one on the upholstery. Who could come home after a long day and relax on that piece of shit?

Matching chairs sat in front of the window facing the sofa and in between, his grandmother had set a delicate table. Its oval dark wood frame and frosted glass insert betrayed its origins in the eighties, out of place with the more formal pieces in the room.

His mother and grandmother shared a taste for ugly furnishings. Although not related, they must have been very much alike.

A distorted chime pushed against his memories. Ryan peered around the room seeking the culprit. Tucked away near a far corner, next to the door that led to the small den he'd already peeked into, a grandfather clock announced the hour, its tune unhealthy. Six already? No wonder his stomach ached. He hadn't eaten since he set off early that morning.

The appliances better work. He hadn't spotted many takeout options in town. Ryan left the living room and turned to the kitchen. Opening the spotless white fridge, he expected empty shelves. A package of cheese slices, bologna, and a note on the top shelf.

October 28th: The lawyer said you'd be here around the first. Thought you might forget to bring food. A.

Whoever *A* was had dropped this off shortly before his arrival. Thoughtful, but weird. He didn't like the idea of people coming and going as they pleased. Maybe he'd change the locks.

CHAPTER 4

Millicent paused at the base of the stairs and hung her coat over the newel post. Judging by the noises traveling down to the living room, Justin was hard at work wasting time. *Zap! Bang! Pow!* It echoed through the quiet rooms. Honestly, that boy could spend eternity staring at the screen in his make-believe world.

She entered the kitchen and cringed. Along the granite-topped counter lay the remnants of Justin's snack. An open jar of mayo, a half loaf of bread—opened and growing staler by the minute—next to an empty package of bologna.

He'd eat her out of house and home, and then what? Carroll only gave her so much to raise the kid, and he ate that in snacks each week. And grateful? Not Justin. Never grateful. He knew she wasn't his real mother, everyone knew, and he reminded her of that every day. If she asked him to do his chores or to get off the computer, he'd give her a belligerent stare and walk away. Why did she think she could raise any child, let alone someone else's bastard?

Because Carroll told you to.

Millicent screwed the lid on the mayo. Yes, although Carroll made it seem like a request at the time. *"Please Millie, it would be a great favor to me if you could take the baby. He needs a decent home and a good woman to raise him proper."* Proper? Yeah, she was doing a great job at proper.

What about his real mother? What the hell was she doing while Millicent raised her boy? Carroll hadn't told her who Justin's mother was, although Millicent had her suspicions. One thing she had no doubt of was that Carroll was the father. That meant that fourteen years ago, it could have been any girl under the age of sixteen in Albertsville. Back then, Millicent had no clue about Carroll's appetite for young girls and believed she'd been special when he noticed her. She'd been half in love with him and willing to do just about anything he asked. Now, she knew better, but no longer had a choice.

She caught her reflection in the window. Millicent Douglas had never been what one would call pretty. Sexy, attractive, cute even, but not pretty. Her blond hair—kept a youthful shade of gold by bi-monthly visits to Amelia—curled about her face. Last year she had given in and allowed Amelia to chop it into a bob. Forty-something mothers did not have long flowing locks meant for young girls hoping to catch a man.

If she wanted to, she could have any one of several men in town, though most of them were married, but she'd had enough of that nonsense. She'd gone out with Tim Reid a couple of times and sensed a growing attraction that could turn into something more, but Carroll warned her away. Of course, she obeyed. It was probably for the best anyway. She couldn't afford to have anything chaining her to this place. Carroll promised she could leave when Justin moved on to college.

"Ma?"

Startled she spun around. "Justin. You scared me."

"You were daydreaming. What's for supper?"

"Looks like you already ate." She twirled the bread bag, tucked the end under—the twist tie long gone—and set it in the breadbox by the stove.

"God, that was hours ago. Where'd you go?"

He peered inside the fridge as he always did, hoping a meal would materialize.

"Mr. Albert asked me to help him welcome Melvin and

Rachel's grandson to town. You remember, I told you this morning."

"Oh, yeah. So?"

"So what?"

Justin closed the fridge and leaned against it, crossing his arms.

The boy didn't look fourteen. Tall and gangly, his voice already changing into a man's, his eyes held more knowledge than a child's should.

"So does he pass inspection or is old Carroll gonna get rid of him too?"

"Get rid of him? I don't know what you're talking about."

"Come on Ma, don't tell me you forgot that newspaper guy that came to write about the old mine closing down."

"Honestly Justin, you've got a vivid imagination. That man was here to do a job. Mr. Albert did not get rid of him. He never planned to stay. When he realized he'd been mistaken about the mine, he left." Millicent turned back to the counter, avoiding his sharp gaze. Sometimes those dark eyes could stare right through her and she worried the boy could read her soul. Just like his father.

"Sure Ma. Lots of mines run without employees. And it was totally obvious that guy never planned to stay. I mean, people who are only passing through always buy up an old cottage and sink a bunch of cash into it to fix it up. That all makes sense to me."

"You don't know what you're talking about. You were nine for crying out loud." Grabbing a cloth from the sink, she busied herself wiping the crumbs from the counter.

"I guess you're right. What does a kid know anyway? So, you didn't answer me. What's Cassidy like?"

"He seems very nice." Millicent didn't have to lie about that. Ryan Cassidy did *seem* nice, attractive, and way too smart. He'd looked them straight in the eyes, his blue gaze burning into theirs then narrowing as he found something he didn't approve of. Just like his father. He read the situation accurately and reacted as he should have. Ryan might prove a worthier opponent than Carroll assumed.

"Is he staying?"

Millicent turned. "You want supper? I suggest you stop badgering me with questions and let me make it. Ryan Cassidy is here to stay, Mr. Albert is happy about it, welcomed him in fact. Now go get in the shower. I'll make you something to eat."

"Why do you always call him Mr. Albert? Why don't you just call him Carroll?"

"What do you mean?"

"I do have eyes and ears, Ma. I've heard him here tons of times and you don't call him "Mr. Albert" then. Why do it now?"

"Because he's your elder and the reeve of this town. It's just respect."

"You're scared of him, like everyone else."

Millicent's heart fluttered. Her cheeks burned before the resentment in Justin's gaze. "I'm not afraid of him. Don't be silly."

"I bet. I hope this Mr. Cassidy has more balls than the rest of this town. Maybe he can make Mr. Albert and the rest of you morons see that he isn't God. He's the reeve of a crappy little town that isn't even on the map."

"Justin! That language isn't acceptable in my house." Millicent threw the cloth into the sink and set her hands on her hips.

"What? Balls? Jesus Ma, I could have said worse than balls." He turned and thundered up the stairs.

She waited until the bedroom door slammed. If Justin wanted to make it out of this town, he needed learn that it wasn't a matter of having balls or anything else where Carroll was concerned.

Carroll didn't scare her, not physically. Justin read something else, something that he was too young to understand. What Carroll knew about Millicent's past could ruin her good name, which was all she had left. Sure, it wasn't much to be proud of, but she'd be damned if a stupid mistake stole that small piece of dignity. The name Douglas still meant something in this town.

Millicent pulled out a chair from the round pine table that nestled into the little nook next to the long countertop and sat to look out the darkened window next to it. In her mind she saw the lights, the stage, felt the groping hands on her naked body. Why behave so stupidly? Not for the money. Her father had all the money anyone could ever need. *Had.* Carroll took most of it long ago.

Millicent sighed. She knew exactly why she did it. For the thrill, the attention… the sex. Up on that stage, men admired her, wanted her, and would pay large sums to have her. After suffocating in this crappy little town for years, Millicent had been someone other than Jake Douglas's daughter. The attention given to her up there had been well earned. Daddy's money couldn't buy the lust shown by those men when she danced. At the time, Millicent believed that lust equaled power. God what a stupid kid she'd been. She'd have continued too and probably would have ruined her life. But someone discovered her little secret.

Carroll had followed her to Timmins after spring break. He must have known she'd hardly attended that private school her parents had enrolled her in. How? He never told her. Millicent rubbed her face, took a shaky breath, and ran her finger over the small J carved into the tabletop. Justin had marked nearly every surface in the house when he was six. She smiled. Where had that innocent little boy gone? Maybe to the same place her innocence had vanished when Carroll stomped every last speck of naiveté from her soul.

That night in an ugly little strip club, her whole world crashed, and plummeted into a downward spiral the moment she looked up to see Carroll Albert standing there, camcorder running. Then he winked, and tossed a twenty onto the stage.

Later he'd taken her home, but not before stopping along the road to get a taste of what she offered the men at the club. He hadn't forced her, at the time she'd been foolish enough to believe that sex gave her the upper hand and she could use it to

RENÉE MILLER

get the tape back.

One week later, her father received a package. The town hall underwent major renovations that year, courtesy of the Douglas family. Her mother lost a long battle with cancer that spring and her father died of a stroke the following winter. He barely looked at his only child even as she sat next to the bed, desperately clinging to his hand while life slipped away from him.

Before closing his eyes for the last time, he looked at his daughter. "Do you know what you've done?"

Millicent hung her head, but his hand found hers. "I couldn't have them finding out. I had to protect your mother from the shame. How could you do that to her, Millie?"

"I'm so sorry. I was stupid."

"Just to keep him quiet, I had to make a deal. What I did was right. There was no other way."

He didn't tell her what he'd done. Millicent hadn't asked either. She learned later, after her father passed. Carroll stood by her until the funeral was over, letting her believe that he cared.

Later, Millicent found the tape, destroyed it, and thought that would ensure her freedom and protect her father's name. But Carroll had other plans. When her father's will was read, she realized what he gave up to protect his town and his name; her future.

The video game sounds started upstairs again, startling Millicent out of her memories and back to her crumbling kitchen. The foolishness of youth had been her biggest mistake. No one was invincible. Carroll Albert had shown her reality, and the lessons hit hard and fast.

During the long, lonely hours before dawn, the temptation to go to the police about Justin's parentage grew unbearable. Common sense would arrive after the sun rose; reminding her that nothing could be done without proof. Carroll held enough to damage her and to hurt Justin. *And I have nothing.*

If only Justin's mother had left something behind—had told a friend or a relative where she ran off to—he might pay a small price for his disgusting habit of molesting young girls. Millicent sighed, fingering the edge of her sleeves. Even if she had told a friend, no one would talk, and the sheep who ran his other operations wouldn't talk either.

RENÉE MILLER

CHAPTER 5

A large desk, a comfortable brown leather sofa, and his grand-father's computer occupied the den. Oddly, the computer sat on the left hand side of the desk, but the dust footprint showed it belonged on the right, closer to the window. Ryan stared for a moment. Someone had moved it. Who? Was it even the same computer? He searched the area around the desk for a sign… of what? Even if he wanted to play detective, he was hardly CSI material.

A light flickered outside the window. Slim shadows drifted along the far side of the barn. Ryan forgot the computer. Dogs? He didn't care to investigate and turned to leave the room. A narrow built-in unit nestled next to the door made him pause, its shelves crammed full of books. Harlequin romances filled the middle shelf, a favorite of his mother's too. Smiling, he inspected the thicker books on the top row. Encyclopedias, dictionaries, and heavy volumes with titles relating to agriculture and cattle filled the uppermost shelf. Ryan skimmed the next shelf. The first book had been set back to front, the spine facing in. Odd. The rest of the books faced the right way. All of them. He pulled the book out and flipped it open. The pages fluttered and settled at either side of a purple envelope, his name crowding its front in loopy script. Another one?

He tucked it into his back pocket and went to investigate the closets. They were as organized as the kitchen. Cleaning supplies occupied one and outdoor clothes filled the other. A tattered plaid jacket hung crooked in the center.

The jacket, out of place among the strict order of the rest of the house, altered Ryan's thoughts. He viewed his grandparents as more than ghosts from the past. For the first time he thought of them as real people. A man wore this coat, risking his wife's ire by carelessly tossing it in the tidy space. His grandfather, a human being with thoughts, feelings, and love for the grandson he'd never met.

Though she gave up very little about her life, when Ryan was a child, his mother mentioned Melvin and Rachel sometimes, and a wistful smile would light up her face. At once she would change the subject, her smile vanishing swiftly.

Ryan closed the door and trailed a finger over the rough wood. Shadows stretched over the narrow hall, swallowing him as he passed the front door. He picked up his bags and dragged them up the stairs.

At the top, near the newel post, he flipped on an ancient light switch, its edges covered in layers of old paint. He stared down the hall. Three doors sat open, waiting for his perusal of the rooms beyond. Ryan took the first and switched on the light. Brilliant shades of peach, yellow, and red assaulted him. He dropped the bags inside the door. "Oh my shit. I'm in floral hell."

His grandmother's love of flowers saturated the room. The rose smothered bedspread nauseated him almost as much as the bright yellow walls.

Across the room, on a vast mirrored dresser, a ceramic vase—too large to fit on a dining room table or the spot it occupied now—collected dust. A mob of multicolored silk blooms gushed in a floral fountain from the narrow opening at the top. Though he turned from the nightmare, his gaze found no solace, flowers…flowers everywhere. Beneath the window, on the opposite wall, nestled a loveseat matching the living room sofa. Next to the loveseat a book—probably the last thing she read—lay opened face down on top of a delicate metal-framed table.

Once his head stopped spinning enough to drive, the hardware store would be his next stop. Ryan bent to his briefcase to retrieve his grandfather's letter. Where would he hide it? The bed? Not the most original idea, but it would do for the moment. Ryan slid his grandfather's letter beneath the mattress and sat on its edge.

Taking a deep breath, Ryan took the second letter from his pocket and tore open the envelope. He pulled out a piece of lavender paper and set the envelope next to him;

Ryan,

Your grandfather has no idea that I'm writing this letter to you. He tries to protect me from the nastiness of life here, but he forgets that I am smarter than he is, and in some ways much stronger.

I know that he asked something of you that we have no business asking. All I can say is that you must follow your heart on that one. Even I am not brave or cunning enough to go against this town. Melvin thinks he is, but I'm afraid they'll get the better of him. If you're reading this, then that is probably what happened. It's unlikely that we died naturally or accidentally. There are no accidents in Albertsville.

If you find their secrets, don't keep them to yourself. They won't like it at first, but you'll be doing everyone a favor by revealing them to the right people. It's what your father died trying to do. I don't even know if this letter will get to you. If it does, remember that nothing is as it seems. A dirt floor has no bottom, the wall is not solid, and an empty space is full. Your grandfather suspects the mill, but he's wrong.

I'm sure you're an intelligent boy. You'll figure it out before long.

I love you, I missed you, and I'm sorry.

Love

Rachel Cassidy (Granny)

P.S. Your mother sent pictures every year. You look so much like my Chad. He was a good man. Believe that.

Ryan's vision blurred. Upset over people he didn't even know. Silly. He folded the letter and slid it next to his grandfather's under the mattress, and then flopped onto his back and into a mountain of pillows.

"Flowers: the real monsters of Albertsville." The blooms made it to the ceiling as well, etched into the white plaster, swirling around a large light fixture shaped like a rosebud.

He closed his eyes. If he held out for the year making as few contacts, and therefore fewer enemies as possible, he could leave with a cool million in his pocket. If he dove in feet first and figured out what the hell was going on in Albertsville, he might lose all of it... and then some.

Were they nuts, paranoid, or just old? Was this monster thing just senile rambling? How could one man hold that much power?

He remembered the way that woman, Millicent, had stared up at Carroll. Her gaze held much more than the awkwardness of a shy person. It held fear. The last man, Farley, looked plain pissed. The bitter hatred he'd glimpsed in those pale grey eyes irked Ryan. Why would a man who obviously didn't like him join the welcoming committee?

Ryan rolled to one side, tucking a hand under his cheek. Carroll's lie about Jeffery calling would have tipped-off him, even without his grandparents' warnings. As the Reeve in a godforsaken little hole in the middle of nowhere, Carroll may as well have been a king. He owned the most powerful position, which raised another question. How did he use that power?

His eyes drooped. Why should he even care what was going on? They'd done nothing for him except cause his mother misery. He'd put in his year and get the hell out of Albertsville. How hard could that be?

A noise drifted through his thoughts. Something moved downstairs. Ryan sat up and strained to listen. Footsteps.

He eased off the bed and moved toward the hallway. Hadn't he locked the doors? He always locked his doors. What if they came back to get rid of him?

"Hello?" a woman's voice.

Ryan relaxed a fraction. He hadn't wandered into some horror movie. He was stuck in a small town where neighbors felt free to come into your house as if they owned the place. A deadbolt, he needed one, or at least a chain. Someone waltzing into his home didn't sit well.

"Mr. Cassidy?"

"Up here," he called, stepping onto the stairs. Whoever she was, she'd get a piece of his mind.

He neared the bottom of the stairs when a small woman appeared in the hall. Curly brown hair bounced in a high ponytail as she walked. She turned toward the stairs and smiled. His mind took back its piece.

She held out a small hand. "I'm Audrey. Sorry, I saw your car and it's pretty early—were you sleeping?"

"No, just exploring." Ryan took her hand, surprised at her firm grip.

"I meant to be here when you arrived, but I thought I had a couple more days. Jeffery said the first. I hear you met Carroll?"

"Yes, and your police chief and some mill guy and a lovely but somewhat skittish woman named Millicent."

Audrey grimaced and folded her arms across her chest, bunching the padded jacket so it hid her slim neck. "That's why I wanted to meet you at the door. I figured a couple of them would be here."

"So, I'm not an exception then?"

"I'm sorry?"

"To the Welcome Wagon. It wasn't just for me?"

Her deep throaty laugh teased his ears, a pleasant shiver tingling right to his toes. "No, that welcome was definitely made for you. They don't waste their time on nobodies."

"Well, at least I'm not a nobody, I guess. Coffee?"

She nodded. Ryan skirted around her and walked toward the kitchen. "I'm not sure what I have here, but everyone keeps coffee in the cupboards, right?"

"Yes, but I don't know how fresh it is. I put a couple of things in the fridge because I didn't know if I'd get back again before you arrived. I've been in a few times to clean the house."

So that explained the note and the uneven layer of dust.

"You've got a few staples like bread, cereal, and sugar, and I made sure the canned stuff in the cupboards was safe to eat too. They didn't keep much."

Her voice trailed off. Please don't start crying. Ryan didn't handle tearful females very well. He never knew if he should tactfully ignore them or offer comfort. Boy, would he love to offer her something. *Way too long without a date, buddy.*

He focused on the cupboards above him. Audrey approached and opened a door above a tiny black coffee maker and reached in. She pulled a duck-shaped jar down from the first shelf.

"Quaint." Ryan took the ceramic duck and set it on the counter.

Audrey moved away, pulling a chair from the small round table in the corner.

How often had Audrey sat in this kitchen with his grandparents, and how much did she know? More importantly, how many scoops of coffee did he need for a half pot again? He dipped the plastic spoon in and struck the bottom. Scraping the coffee grinds away from one side, he unearthed a hairline crack at the outer edge. A little voice inside his head warned him not to dump its contents. Audrey might not be trustworthy. Remembering her full lips curving into a hesitant smile at the stairs, he hoped she'd turn out to be a friend; maybe even one with benefits.

Ryan doled a third scoop into the filter and replaced the lid.

"So, are you staying?"

Startled, he nearly dropped the jar. "Yeah, I think so. Why, did you think I wouldn't?"

After much fumbling, the machine offered a faint gurgling noise. Success. He turned to meet Audrey's gaze.

She looked grim.

"What?"

"If you're going to stay, then I should give you a bit of advice. Fair warning I guess you could call it."

"Okay, I'm all ears." Ryan leaned against the counter.

"Let's wait for the coffee."

The sounds of the "Great Canadian North" filtered through the window. Ryan stood next to its large panes fighting the urge to get in his car and drive away. The calls outside sounded alarmingly like a pack of wild *somethings*. Eerie howls filled the occasional silence… wolves? Ryan had never actually heard a wolf in his life. Well, not outside the Discovery Channel. He opened his mouth to wonder at the proximity of the howls, when a low wail joined the chorus; a noise he could only compare to a dying cow, bawling in agony. He looked to Audrey.

She giggled. "That's Larry."

"Larry?" Larry better not be a man.

"There was no mention of him in the will?"

"No, should there have been? I don't think I'm going to stay long if Larry is a stipulation of my inheritance. He sounds…sick."

Audrey laughed, holding her middle and snorting between guffaws.

Ryan frowned as she met his gaze, her green eyes moist. He didn't find the idea of inheriting Larry funny at all.

She sobered. "I'm sorry. Your face was just so—Larry is a moose. He's been hanging around for the past couple of years. Melvin fed him one winter and that was it. We still feed him now and then. When he deems our offerings worthy he accepts them, and he stays in the barn if it suits him. No one gets real close to him, but sometimes if he sees the lights on he'll peek in the windows."

Ryan turned to the large window that occupied the far corner of the room. His own image reflected back. Beyond the deck, the barn and the field lay camouflaged in darkness. No moose. His heart skipped a beat as he thought of Larry tapping the thin glass with his antlers. He imagined the glass shattering, and then he'd have a wild animal in the house, one with sharp antlers and feet bigger than Ryan's head. Moose killed more people every year than bears.

"As long as he doesn't knock and break a window, or attack me when I go out to my car, I guess I'm okay with that."

"You're perfectly safe. He's never broken a window and he stays away from people. The closest he's come is to stand outside or walk on the deck. He's harmless."

"Sorry, I'm from the city. Our wildlife is pretty limited. I might be lucky to see ducks at the park or a stray cat or two in the parking garage. Cats can be frightening sometimes, especially when they're hungry… or pissed. But I've never encountered a moose. Isn't he scared of the wolves?"

"No, the wolves are way out in the back forty. They don't approach the house. Well, not that we know of. I know they sound close, but I think I've seen a wolf in town twice in my whole life."

"Only twice? That's a relief." He wasn't sure what a "back forty" was and he didn't want to ponder it too much. The idea of wolves in town—ever—made him nervous enough to force him from the window to the chair opposite Audrey at the table.

Larry made another guttural wail. Ryan raised his cup.

"Right, I was going to fill you in before Larry interrupted," she said.

"You were. Although I don't think anything you tell me at this point could be more fascinating than a moose at my door or wolves in my back forty. But feel free to try."

"I think you'll see that Larry is the least fascinating creature in Albertsville. How do I say this? I guess it's best to just come out with it. Carroll is dangerous, and not because he has money. He's unscrupulous and evil. I'm not exaggerating for effect either."

"I assumed the locals might be dishonest. My grandparents left me some letters. So, the Reeve is a crook and a liar. That's a surprising thing to know about a politician."

"Okay smartass, a dishonest politician doesn't surprise anyone. Carroll's father ran this town for years. Jarrod Albert was bad. We thought he would be the worst thing that ever happened to this town. Boy, did we have a shock coming. When

Carroll took over about ten years ago—after his father's sudden heart attack that no one believes was a heart attack—he decided that bribery didn't quite meet his needs. He wanted more than wealth. Actually, his whole adult life he's been preparing to own this town. He expanded on his father's misdeeds and his wealth on a level I can't even describe.

"Twelve families founded this town. You'll get to know them eventually. There's the Alberts, of course," Audrey counted off on her fingers as she spoke. "And then the Raymonds, Smiths, Chamberses, Douglases, Swifts, Perrys, Reids, Jamiesons, Joneses, Bakers, and Cassidys. Before the town was established, each had his own piece of land. Now, eleven are left, but only one man owns nearly everything. Carroll Albert. He will lie, cheat, steal—even murder anyone who gets in his way."

"Why isn't he in jail? If you know, I'm sure other people do. Murder is one of those things that law enforcement notices."

Audrey's cheeks reddened and she stared into her cup. "If anyone knew what goes on here, most of us would lose everything. Carroll has manipulated everyone into a corner. It's easy for you to say that no one can force you to lie or keep secrets, not a whole town certainly, but you don't live here. You don't know how far his power reaches. We do."

"Why don't you leave?"

She lifted her face and shrugged. Her eyes welled with tears. "It's that simple, isn't it? Leave."

"What? I mean it. Why not just go? He can't control you if you aren't here. He wouldn't have any power without people to manipulate. Just get out, forget him and this place."

"We've all grown up here. The idea of uprooting families, leaving a guaranteed job with a lower cost of living is senseless. They couldn't afford to go even if they wanted to. There are things, events that have made it impossible. If anyone knew… they could lose what little they have left. Plus, the minute they step over the town line, if they even make it that far, they'd disappear. Carroll has eyes and ears everywhere."

"Come on, what the hell could an entire town have done that would allow him to toss any one of them in jail? Seriously, this sounds like a bad movie. Worse than a bad movie, like one of those miniseries on cable… on that women's network. When's the white knight coming in to rescue them all? I hope that's not the role you expect me to play. No fucking thanks."

"I never asked you to do anything."

"Don't you see how crazy what you're telling me sounds? If he's guilty of a crime as serious as murder, then that trumps whatever you might risk in blowing the lid on him. Unless you've murdered someone. Is that it? Albertsville is a hotbed of serial killers? Shit, if I knew someone was capable of taking a life, I'd want him locked away, not shaking my hand and kissing my babies."

"It's not that we've killed anybody and I doubt we'd go to jail. Not all of us, anyway. I can't explain because you don't know this town. It's more complicated than that. You'll see. I give you a week at the most, and you'll understand what I'm saying. Until then, just don't make a lot of commotion and you'll be fine. He may end up liking you, but I doubt it. Your name isn't one of his favorites. Melvin and Rachel almost had him."

"What do you mean?"

Audrey chewed her lower lip.

Suddenly she's reluctant to share? Ryan leaned back in his chair and stretched his legs out in front of him. His foot touched the far leg of the small table.

"Melvin gathered a lot of evidence before he died, but he didn't move fast enough to do anything with it. I imagine his records are gone now in any case. Rachel told me the week before she died that she thought something would happen. Someone had been in the house while they were gone. Then people in town started avoiding her. I told them to leave, to forget the whole thing; but Mel wouldn't let go."

"In her letter my grandmother mentioned that she and my grandfather might die under suspicious circumstances."

"Fred, the police chief, filed the report, signed the death

certificate, and sent it off before their bodies had turned cold. It was a clear night, not a snowflake, or a raindrop, not even another car around. According to Fred, Melvin drove into a tree, killing both of them instantly. We never saw the bodies. Tim, the coroner, said they'd been sent for cremation."

"I know, they said it was something like blunt force trauma to the head, for both. They figured the tree—"

"Bullshit. No one was allowed near this house or near that section of road for a week. They cut the tree down and the car is gone. Why? Because Carroll, Fred and that dipshit Farley were in here cleaning up the evidence your grandfather found, and creating their bogus accident report."

Sure they were rednecks, but even rednecks couldn't get away with this shit. Fred Smith was not the only cop in town; the rest would question him whether he was Chief or not. Farley Swift didn't look smart enough to pull off such a caper and keep his mouth shut. To Ryan, he seemed the type that told his story after a drink or two. And then there was the government. Didn't they have regulations, procedures that made it impossible to doctor these things as Audrey implied they had?

Ryan rubbed his eyes. "I don't know. It's kind of far-fetched. Maybe they really did lose control. Maybe my grandfather had a heart attack, or a stroke. They were almost eighty. Is it possible that you're a bit paranoid? Often when people believe something enough, they manufacture facts or events to fit their theories."

"You'll see." Audrey picked up her cup, her gaze drifting once more toward the window.

She seemed an intelligent woman, strong willed and definitely not the type to keep her mouth shut against the murder of people close to her. If Carroll did kill his grandparents, he had to have something serious on Audrey to keep her silent.

Ryan fingered the chipped enamel on the handle of the cup. "What does he have over you?"

Dots of color formed on her cheeks. "Pardon?"

"You said he held almost everyone under his thumb, I'm wondering what you could have done or what you might lose that's so terrible you'd stay silent about the deaths of two inno-cent old people—that you claim to care about."

Audrey shifted her gaze to the window once more, al-though Ryan suspected she didn't see the inky darkness or the stars that scattered across the night sky. She fidgeted with the rim of her cup, running her fingers around it, sliding down and then repeating the motion again.

Ryan's followed the movement down the mug—another flowery item in the house—and caught a slight tremor in the slim fingers. "Is it that bad?"

"No, he has nothing on me or over me. Not really."

"Why then?"

"Just stupidity really. Partly my fault. I'd told my dad about something that happened and he went straight to Carroll."

"That has nothing to do with you now. Are your parents still alive?"

"They died in a fire when I was eighteen. Something hap-pened to my mom and—it doesn't matter. The point is my dad's temper got the better of him and Carroll decided they were a liability he couldn't afford anymore. I can't prove that of course. I just know it. Carroll couldn't touch the trust they'd set aside for me, thank God. He took our house and any money left in their bank accounts for what he called back taxes. He probably set the fire himself. That land has been in my family since Albertsville was founded. Now, it belongs to Carroll."

"You don't have anything?"

"Oh, I had enough in the trust to open a hardware store and buy a small house. I'm okay. Your grandparents took me in for a while, helped me get through school. The store is small, earns just enough for the ends to meet, but it's mine. By the time I considered leaving, I had another family to consider; Melvin and Rachel. Your grandfather worked for years to find out what Carroll did, but even he hesitated over bringing the rest of us down."

"I see."

"No, you don't. But you will. I can't prove what happened

with my parents but I keep hoping one day Carroll will slip up. So far he's proven far too smart for me."

Larry wailed outside. This time it sounded farther away, closer to the barn. Ryan smiled. A pet moose.

Audrey pushed her chair back and stood. She straightened her sweater, which had moved over her hips to reveal tight-fitting jeans. "It was nice meeting you. It's not my intention to scare you away. Stay if that's what you intend to do, but I had to make sure you know what kind of people run Albertsville." She offered a thin smile.

"I'm not scared at all. Curious, maybe, but I see no reason for fear."

"Not yet. Anyway, I'll see you tomorrow. I'm sure you'll want to start working on this place soon. You can open a tab at the store. I'll charge everything to the estate."

"Thanks. I appreciate that."

"Yeah, I'm not crazy about Rachel's affinity for flowers either. But Chad used to bring her flowers every day. After he died, I guess she tried to fill the void somehow. Roses remind her of him. Silly."

"Not silly. Nice. Although, I'd have preferred that he brought her something like high-end electronics or maybe beer. That would have worked better for me."

"I'm sure." Audrey smiled and turned to the hall.

Ryan followed, his gaze drawn to the way her hips swayed as she walked. She turned and he belatedly looked to her face. He searched desperately for something to say. "So, I'll see you tomorrow?" *Dork*.

"Yes, tomorrow. And promise me you'll stay away from the others. I think given enough time, and enough rope, you could hang yourself very well."

"I don't know what you mean."

Audrey winked and opened the door to step out onto the deck.

Ryan reached to push it closed. He flipped the switch next to the door, illuminating the path to her truck.

She climbed into an old black rust bucket. A smile played

on her lips and she waved before firing it up.

How did he not hear that beast roaring and whining like that when it pulled up the drive?

After the rear lights of Audrey's truck flashed once, twice, and then vanished on the first bend of the road, Ryan remained by the window, gaze unfocused, his mind churning. Eventually he moved from the window and climbed the stairs.

Even if Audrey had blown the Carroll situation out of proportion, it wouldn't hurt to dig a little. If there were a shadow of truth to the theory that Carroll murdered his grandparents, He would find out. He wouldn't sit idly by and worry about ruining the town either.

CHAPTER 6

The calls of Larry the moose had continued until midnight, interrupted now and then by the wolves. The back forty sounded awfully close to his front yard. According to Wikipedia, the term actually referred to uncultivated land on a farm or a ranch. The wolves could easily mistake the entire property as home territory.

After rising early, he stumbled to the kitchen. As the sun climbed over the horizon, it lent an orange glow to the yellow walls of the room. Ryan stood at the window to watch the pale light creep over the fields and found it strangely comforting. He couldn't wait to sit down to write.

The untouched beauty of a sunrise untainted by smog, the silence of a morning undisturbed by horns or sirens, everything filled him with an inner peace he couldn't recall ever feeling anywhere else.

But no matter how peaceful his inner self might be, he wasn't sufficiently awake to do anything of any real importance. Coffee first. Everything else later. He moved about the room that was slowly growing on him, despite his aversion to organization.

His grandmother's store brand brew filled his nostrils and calmed his caffeine-deprived brain. The strange shallowness of the duck jar tickled at his brain. He'd investigate it later, when his mind had time to wake up.

He rummaged through the many drawers that ran beneath the counter, searching for a notepad and pen. Sadly, all he managed to unearth belonged to his grandmother. He'd feel real manly walking into Audrey's hardware store carrying a list written in purple ink atop a bed of happy flowers.

Too lazy to walk to the den to search the desk, he sat at the small table to begin his list while the percolator bubbled and hissed. Paint. A gallon for each room should suffice, and paint brushes, tape, and drop cloths... maybe Albertsville had a painter.

A shadow passed over the page. He froze, terrified to startle the inquisitive dark-eyed beast that peered back at him. Larry the moose huffed, fogging up a small circle of glass before leaving the window and lumbering out of sight. The breath Ryan held hissed from his mouth.

Perhaps he'd better look into Animal Control as well. Slipping the list in his pocket, he strode to the hallway. He peered around the door, and searched the deck for signs of the moose before running out to his car.

The winding drive to the road proved uneventful with no moose or wolves darting into his path. Not a single car passed him on the way into town, but Albertsville bustled with activity as Ryan drove down the main street searching for the hardware store. Damn, he should have asked Audrey for an address, or even the store's name.

He laughed. The town boasted one paved street. How hard could it be to find anything?

People bundled in thick parkas and camouflage hats and coats—even camouflage pants—roamed the sidewalk, getting in and out of vehicles parked along the way. Most of Albertsville drove pickups and SUV's. The car made him conspicuous, a sissy in the face of tiny, grey haired women driving monster trucks.

How did they afford these vehicles anyway? Surely a single mill didn't produce that much income. They used to have a mine here, but he'd read somewhere that it closed.

The familiar red and yellow double H's of the Home Hardware chain couldn't be missed. Ryan pulled to the side behind a blue Chevy Blazer. Its bumper sticker told him to honk if he liked beaver. Smiling, he shifted his car into park and took the key from the ignition.

He pulled his jacket tight against the brisk wind and opened the door. The sun was deceiving. Although it got just as cold in Calgary, the winds didn't feel as bone-rattling.

Nestled between a dentist's office and a florist, Audrey's store fought for room. The shops had been sandwiched so close they resembled one long building. Perry's Home Hardware, written in yellow atop a red backdrop, hung over the door. A small-paned window displayed snow shovels and ice salt on the left, and a monstrous-looking snow blower covered the right side with a sign warning customers to be ready for "Old Man Winter" propped in front.

Ryan opened the door to a loud clang from an overhead cowbell. The storefronts were narrow but inside they ran deep. Narrow paths divided the store's three long aisles, where red signs hung from the ceiling listing the contents of each section. Product hung in neat rows with less than an inch of space between each. Below them sat bins of bulk screws, paintbrushes and other items.

He could probably eat off the white-tiled floors that reflected the fluorescent lights. At the front, to the left of the door, was a tiny counter covered in red Formica. A cash register and a computer sat at one end and a key rack on the other.

"You came," Audrey's voice came from somewhere behind a stack of boxes blocking the middle aisle.

"I said I would."

She poked her curly head around the side of the cardboard tower. "Sorry, I've only got so much storage space upstairs, so I'm trying to figure out how I'm going to put this washer fluid out and not have to carry any of it up. I think I might have ordered a bit too much."

"You do have a lot of it."

"Well, it's the special kind for cold weather. It'll sell, but only after it gets real cold. Until then, I need to store it. Once it snows, I may not get a delivery for a while. These roads are a bitch most of the winter, so it's a tough call."

"Really? I hadn't thought of that. It gets that bad up here?" The idea of being stuck in one place for an indefinite amount of time made his skin crawl.

"When we say snow, we don't mean flurries. It's usually either a big dump or nothing. It takes a while to clear the roads and the ice is terrible. I only get maybe one truck every three or four weeks between December and March."

"Wow. That's going to make for a long winter."

Audrey laughed; the soft sound sending shivers down his spine.

"It's not that bad, but from a business point of view I have to prepare for the worst. So, you've got your list?"

He handed her the scrap of paper. "Please don't comment on the paper."

"Nice ink. It matches."

"Yeah, I hope you have regular pens and paper here. The kind normal people use."

"I do. But I think this is nice."

"Not really."

Audrey scanned the list and nodded a couple of times.

Ryan turned to the window.

A woman stopped and stared openly at him for a moment. Her dark eyes widened initially, but then they softened and gathered a curious light. Suddenly, her face changed and she moved away. She waved, almost as an afterthought.

He raised a hand to wave back, but she was gone.

"That was Amelia." Audrey said.

Ryan turned. "She looks nice."

"She's okay. She moved here about five years ago, after meeting and marrying Ferris Jones. Amelia isn't the smartest. She suffered some kind of head trauma as a kid and it short-circuited a few things in her brain. They met at a family reunion; her mother and Ferris's dad were second cousins. But

Ferris loves her and they thought the connection was distant enough, a sad story really. They found out a while back that Ferris's dad was her father too. But we all pretend we don't know. They're good people. A little strange, but aren't we all in some way?"

"I guess. Half-brother? That's... icky."

"Well, they didn't know at first. And they can't have kids, so whom are they hurting? The Jones line will end with them. What would you do if you loved someone enough to marry her and then found that out? I'm not sure. I guess we'd all like to think we'd feel differently about a relation, but you can't dictate what your heart wants. Anyway, I'll get your paint started while you look around for the rest of this list. Are you sure you want to paint everything white?" She curled her nose a little.

Ryan laughed. "Any suggestions?"

"Do you trust me?"

"As much as I trust anyone I barely know."

"Well, trust me on this. You can't paint that house white. It's just not right. An old place like that needs color. Anything you don't like, I'll return for your boring white."

"Okay, but I don't like anything really bright like red or orange. And I hate pastels. They hurt my brain."

She rolled her eyes and walked to the back of the store. Ryan wandered the aisles looking up at the signs and then to his list. As he crouched to the bins full of rollers and brushes, the bell on the door clanged.

Shuffling feet moved around the front, near the counter.

Ryan stood, peering around a bucket of extension poles.

The woman from the Welcome Wagon stared around, her fingers stroking the tattered edges of her blue scarf.

He stepped out from his position and waved. "Hey, Millicent, isn't it?"

"Mr. Cassidy, I thought that was your car outside."

"Hard to miss since I think it's the only one in town."

"Not the only one, but there aren't many. Cars don't fare well up here I'm afraid. Not in the winter. Plus, many of us are either farmers or loggers so we need our trucks."

Ryan leaned against the small counter. His arm brushed a box of utility knives, and he pushed them back. "Is that all anyone does?"

Millicent blinked. "I'm sorry?"

"The mill and the farms. That's all people do for money? What kind of mill would pay enough to keep people in SUVs and build a town hall like you've got here?"

"I'm sure I don't know." She fiddled with her scarf. No luck.

He tried a new approach. "Isn't there a mine around here?"

"A mine...oh, you mean the old mine. It's not operating anymore. Carroll bought it."

"Really, so everyone works at the mill?"

"No, there are stores as you can see, and the farms do well. Why do you want to know?"

"Curious. Audrey is just mixing some paint for me. She'll be up soon."

"Oh, actually I was going to stop by your house later but when I saw your car, I hoped I could save the trip." Her face reddened.

"What can I do for you?"

"There's a meeting tonight, at the town hall. You know where that is?"

"How could I miss it? The big palace at the end of town?"

Her short laugh sounded unnatural. "Yes, that's the one. Most of the town usually shows, and I thought it would be a great opportunity for you to meet everyone."

Ryan gazed at her in silence.

She moved her hand up to fidget with the straps of her oversized black purse.

"I'd think as the new guy, I'd hardly be welcome at a town meeting."

"Of course you would. It's *important* that you go." Millicent's smile vanished.

In her dark eyes, Ryan saw a desperation that set his nerves on edge. She was trying to tell him something without telling him. He hated when people talked in code, especially when there was no one around to hear them. "Why?"

"Why what?"

"Why is it so important?"

"Trust me, it is."

Ryan chewed the inside of his cheek. No, he wouldn't let her off that easily. "Sure, but I need something from you first."

Millicent glanced to the window and back. "What?"

"What happened to my grandparents?"

"I don't know."

"You're lying."

Millicent straightened and lowered her hands. "I am not a liar, Mr. Cassidy. I don't know what happened to Melvin and Rachel. They said they crashed into the tree. Do I believe it? No. Does anyone? I doubt it. But unless you get to know this town, you may never know the truth."

"And this meeting will give me clues?"

"It might. You need to know who is who around here. Please, come out tonight. It's at seven. You don't have to speak, just sit at the back and observe. I think you'll be glad you did. If you're interested in the mine, check it out some night. Just don't get too close." Millicent turned and pushed through the door.

The bell clanged as it closed behind her.

Audrey's footsteps sounded from the back of the store.

Ryan turned in time to spot her frown as she approached him.

"Was that Millicent?"

"Yes."

"Did you tell her I'd be right back? I swear, sometimes that woman has no patience at all."

"I did. But she wasn't looking for you. She was looking for me."

Audrey paled. "Why?"

"I guess I'm going to the meeting tonight."

"I think that would be a bad idea."

"Which is why I have to go."

53

"Julia!"

Two goddamn hours until the meeting, an important meeting, and his wife was missing in action. She knew how he prepared for meetings, and yet he always had to search her out.

Carroll buttoned his shirt, glancing at his watch. Anger rose into his chest, burning there when he realized he'd missed a button. He growled.

The bedroom doors opened.

He turned from the floor-to-ceiling mirror that covered the wall.

Julia stood in the threshold, her face red and her arms crossed over her chest. Her pink yoga pants and matching jacket hugged her body like a glove. Christ she wasn't even ready yet.

"You hollered?" she asked.

"Don't take that tone with me. You know what day it is."

"Yes, it's Wednesday."

"It's meeting day. Stop playing games and get in here." Carroll turned back to the mirror. He watched her expression flit from irritated to fearful and back to irritated again as he grabbed his tie from the rack on his dresser and looped it over his head. Let her stew, she had a duty and she'd damn well honor it. He tugged at the tie, wincing as he yanked the knot top tight. Righting it, he examined his reflection, running a hand through his hair.

He caught Julia's eye in the mirror and raised a brow. She remained rooted to her spot just inside the room, but lowered her arms. She'd argue. She'd bitch. But that's what wives did. In the end, she'd do as she was told and please her husband. Just as he'd trained her to do.

"Carroll, I really don't have time for this. I have to get to the hall and help Millicent with refreshments. Before that I have to pick Mickey up at—"

"You don't do a fucking thing until I tell you to do it." Carroll spun, fists clenched at his sides. He took a breath and closed his eyes. She would not ruin his mood. Patience would be paramount tonight. To be patient, he needed a clear mind. Opening his eyes, Carroll smiled.

Julia's face reddened, and her body tensed.

Here it comes, her token rebellion. Every damn month he endured the same shit.

"Why don't you call one of your little girls? I know how you prefer them. I don't understand why you insist on pretending you still want me. It's not like I care."

"Get over here." Carroll pointed to the floor in front of him.

Julia did not move. "This is silly."

Carroll sighed and looked to the ceiling, his finger still pointed to the floor. When he'd married Julia she'd enjoyed pleasing him, did whatever she could to make sure that he was happy. Her attitude changed after finding Lindsay Chambers in his office. It wasn't as though she caught him doing anything inappropriate. If she'd arrived a little earlier she might have. She made her assumptions and now this is what he dealt with.

"I don't want to have to reevaluate our marriage… or your usefulness. Do you want that?" He leveled a pointed glare at her.

Julia paled, and her hands came together in front to worry the zipper on her sweater. She shook her head and stepped into the room. "I feel as though this is all you want me for. Why don't you ask me for anything else?"

"You know that's not true. I love you. Have you forgotten who was here when you needed a shoulder? I comforted you, supported you in your time of need. I helped you when no one else would. I know you loved him more than me, and I ignored that because I care for you. Do you know how it feels do know your wife imagines your brother every time you touch her? I love you enough to overlook that. What more do you want? I don't ask you for much more than this. Is it so bad to make me happy?"

Julia shuffled toward him, stopping a few feet away. She looked to the bed, and back to him. Carroll smiled, a loving and encouraging smile intended to make her relax. His fucking brother. What a joke. She loved that fool with the devotion only an idiot was capable of. The truth is that Julia had been the prize in a hard-fought war. His brother—half-brother—had always been the favorite. Their father bestowed all of his attention on the younger son. Carroll had fought for years to gain his father's interest until he realized he'd never have it while Randy lived.

The deciding moment came when Randy brought Julia home and announced their engagement. Carroll had tried and failed to capture her on more than one occasion. He'd been furious. Randy knew how much he wanted Julia, how hard he'd worked to win her over. Still, he'd gone after her and proposed. He didn't do it out of love. Randy did it to spite him.

No one made him look like a fool. Blood or not, he wouldn't be laughed at. He smiled remembering Randy's face as he realized his brother's intention. Carroll never finished last.

Julia needed to be reminded of her place. One of these days, he'd lose his patience and she'd find out what he really preferred. But that's not how one treated his wife right before an important meeting. He had to be calm, controlled, and he couldn't afford to let his emotions get the best of him. The people might feel the energy, and react accordingly.

Julia knelt on the soft carpet at his feet. He smiled, burying his hands in her hair. She reached over to pull down the zipper and open the button of his pants. Her hands paused for a moment. Carroll curled his fingers into her hair, tugging gently. Julia pushed the pants over his hips and then her mouth enveloped him.

CHAPTER 7

A bitter wind blew through the darkened parking lot, shaking his little car. Many people passed, turning to stare openly before continuing inside the municipal building. Ryan had christened it the Taj Ma-Albert.

Audrey tried to convince him not to come, saying that it would be a nonsense meeting. She warned that Millicent had probably been ordered to get him to go, for reasons known only to Carroll.

Ryan came anyway, wanting to meet the town and get the uncomfortable bullshit over with. Judging by the stares he'd received in the fifteen minutes he'd sat waiting for Audrey, he made the right decision. They wondered about him, stared, gawked and whispered as they passed. Why not satisfy their curiosity?

The fancy lights adorning the front lawn of the Taj Ma-Albert illuminated the parking lot as well as the building. People shivered as they rushed inside. Ryan turned the key and cranked the heat to keep the chill of the night from turning him into a Popsicle.

A horn blared, or rather it coughed, somewhere to his left. Audrey's battered old truck took up two spots near the end of the lot. The hinges screeched as she opened the door, climbed out, and slammed it shut.

He pulled the keys from the ignition as Audrey stopped just beside the car.

"Still want to do this?" she asked.

Ryan stood and closed the door, pressing the black device on his keychain to lock the car. "Yep. Come on, how bad can it be?"

Audrey raised an eyebrow and walked past him.

Ryan followed, nodding at a couple emerging from their truck; a clone of Audrey's but with a red cab and a blue bed. They lowered their eyes and did not return his greeting.

He raced up the steps behind her, shivering as the big doors closed. Ryan struggled to keep pace with Audrey's brisk stride as she moved through the foyer of the building. Trying to stay close, but unable to stop himself from staring open mouthed at the décor, he broke into a trot. She disappeared around a corner.

The white tiled floors shined, blinding under the fluorescent bell lights that hung high above in the arched ceiling. Dark paneled walls matched a desk curved in a half moon to the left. To the right a display of town artifacts, set in glass cases above a large wooden base, covered the entire wall. The rough wood looked out of place with the spit and polished shine of the rest of the hall. He'd have to check it out, but not tonight. Audrey was on a mission.

"Hey, wait," he called. Rounding the corner, he nearly ran over her.

Audrey stood, arms crossed over her chest, a tight smile on her lips. "I want to get a seat at the back. It's probably filled up already. Unlike you, I like that people here barely notice me."

"Why are you so bent out of shape? It's not like I asked you to chaperone. I've been wearing big boy pants for a while now. You could have stayed home, unnoticed."

She sighed and turned, walking down the narrow corridor to a double set of doors near the end.

He followed.

"I couldn't let you come alone. They're up to something. I

understand that you want to meet people. But really, in this town, the less you know about them—and the less they know about you—the better. Safer. Just get your year in, then get out and forget this place."

"What if I don't want to forget it?"

Snorting, Audrey opened the door and waved him inside. Heads turned to stare as he entered the room. Audrey slipped behind him and took a seat in the back corner.

Ryan nodded at the gawkers as he shuffled through the narrow space between the chairs to join her.

Compared to the city meetings held in Calgary, Albertsville's municipal hall was small. It seated fifty people comfortably, but they'd jammed folding chairs into two thirds of the room so that double that number could attend. A long conference-like table sat atop a stage a few inches off the floor and filled the section of the room not crammed with people. Behind the council members who sat at the table, facing the crowd, a Canadian flag hung on the paneled wall. Flanking it were pictures of the Queen and the Prime Minister. Just to the left, over a bookshelf filled with multicolored binders, hung a slightly smaller picture of the Reeve. The man himself was not yet present.

Ryan glanced at his watch as he took his stiff backed chair next to Audrey. "I thought this thing started at seven. It's going on half past."

She laughed. "Take a look at the agenda; it's posted in the foyer. They schedule meetings between seven and eight, never at a specific time. I've never heard him say so, but I think Carroll likes to keep people waiting. It makes him feel important."

"Oh."

The other four council members, three of whom he'd met in front of his grandparents' house, sat behind the table, shuffling papers and whispering among themselves. Only Millicent sat apart, a file on the table in front of her, glancing up at the crowd now and then. She searched the faces, her eyes flicking over a row at a time before moving back to her folder.

Seated next to Millicent, a large man of about fifty, with a flat face and sporting a tattered plaid shirt, no tie, seemed out of place next to the other council members. His eyes, although a tad on the intense side, were kind, and laugh lines fanned around them. He spoke to Fred Smith, waving his hands around. His cheeks and nose reddened as he grew more agitated.

Fred said nothing and shook his head, a smile playing on his mouth. He then shifted his gaze to Ryan's.

Tiny fingers of ice tap-danced up his back.

The police chief's smile froze in place, his brown eyes narrowing for a brief moment, but he recovered, and nodded before turning back to the man next to him.

"Who's that guy?" Ryan asked.

"Farley?"

"I know who Farley is. I mean the one talking to the police chief. The guy wearing plaid shirt."

"Oh, that's Ira Raymond. He preaches at the Presbyterian Church, St. Andrews, behind the grocery store. It's the only church in Albertsville. We used to have a Catholic church too, but it burned down about ten years ago. Someone smoking in the confessional they said. The priest, a dear sweet man everyone adored, moved to Timmins. I guess they just never felt the need to rebuild and send another."

"Or Carroll Albert saw no need. I take it he's not a Catholic?"

"See? You learn fast. Ira's okay. I think he's sleeping with the organist, Janice Noel. But I'm just guessing. It's like one of those "worst kept secrets" kind of things. Ira is always making eyes at her. I might be wrong though."

"Nothing wrong with a reverend finding love is there? I'm not sure what the rules of the Presbyterian faith are, but I thought the Catholic Church was the only one that restricted their clergy in that way."

"I think his faith is okay with love and marriage, but not when it's adulterous."

"He's married?" Ryan shifted his gaze to the Reverend who

still spoke to Fred. His face completely flushed now, but his shoulders slumped. Whatever it was he tried to convey to Chief Smith, he'd almost given up.

"No. She is."

"Oh." Again he couldn't think of an appropriate retort. This place was a fucking soap opera—The Frozen and the Illiterate. He chuckled. Reeve Albert would be the redneck's answer to Victor Newman.

"What?"

Startled, he turned to Audrey's frown. "What?"

"What's so funny?"

"Nothing. You wouldn't find it amusing."

"Try me."

A door at the front of the room, one he hadn't noticed next to the Prime Minister's face, opened. Everyone hushed as Carroll Albert strode through. His dark gaze scanned the room, settling almost immediately on him.

Ryan smiled and nodded. Someone must have warned the Reeve of his presence.

Carroll returned the gesture, although his lips thinned to an irritated frown.

He had to give Albert credit, the man had presence, a certain x-factor that would be hard to resist. Tall, with an athletic build and a smile that probably sent more than a few female hearts racing, he knew how to grab attention. Ryan imagined that his charisma, combined with the fear that was palpable in the room, made him seem almost Godlike.

Carroll took the center chair, the comfortable one.

Fred stood, effectively shushing the murmuring crowd. "Please stand."

Ryan rose with the crowd. Shit, did they have to pledge allegiance?

Fred placed a hand over his heart and the rest of the council did the same. The crowd sang the opening lines of the Canadian anthem.

Ryan glanced at Audrey. Eyes forward, she ignored him and sang along. He cringed at the mishmash of voices. They'd never make a choir. A handful of shrill voices rang out over the mostly monotone crowd. He resisted a very strong urge to cover his ears.

Once they'd thoroughly shredded Oh Canada, the crowd sat and Carroll called the meeting to order.

As the council members motioned and seconded repeatedly, Ryan took the opportunity to scan the crowd. Most appeared dressed in their Sunday best, plaid or denim dress shirts buttoned to the collar on the men, muted sweaters or white blouses on the women. Everyone wore some form of black pants and he shifted uncomfortably in his seat. He turned his gaze to Audrey and noted for the first time that she too wore a pale pink sweater and black jeans.

"You might have mentioned the dress code," he whispered.

She smiled and winked. "You didn't ask."

Ryan's lips curved. No, he didn't ask. He sat in his battered old sweatshirt and blue jeans, underdressed in a group of people with whom that shouldn't be possible.

Millicent stood and cleared her throat. "Before we move to the first item on the agenda, I'd like to welcome Ryan Cassidy to Albertsville."

Ryan stiffened at his name.

"Thank you, Millie. I think that's a wonderful idea." *Wonderful* sounded strangled as it passed Carroll's lips.

"Could you stand, Ryan, so everyone can see you?" Millicent blushed, but she smiled.

He stood and gave a slight bow before sinking back down into his chair.

Audrey leaned close to his ear. "See? Bad idea."

"He's a little shy. I'm sure everyone will make him feel comfortable. He'll be with us for a while, settling Melvin and Rachel's estate. Is that correct, Mr. Cassidy?" Carroll pinned him with a friendly smile.

"Yes, but I'm thinking I might stay. I haven't decided yet. Thought I'd wait until spring before I made any firm plans. I've always wondered what a farmer's field looked like right before harvest. Maybe I'll do some planting of my own...

although, I'm sure the soil isn't nearly as good as my neighbors. It's been neglected for so long."

The councilors sobered at this. Only Carroll's smile remained fixed. The others glanced at the Reeve and back to Ryan.

"I understand you must stay for the year, but I'm sure you want to get back to city life once everything is settled. Running a farm is a lot of hard work. You don't even have working equipment. As much as I love my town I have to say, once you've seen one bale of hay you've seen them all."

It was Ryan's turn to smile. "Not for this guy. I enjoy a challenge. Maybe I'll get lucky. Besides, the mountain air agrees with me and you've all been very welcoming."

"Indeed." Carroll turned to Millicent, who shrank into her chair. "Well, nice to have you... however long you're here. What's on the agenda, Fred?"

"Not much. We have to set a date for the upcoming election."

Audrey had been right. It wasn't a coincidence that he'd been asked to attend this particular meeting. Ryan caught Millicent's intense stare. Her eyes were desperate, questioning. What did she think he could do?

"So, to clarify," Carroll interrupted his thoughts. "If you're interested in running for council, you've got until the end of November to get your paperwork into this office. You must have your motion seconded to be valid."

Ryan raised his hand, ignoring Audrey's elbow to his ribs.

Carroll nodded, his face paling.

"Is this only for council? The election I mean. Is your position open as well?"

"Yes, of course it is. Are you running?"

Snickers rippled throughout the room and Ryan's face warmed again. Right. Nice joke. No one would elect the new guy, and politics weren't his forte. "No, I just wanted to clarify. Some municipalities run their council elections separate from mayoral, so I wanted to make sure I understood. This election is for the whole shebang, so to speak, and anyone who might want to make changes, or shake things up a little, can run for council. Am I right?"

"Yes, anyone who wishes to run can do so, for any position. But you have to be nominated. Someone has to back you up, to put it simply. At least one other resident has to want you to run. Is that clear enough?"

"Yes. Thank you."

Carroll turned to the crowd and continued speaking, his voice droning in the back of Ryan's mind. The wheels turned, making an awful racket in his head.

"Don't you dare," Audrey whispered.

"What?"

"You cannot run for council, it's ridiculous. You've only been here a couple of days. No one would elect you anyway. The council is made up of the founding families, always has been."

"I hadn't considered it," he lied. "But, according to what you said the other night… yes, I'm from a founding family."

CHAPTER 8

The fluorescent light over the council table hummed and flickered. Carroll hated fluorescents. The light cold and unflattering, but he he'd tried to be economical. He needed certain luxuries that weren't in the official budget, so some areas had to be sacrificed.

The last of the town's residents finally left after guzzling lukewarm coffee and tea, while gorging on the sweets put out by Millicent and Julia. He sat back in his chair, hands behind his head, eyes closed. As he thought about his next move, nervous coughs, a shifting body to his left, and Fred's cracking knuckles filled his ears.

He'd dismissed Ira, useless fuck that he was, and then Farley had muttered something about the mill and cleared out soon after. Farley never stuck around to field the shit when it flew. Carroll let him go only because if a job needed doing, Farley wouldn't hesitate.

He opened his eyes and turned to Fred. "So, Mr. Cassidy isn't as stupid as we thought."

Fred twirled his pen, set it down, and scratched his widening gut.

The sight made Carroll cringe. God, the man needed to take better care of himself. He would have to start reminding him of how the chief of police should carry himself. It certainly wasn't like some redneck alcoholic with a penchant for sweet rolls. Could Fred even pursue a convict if the need arose? Carroll sniffed. Good thing he could shoot a moving target.

Fred shrugged and cracked another knuckle. "Seems pretty dumb to me."

Carroll looked pointedly at his hands, and curled his lip.

Fred stilled. "I mean, who would think about running for council after a couple days in town? He's just trying to stir shit."

Fred's chatter grated on Carroll's nerves as much as his cracking bones.

"I don't know. I think he might be trying to fit in." Millicent's voice was quiet, hesitant.

Carroll stared and she looked away, shifting further behind Fred's girth. "Really? Millie, I hate to think you're hot for this boy. Shame on you. Old enough to be his mother and you're thinking of getting in his pants."

"That's not—"

"No?"

She closed her mouth, shaking her head.

He stood. "I don't believe you. I think you're allowing the prospect of a little roll in the hay with Chad's son cloud your judgment. I'm not sure that cock size is a genetic thing, love. Junior may have missed the boat on that one."

"Nice. Thanks for the vote of confidence. Jesus, that's disgusting. I just think you're paranoid. He just got here, and he knows nothing. He asked me about the mill and—"

Fred tapped the table with his keys. "Sometimes it pays to be paranoid."

"Right. Fred is absolutely right on. What you call paranoia is what I call covering *my* ass. He wants to know about the Mill? Maybe he wants to check out the fields too. Shall we show him all of it? We've missed something at that damn house. He knows too much. Just trying to fit in, my ass. Jesus Millie. When did you get so stupid?" Carroll walked around the long table toward the door to his office.

"Are we done then?" Millicent asked.

"For now. I need to let things stew a bit before I make my next move. You, my dear, need to start thinking like a predator. I'd have thought you would have had enough of playing prey."

Fred snickered.

Carroll pushed through the small door to sit in silence for a while. His mind worked furiously as he moved to turn on a little lamp on his desk. The shadows scurried away as the lamp's golden glow cast its light over the small room. Slipping his hand beneath the desk's edge, he pressed a small switch next to the drawers. A faint snap echoed from the door.

Turning he pressed a button hidden behind a tall grey filing cabinet. The picture of the Queen quietly slid open above his head to expose his treasure trove. The safe had cost a small fortune, but he didn't mind the expense. The company he'd contracted in Toronto had been discreet and well worth the money. Their men even pretended to be builders finishing up a botched electrical job so that no one suspected anything amiss.

Carroll pulled out a large leather-bound book and flipped it open. He'd marked several pages for quick reference. Even Fred knew nothing of his little hiding place and he aimed to keep it that way. This office was his and his alone.

Perry. He scanned the lines on the page. The Perrys had done nothing to boost this town in a long time. True, Audrey was all that remained of the once proud family, and he now owned their share of the town, but that didn't release her from her responsibility. She would be the perfect weapon against Ryan Cassidy.

Sal's Bar and Grill hummed with activity as Ryan and Audrey pushed through the doors, which teetered precariously on their battered hinges. The patrons, seated at low tables scattered around the room, looked up as they entered. Many turned away, but a handful continued to gawk.

"Maybe we should call it a night," Audrey said.

"Crazy talk. Let's get a drink and find a spot to sit."

"It's Wing Night. I don't know if you noticed, but Sal's has no spots to sit on Wednesdays."

Ryan smiled and walked to the tiny bar at the back of the narrow room. A man wearing a black shirt and pants—covered with a red apron with "Sal's" emblazoned in white on the bib—stood behind the counter wiping a glass with a battered rag. He frowned as Ryan approached and set the glass down before moving toward them.

"Busy spot," Ryan offered.

"Only on Wednesdays and Fridays. The rest of the week it's like a morgue in here." The man's voice was rough, as though he'd swallowed a mouthful of gravel and it lodged in his throat.

"Hey, Sal." Audrey pushed ahead of Ryan and climbed up on a stool. It wobbled, the legs shivering as though they might snap in two under the weight of her small body.

"Miss Perry. What will it be tonight? Gonna go suicide again?"

"Nah, this city boy wouldn't survive that, just plain hot wings tonight. Maybe a half order of your honey garlic too. Just in case he left his balls in Alberta."

Sal winked and then turned to the doors behind the bar, opening to a large grill and a mound of dishes in a grease-spattered steel sink.

"We have hot wings in the real world too, you know?" Ryan said.

"Sure, but not like these. Even the locals can't eat them. Except me, of course."

Ryan snorted and took the stool next to her, testing it first for reliability. The crowd slowly resumed its previous hum, although a few looked his way as they spoke. Carroll and the rest of the council were noticeably absent.

Someone tapped his shoulder and he turned. His knees pressing into Audrey's in the tight space sent a tiny shiver through him. A tall man, frighteningly pale and thin, stood behind him. The dim light of the bar cast shadows over his already sharp features, like the readers of the ghost stories he'd heard while at Scout camp. They'd put a flashlight to their faces and the shadows distorted their features as they did this man's now.

"I just wanted to introduce myself. Kim Farrell. I manage the Mill. I helped your grandpa clear the west field a couple years back. Good man, Melvin was. Sad to see him go like that," he spoke in a rush, his voice softer than Ryan expected.

"I wish I'd known them, but nothing can turn time back no matter how much we want it. Nice to meet you, Kim." Ryan offered his hand.

Kim grasped it briefly in his bony fingers, and then resumed his stance, hands in the back pockets of his baggy black pants. He gazed across the bar.

Ryan followed his gesture to a burly man who sat at the end of the bar nursing a beer. He spoke to no one, scowling at his glass and fidgeting with a coaster.

"Well, just thought someone should say hello to you instead of just staring. They aren't so bad here, just a little backward sometimes. You be careful who you talk to and you'll do fine. Some aren't as friendly as they make out to be. In fact, other than Audrey, I'd be wary of anyone who acts like your friend."

His gaze met Kim's. "I've realized that already and it's barely been a couple days. Are you someone I should be wary of?"

"Nah, I keep to myself mostly. Got my reasons and then some. We won't be sharing a beer or nothing. Promise. You take care. Nice to see you, Audrey," Kim nodded to Audrey and turned, walking around the bar to sit next to the large man that he'd stared at only moments before.

The big man turned. His eyes bored into Kim as the smaller man spoke. Their shoulders touched as they talked and Kim caught Ryan's stare briefly before he averted his gaze back to the bar top.

"Who's that with the mill guy?" he asked.

"That's Calvin Chambers. I'd stay clear of him if I were you."

"Why?"

"Very troubled. He and his wife, Anita, they've got a few kids, very little money, and he's always in here or at the Mill. They used to be so in love, years ago. His family has lived here from the beginning, hers too. He started at the mill when his father died, and everything seemed to go downhill from there. He and Kim are virtually inseparable. There are rumors, but…"

"Rumors? What, like a bro-mance?"

Audrey raised an eyebrow.

The light switch flicked in his head. "They're *gay*? No. Get outta here. That big scary guy? Bullshit. I don't believe it."

"Like I said; rumors. And gay doesn't mean you wear a big sign or anything. I don't know if it's true, but Calvin and Kim seem to toe the line with Carroll better than most. He says jump, they ask how high. Kim's a nice man, and I know he's a little, um… adverse to female company. Calvin, I don't know. He can be okay, but about ten years ago, I guess it was shortly after Chad's accident—your father, I mean—he changed. I don't know, I guess there could be explanations, but I never considered it much. People here change overnight, depending on what Carroll has planned for them."

Ryan held his tongue as the wings arrived.

Sal set down two plates, and a stack of napkins. "Drinks?"

"Coors for me," Audrey said and turned to Ryan.

"The same."

Sal went to the dented steel doors behind the bar and took out two bottles, twisted the tops, and set them in front of the plates on the bar.

Ryan tipped the bottle to his mouth. The cold bitter liquid ran over his tongue. If he were home, he'd be tempted to chug a few and obliterate the stress of the past couple of days. He sighed as he set it back down, resisting the urge to polish off the rest of the bottle.

Audrey laughed. "Needed that, eh?"

"Definitely. I think I'm going to start taking notes for my first novel. It's sure to be a bestseller."

"Notes on what?"

"This town. It's better than a soap opera. You've got a power hungry town official lording over a town full of terrified residents. I suspect he might be some kind of monster, but I'm not sure yet. Either way, I may have to play him down a bit; he's a little cliché. Then there are the individual stories, let's not forget those. Reverend and the organist, the mill manager cavorting with the lumberjack, the crazy lady and her brother— I'm just breathless waiting to hear the rest. Oh and let's not forget the lovesick Larry. I mean every soap opera needs a lonely old moose."

"It's not funny."

"Didn't say it was. It's pathetic really." Ryan picked up a wing, his eyes burning at the tangy aroma of the barbeque sauce that covered them.

"You can't write about them."

"Why can't I? Is there a law against it? Fiction is fiction. No one knows where an author draws inspiration from. Not unless he tells them, and I don't plan to do that."

"You're a writer?"

"I'm a reporter. I mean, I was a reporter. Fiction is my hobby, although I haven't actually finished a manuscript yet, just lots of starts and a couple hundred short stories. It soothes me. Never considered trying to get published till this came up. Now I've got tons of time to think about it." Ryan bit into the wing. Warm grease dripped down his chin and the sauce bit his tongue. He grabbed a napkin and wiped his mouth.

Audrey smiled. "Hot?"

"A bit. I like it hot."

She scowled and picked up a wing.

Ryan frowned when she bit into it and not a drop of greasy sauce marked her mouth or her chin. She ate as though starving, finishing the wing in seconds and then reaching for another. Why was it that women like her, the ones who looked so small and fragile, often ate like starving refugees?

They ate the wings in silence. Ryan let Audrey have the barbeque while he polished off the honey garlic. Not because he couldn't handle the hot wings, but because she seemed to like them so much and ate three before he finished one.

"Excuse me," a woman's voice.

Ryan turned and set his chicken down to greet the source.

A squat woman scowled at him. Ryan guessed she might be in her forties, although the deep frown lines and her pale skin made her appear older. She stood clutching a battered red handbag in front of her ample chest. Her body trembled, and white knuckles wrapped around the worn handle of her purse.

"Hello—"

"I don't have no intention of being friends with you, Mr. Cassidy. You can save that cocky little grin for another female. One that falls for that sort of thing. I just wanted to say something, so it's clear and we can go on about our lives without any trouble. You understand what I'm saying, Mr. Cassidy?" She spoke his name as though it tasted foul on her lips.

Well shit.

Audrey kept her face averted, focused on wiping her hands.

Back to the woman Ryan smiled again. "All right. I'm all ears."

"I know your type and I don't like it. I don't like the problems you're causing already. You think you can come in here and charm everyone with your baby face and that butter-won't-melt smile, but you're wrong. What was that bullshit at the meeting? Trouble, that's what. Some of us have a brain in our head and we remember where you come from. Your mother was a conniving little slut and your father no better than a pedophile. White trash. That's what you are. Melvin and Rachel used their money to gain respect. Cassidys always did feel they were better than anyone. I don't care if your great granddaddy helped found this town; none of them were worth shit. Lord knows there was nothing about your parents that's respectful. Weren't even married."

Audrey choked and sputtered. Grabbing her beer she swigged down half the bottle before she set it down. She still didn't look at Ryan.

He raised an eyebrow at the woman, startled at the outburst. "I'm sorry you feel that way, ma'am. I'm afraid I can't speak for my father or my grandparents as I didn't know them and I have to give you the benefit of the doubt. Perhaps they were all jackasses, I don't know. But I can speak for my mother, and I'll politely ask that you never let her name pass your lips again. I promise you won't have to tolerate my cocky smile or charm if you do."

"You're nothing special. My husband would wipe the floor with you if I told him to. Just get out of our town and leave things be. I can tell you're up to no good. We got enough problems without some city boy coming in and making it worse. Do us all a favor and go back where you come from. You Cassidys are nothing but trouble, every one of you. This is your only warning. You cause shit in this town and you wind up at the wrong end of a chipper just like your daddy." She spun away and marched to the door.

Ryan sat speechless. He felt the eyes on him, but didn't bother to look around at the other patrons. How many more hated his family as much as she did? Suddenly the stories weren't so amusing, and he understood why his mother told him that the only thing waiting for them in Albertsville was ignorance and hate.

"Sorry. I probably should have said something but I think you handled her as well as I could have." Audrey stood, wiping her hands on a napkin and then shrugged. "I did warn you."

"That was?"

"Anita Chambers."

Ryan caught the brooding stare of the crazy woman's husband seated across the bar. From the seat next to him Kim stared open-mouthed, eyes wide.

"She didn't bother me, really. You get people like her no matter where you go; bitter, miserable souls who can find nothing good about anyone. What concerns me is that her husband might feel the same. That's a big man; a big, angry man. I don't need that kind of attention."

"You're silly." Audrey threw two twenties on the counter and slid off her stool.

"We're going?"

"I've had enough, haven't you?"

"Yeah. Thanks for dinner." He stood and let her to lead the way to the doors.

Heads turned as the left, and Ryan breathed a sigh of relief when the doors closed.

"You see that?" Calvin Chambers pointed his chin to the doors.

Kim nodded. "Yeah, I don't think he's so bad. Seems nice and honest to me. That's not something we have in abundance around here."

"Like you'd know. He looks like his old man. That's probably why you're partial to him. You always made eyes at Chad." Calvin took a swig from his beer and glared at the door. He hated that his gut still burned with jealousy over the man. Chad was dead. Calvin had seen it, listened as the cocky prick took his last breath. He shouldn't care, shouldn't even want to care. But he did.

"I didn't do anything like that. Chad was the only one in this town who knew what I was and was still kind to me, didn't treat me any different because of it. Everyone else makes their speculations, but they don't know for sure and they treat me like shit because of rumors. Besides, I don't know why you hated Chad so much. He tried to do something for us, and he got killed for it."

"They don't hate you cause you're g—because of that. They hate you because you took over for Douglas at the Mill. They all loved that man. That's all. They'd have hated anyone who took that job. That's why I turned it down. Chad wasn't helping no one but himself. He didn't give two shits about you or me. All he wanted to do was nail Carroll. Asshole would have fucked us all to see it happen. You're too soft sometimes."

"Whatever. Bunch of fucking rednecks."

Kim's flushed cheeks and trembling hands—as he toyed with the coaster—tormented him. Those long fingers stroked the cardboard and his pants tightened. Jesus, why did he let a man do this to him? He hated this weakness, this sin he was forced to live in. The devil introduced himself years before, but he'd pushed him away. The day he'd met Kim Farrell the bastard moved in for good.

He had stayed late that night to help Kim fix a busted belt on the big conveyor, and then Kim invited him back to his place for a beer. He went, telling himself he was only being nice. Kim was the new guy and maybe if he proved to everyone that he was okay, they'd lay off. Stop being so nasty to him. But Calvin had known better, even as he whispered the lies to himself. He'd known as they drove home from the mill, as he'd inhaled the musky scent of Kim's aftershave mingled with the heady aroma of wood shavings and sweat. For most of his life he'd been telling himself that his longings weren't right. Men didn't like other men like that. But Kim laughed about something and turned. They'd shared a look, a long, silent stare that said more than words ever could have as Kim unlocked his door and let him pass.

As he entered the dark house, he tried to think of the day he'd exorcised the demon from his soul. Tried to remind himself how hard he'd worked to be normal. He'd gone to church camp for the last time at thirteen and realized how awful and dirty he could really be. The other boy had cried when he told him that they'd made a mistake, and he'd vowed never to let the devil take him like that again. He'd fought the urges, and buried them deep down in the secret part of his soul he never visited. But Kim, well, he'd never felt such an emotion for another human being before. When he was a boy, he could excuse it, blame it on hormones. Now... Damn him to hell. Now he was trapped, loving a man in a way he had no right doing.

Kim stood and reached into his pocket to retrieve a couple of bills. He laid them on the bar and picked his coat off the stool.

"You going home?" Calvin asked.

"Thought it might be time. You?"

"Nah, Anita's there. She's in a right bitch in case you hadn't noticed. Don't know why she gives a shit about that kid. Not like his old man ever done anything to her."

"Maybe if he had, she wouldn't be your problem anymore."

Calvin snorted and pushed off his stool. Kim sat down again to wait, as he always did. Calvin wandered to the door, pausing here and there to chat with neighbors and coworkers as he did.

He felt the stares, but dulled by the ache in his gut; the agony of waiting before Kim joined him. People waved as Calvin left, and he told himself the knowing smiles were his imagination. Only two people knew his secret. He'd paid Carroll Albert more than enough to ensure it never got out, and he'd keep paying until he died. Turning back, he nodded to Kim. He pushed through the door and continued through the path behind the bar toward Kim's house. He lifted a hand to his chest, his fingers seeking the key threaded on a thick chain and hidden beneath his shirt.

CHAPTER 9

Large wet flakes pelted Carroll's face. He rapped on Audrey's door. Grey clouds, heavy with precipitation covered the dim light of the morning. He cursed, knocked again, and then pressed the bell.

Glaring at the piece of shit parked in the driveway, he leaned to peer in the window next to the door. Dark. She could not be sleeping. She liked to be up and out the door before dawn to jog while no one roamed the streets.

He should have gotten rid of the mouthy little bitch along with Melvin and Rachel. She'd never been a team player anyway, and buddying up with those two troublemakers didn't help her cause. Had she confided her suspicions to anyone yet? The question bothered him for a while. He'd almost taken her out just to be safe, but then her attitude changed.

Still, women could be unpredictable. Just when you thought you'd handled them, they went crazy, blabbing things that got them into hot water. Carroll found it best to keep a woman busy and her lips from flapping. If Audrey stayed in his town, she would have to stay busy.

He rapped on the door again. The aluminum frame rattled on its hinges. Her silence stretched his patience to the limit. A thump sounded inside. He tucked his hands into his parka. The snow melted as it fell on his head and trickled down his face. "Fucking bitch."

Audrey's pale face appeared in the window. She frowned but the lock turned. *About time.* The interior door opened. Audrey stared from behind the screen door, but didn't move to open it.

"Can I speak to you?" he asked.

"Sure."

"Can I talk to you inside? It's rather wet out here."

"I'm not dressed."

Oh, for the love of Christ. "I didn't come here to seduce you. You're hardly my type. We need to talk. That's all."

Bundled in a worn blue robe, with her curly mop of brown hair piled on top of her head, face free of makeup, Audrey looked about twelve years old. He reconsidered his promise. She'd probably be like a ripe young virgin, despite her thirty-two years. In fact, Carroll didn't recall the girl ever having a boyfriend. Perhaps she'd never experienced a man at all. She stared. Oh, if she only knew the direction of his thoughts, she wouldn't be so cool.

"Well?" he prompted.

"Fine, but I have to get to the store soon. So make it quick." Audrey flipped the lock and walked away.

Little bitch thought she could treat him like some regular Joe? Fat chance. She wasn't scared enough. Fred suggested a few deliciously cruel ideas when they'd discussed how to keep her quiet. But she hadn't done a thing, so he'd filed Fred's suggestions away for later. Perhaps Miss Perry required a little lesson before he made her help him deal with Cassidy.

He yanked the door open and followed her inside the dark cottage, stepping into the tiny living room and toward the light that shone in the kitchen at the back. Carroll curled his lip. The entire house could hear you shit in this pathetic little place. Disgusting.

He brushed the snow off his coat, leaving a trail of slush as he clomped into the kitchen.

Audrey turned from the counter and looked pointedly at his

feet. "You always walk through people's houses with your wet boots on?"

"I don't have time—"

"Right. Let's get it over with."

Carroll crossed the short distance between them. "I think you've forgotten who you're speaking to. I think that you've been making googly eyes, dreaming about fucking Mr. Cassidy, and now you think you're something special. Let me remind you how things work here. You are nothing. You're here because I let you be here. I could have you gone with a word. You owe *me*, not him."

Her green eyes widened, but he didn't see enough fear in their depths. She'd paled, but her shoulders remained back, her jaw set at a stubborn angle.

"Please don't hold anything back, Carroll. Tell me how you really feel."

Carroll pressed his lips together. The little kitchen boasted bright orange walls decorated with roosters. Rooster clock, plates, dishtowels, and even rooster placemats on the small round table jammed into the corner. Didn't matter how much money or intelligence someone had, low class always showed through. He turned back to Audrey who leaned against the counter. He smiled, moving so that his body pressed against hers. She stiffened and he imagined the moisture from his coat seeping through her housecoat, chilling her bare skin and hardening her nipples.

Carroll could almost taste the salt on her skin as he inhaled her scent. There's the fear. "Why are you spending so much time with Cassidy? I thought you agreed you'd convince him to leave, not get cozy with him."

She sighed and set her cup down on the counter. Carroll shifted his gaze to the parted neck of her robe. She wore nothing beneath it and heat surged through his groin. He could take her right now and she couldn't lift a finger to stop him. Maybe he'd find out if Cassidy had given her a go.

Audrey lowered her arms to her sides. "I am trying to get him on your side. That's why I went over there. And I haven't spent much time with him. We talked his first day here, and then he came to get some paint and supplies later. He followed me into the meeting the other night. He's curious about a couple of things. I don't know what to tell him."

Carroll couldn't quite say how he knew she lied, but his bullshit alarm shrieked in warning. "You don't? Well, I'd tell him to mind his damn business. Tell him whatever will get him to leave. But I don't think you want any of those things to happen. You're either lying to me or you're not trying hard enough."

"He wants his inheritance. I think if you just let him be, you'd find he's not such a threat. He's not what you think he is. That's the problem. The more he's pushed to leave I guarantee he'll become more determined to stay. If we just leave him alone, he'll probably get bored."

Carroll reached up to run his fingers along her jaw. She shivered as he trailed down her neck to the V in her housecoat. Her heart pounded a nervous staccato beneath his fingertips. "I doubt he'll ever get close to bored. You are strangely attractive, you know? Because you've been a good girl, I've left you alone. Maybe that was a mistake."

"You can't do anything to me." Her words came out on a breath, barely audible.

"I can't? Get him out of here by Christmas or I'll have to rectify the error I've made in ignoring your presence in my town. You contribute nothing, have never done anything to make this town better, and I can't allow that anymore."

"I'll do what I can."

Carroll leaned down, brushing his mouth across hers. Her lips parted and her body stiffened against him. Flicking his tongue against her lower lip, he smiled at her sharp intake of breath. He lowered his hand to her hip and pulled her closer. "You'll do more than that. Find out what he knows and what he plans to do about it."

She swallowed.

Carroll's gaze moved to her throat. Her skin bloomed under his scrutiny. "You know, I've never noticed how green your eyes are before, Audrey. You're blushing. Why is that?"

"I—it's warm in here. Stop trying to scare me. I'm too old for you."

He squeezed her bottom and she pulled away, but the counter prevented her from escaping his body. "Usually, I'd agree. Most women your age are used up, withered and dry. You're different though, so tiny, soft and untouched. Have you ever had a boyfriend? A lover?"

"That's none of your business. I said I'd do what you wanted and I'm trying. What you're doing right now amounts to rape. I don't want you to touch me."

"I don't have to rape anyone. You're quite mistaken. I seduce women and when I'm done, they beg for more. I always leave them quite satisfied. I bet you're anticipating my touch, yearning for it, despite your little act. Imagine my lips on your body, my tongue licking, tasting places no one's tried. You'd press my face into you, and you'd moan for more. Of course, I'd oblige. I bet you taste so fucking sweet. What's wrong, Audrey? You're panting like a bitch in heat."

She tried to turn her face but Carroll captured her chin in his hand, forcing her to look at him. "Don't be ashamed because you want to feel me inside of you. You're hot right now, aren't you? Are things getting damp under that rag? Hmm? I bet they are. You can be honest with me. We're both consenting adults after all. Maybe I should check. It's normal for a woman to want sex, especially a woman who hasn't had a man show her what her body is for. I'd teach you things you haven't even imagined. Would you like that?"

She shuddered as his hands moved to the front of her robe, toying with the tie that held it closed. She turned her head from his mouth and closed her eyes.

"Please just leave. I don't want you, and I never will. I want you to leave me alone." Audrey's voice no longer held its edge of steel. It faltered, no more than a whimper.

"No you don't. Stop lying to yourself. If you don't get rid of Cassidy, I'll come back. Then we'll see how much you don't want my touch." Carroll bent to press his mouth against her neck, and slipped his hands inside her robe to feel the warm skin of her stomach. He lowered them through soft hair before he slipped a finger insider her. Just as he thought. Women couldn't deny this. Audrey recoiled as he moved his finger, raising her hands to his chest to push against him. Just like a virgin.

He backed away, slowly licking his fingers as he inhaled her scent.

Her face flushed.

He chuckled.

She kept her gaze on the faded tile at her bare feet.

"I want him gone. I don't care how you do it." He turned and strode out of the nauseating kitchen and to the front door.

He paused on the front step to gaze at the swirling haze above him. His smile faltered. The snow had grown so thick he could barely make out the sky for all the whiteness. It was too early for this kind of weather. But he couldn't control Mother Nature, no matter how much he wished he could.

Carroll whistled as he strode to his Hummer, parked on the curb. Cassidy would go, whether Audrey did her job or not. Carroll didn't care if he went on his own, or in a box, he'd be gone by Christmas. And Audrey… he opened the door replaying in his mind the way she'd tightened around his fingers.

Audrey hugged her robe tight, shivering as the SUV's engine roared outside. She stood against the counter, her gaze on the puddles left by Carroll's boots. When the vehicle's sound faded she sank to the floor.

His eyes, the way they'd changed as he drew closer, darkening from blue to almost black when he pressed his body to hers, refused to be banished from her brain. His hands on her body, inside… Then his breath on her face. She shuddered again. How long until he just took what he wanted? She hoped he'd forgotten her by now, had avoided him all this time and remained apart from everyone else for just that reason. Now she'd allowed herself to be as wrapped in his bullshit as everyone else. Her stomach churned as she recalled her body's traitorous reaction to his hands.

Unable to move from her spot on the floor in front of her counter, she hugged her knees to her chest. The memory of what Carroll Albert would do if he thought you might not be loyal had haunted her dreams for many years, long after her parents died. She should have left.

Audrey snorted, blinking away the tears that threatened to spill. Like she could have left, despite what she'd told Ryan. She might not have taken money from Carroll, but she turned her head to everyone who had, and the things he asked them to do in payment for his generosity.

The evening she'd first encountered Carroll without the presence of another adult, had been warm and full of promise. Crickets sang in the fields and mosquitoes swarmed as the sun set over the pastures. Audrey had been exploring. The rest of the town celebrated the Canada Day weekend at the Douglas place. She'd wandered off, bored and itching to dig into the new Stephen King book she'd snuck home from the library. Audrey had told her mother she felt a little sick and wanted to leave. Her mother looked like she might say no, but her father—who believed at fifteen independence was important—had told Audrey to go on. They'd be home soon.

Fiddling with the worn tie of her robe, Audrey smiled at the memory of her parents. They'd waved as she walked away; believing nothing could harm their smart, responsible daughter. She remembered walking past the Cassidy place, wondering if Melvin and Rachel were okay. Their son had died only a short while ago, and they'd retreated to their farm saying little to anyone. Audrey didn't know the details at the time, but she knew from conversations her parents had late at night when they thought she was sleeping, that Chad Cassidy hadn't fallen onto the conveyor as Farley claimed. But no one else had been there, so no one disputed it. Audrey thought she'd heard rumors that Calvin Chambers had been scheduled to work that night, but those rumors died a fast death. Just like most of the rumors in Albertsville.

The lights in the rambling farmhouse were off so she continued through the fields toward her own house. She crossed the Alberts's yard a short time later. The pool house light was on. She hadn't seen the new Reeve at the festivities in town. She'd seen his family, and the rest of the council, but Carroll Albert had been absent.

The rumor at school was that Carroll offered special deals to girls who were nice to him. He got them cool jobs—like cleaning his house, working at the Municipal Building and even scholarships to college—but he liked a little in return. Audrey didn't know if all that was true, but some girls suddenly had nice clothes and neat jobs now and then. Her fifteen-year-old heart fluttered at the thought of doing what the girls described with the Reeve. He wasn't gross like the other adults his age. He was kind of cute, like a movie star. Though, Audrey couldn't imagine him wanting to date a young girl. His wife was beautiful and he could get into trouble for that kind of thing. He seemed smart enough to know that he'd risk his reputation and his position as the town's leader by doing what those girls said he did.

Audrey shivered, hugging her body tighter as she remembered walking through the yard, believing her naïve thinking was logical. Only a kid would believe someone like Carroll would worry about being caught.

She'd paused. A cry, then choking sounds from inside the pool house. The Reeve was supposed to be in town, but maybe he was sick. Audrey wavered, her feet pushing her to keep moving, but her curiosity drew her to investigate the little hut next to the kidney-shaped pool.

Curiosity won, and Audrey stepped to the door. She raised her hand to the brass handle, but the door swung in before she touched it and Carroll Albert stood, frowning.

"Can I help you—Audrey, is it?" he asked.

She looked up at the Reeve and shook her head. "N—no, I heard a noise. I wanted to make sure you were okay."

He'd smiled then, and Audrey's teenage heart fluttered struck again by how hot he was for a grown up.

"That's sweet. As you can see, I'm quite all right. Would you like to come inside the house for a minute? Shouldn't you be at home? It's getting dark."

"I was just going. Thanks." Audrey turned to leave but he grabbed her arm. She looked at the door. Closed. She tugged her arm but his hand tightened and he didn't seem so cool anymore.

"No. I need to talk to you. Don't be afraid. You're always so quiet, flitting here and there, and I never see you unless you're at your mother's side."

"You probably want to go back to... what you were doing."

"I'm finished. Come to the house with me for a bit. I'll just shower and take you home. I won't bite, unless you ask me to" He winked, moving his hand to hers and gently pulling her toward the house.

Audrey rubbed her arms. She could still feel his fingers biting into her bare flesh. The next morning she had to cover the tiny bruises he'd left. Although his hands were rough, and fear crept slowly into her belly, urging her to run, to fight, Audrey had followed him, knowing it was a bad idea but afraid to anger him. Something about Carroll Albert made her want to keep him happy, to make him like her. She didn't know why, she'd never cared if people liked her before. Her body trembled when he looked back and winked at her, and her palms felt cold, but sweaty like when Charlie Dawson had smiled at her in math class and asked to borrow her pencil. She'd wiped her hands on her shorts, hoping Carroll didn't notice.

The wind howled outside. She should lock the door in case Carroll came back, but couldn't move from her spot on the floor, the memories unfolding too fast to stop them.

That night inside his house, her eyes had rounded at the opulence of the furniture. She turned to Carroll's soft chuckle.

"Come on, I'll show you around," he'd said and pressed a hand to the small of her back.

Audrey had followed him upstairs, and he'd pushed open doors as they passed through the long hallway. Three bathrooms and four bedrooms later, they'd arrived at a double set of doors at the very end of the hall. He opened them and ushered her inside. His room.

Audrey closed her eyes as the memory of that night flooded back. She slipped her arms back to her knees in an attempt to stop her body's instinctive tremor. Warm moisture trailed down her cheeks, a cruel reminder that she'd fooled herself into believing that he hadn't hurt her. She didn't want to remember, had avoided Albert as much as she could so that she never had to. Now, it wouldn't go away.

He'd shut the doors. His smile vanished, his eyes narrowed and he'd dragged her against him. She cried out and he silenced her with his mouth. His hands had roamed her body, cruelly pinching and squeezing and she'd gagged when he thrust his tongue into her mouth. She'd pushed at him but he'd been so much bigger, still was so much bigger.

"What did you see?" He slipped the strap of her tank top down, and sank his teeth into her shoulder.

"Nothing. Please let me go. You're scaring me."

But he didn't release her. Instead he'd put his hand down the back of her shorts. "What have we here?"

"Don't—" She pushed at him and he moved his hand around to her stomach, yanking the button open on her cutoffs and forcing his hand inside.

"I asked you a question. Maybe you want me to show you what I've shown your friends. Is that it? Were you jealous? Thought I didn't notice you? I don't want you to feel left out."

"N—no. I'm sorry. I want to go home."

"I'm not through yet. I'll take you home, but you have to do something for me first."

Audrey's heart had pounded in her chest, so hard she thought she might die of fright right there. His fingers slipped down and she'd frozen, unable to move, unable to do anything but stare at his face smiling down at her, his eyes knowing. She wanted him to stop, but her body leaned into his touch. Sickened she'd closed her eyes and cried.

"Now, what did you see?" he'd asked, lowering his mouth

to her face, brushing her chin, then her neck with his lips.

"I didn't see anything."

"You're lying." He pushed at her shorts, shoving them over her hips.

"I'm not. Please, Mr. Albert, I don't want to do this."

"I'm not partial to whiners, and you're beginning to wear on my nerves. You don't want me angry with you, do you, Audrey?"

She'd shaken her head.

He released her, moving to the door before turning to pin his dazzling smile on her.

Audrey hiked up her shorts and risked walking toward him. As she passed into the hallway his hand touched her arm. She turned, still unable to look at him.

"You saw nothing, just like you said. If I hear that you did see something, I'll give you what you're asking me for. Mommy and Daddy won't have anything to say about it either. The dead don't tell stories. Clear?"

Audrey nodded and he let her go. She'd hurried down the hall and nearly fell as she barreled down the stairs and ran through the patio doors to the yard. She'd ignored the pool house and ran home.

Kelly Thompson missed school that week. Two weeks later, the principal announced that Kelly had run away; anyone who knew her whereabouts should come to his office immediately. No one knew where she went. Fred wrote the whole thing off as a rebellious teen taking off and Audrey made herself believe him. But now, as she sat on her kitchen floor, the memories of that night haunting her, she admitted that in the fleeting moment before Carroll had shut the door to the pool house, she'd seen the body of a girl on the folding bed. Kelly hadn't run away.

CHAPTER 10

Howling drifted to Ryan's window from somewhere behind the house.

"Damn wolves." He stretched and glanced at his watch. Jesus, he'd slept the afternoon away.

Another long howl broke the silence. Maybe he should get a rifle, or at the very least a pellet gun. Surely everyone out here owned a firearm. They probably knew how to use it too, unlike him.

His muscles protested at his hasty attempt to move. He'd started painting in the bedroom before the sun rose that morning. When he went downstairs to clean up, large flakes floated down to wrap the deck in a thin white blanket. Ryan watched awhile, finding comfort in the soft rhythmic pattern of the snow.

Admiring his new grey-blue bedroom, he congratulated himself on a job well done. It looked a damn sight more mas-culine than the peach.

He shifted to sit on the edge of the bed and turned to the window. About an inch of snow piled on the ledge. "Shit."

In the few hours he'd slept, the snow had coated the entire field, sparkling in the waning light. Ryan turned, grabbed his sweater from the chair, and headed to the door. More coffee, and then he'd go see how bad the lane was.

He made his way down the steps, sleep still clinging to the corners of his brain. Shadows crept over the walls of the kitchen, making him long to climb back into bed. Instead, he went to the cupboard and pulled down the duck. The lid tilted as he set it down, revealing the bottom of the canister. Ryan tapped the scoop against the side. A hollow clang echoed back. "I forgot all about you, little duck."

Dumping the remaining grinds onto the counter, he tipped the duck back over. He reached down and pulled a drawer open. Hadn't he seen a...*there it is*. From inside the drawer, he rescued a tiny blue penlight, pressed the switch to test it, and shone its beam inside the canister. A tiny crack ran around the perimeter.

He leaned across the counter, pulled a knife from the block and then inserted its tip into the crack. The bottom shifted as he ran the knife around. "Damn."

A bundle of papers, sealed inside a plastic bag, occupied the hidden space. For reasons Ryan didn't understand, he wasn't eager to examine its contents, even though it could help to make sense of the crazy-talking people of Albertsville. After a deep breath, he grabbed the bag. Probably pictures of Larry and Melvin or something silly like baby pictures of his father.

From the bag, he pulled out a stack of yellowed paper and several photographs. More mystery? He fanned the pictures, some relatively sharp, others faded and dog-eared. In the first shot, a younger Farley pointed at the photographer outside the mill. The next showed the same place at night, with shadows crowding an upper window and a red circle staining the snow. There were photos of marijuana fields and sheds. Is this what they think they're hiding?

The last image was faded and torn at the edges. Ryan held it close to his face. A building, lined with tall fences. In the background a large and very deep crevasse, mountains of white sand piled behind it. The mine?

He set them aside with the rest and turned to the handwritten pages. Dates, times, and names. None of it made any sense to Ryan. Some of them were more than fifty years old. Ryan set the first page behind him and read the second.

Melvin

I know where you've been and what you've done, but your little story is missing some pieces. You're terrible at hide and seek. Stop the nonsense. Bad things always happen to good people. I'd hate to see you end up like Chad.

It wasn't signed, but Ryan didn't need to see a signature. His grandparents had found something and paid the ultimate price.

Ryan's attempts to drive down the farm's winding lane without shoveling proved interesting. His car didn't slide and he avoided slamming into a tree, but he almost became stuck a couple of times, the car's wheels spinning before gaining traction and lurching forward.

The trees that lined the drive had turned from green to white. Their branches drooped under the weight of the snow, making the winding laneway feel even more cocoon-like than they had on his first trip to the house. The eerie silence, punctuated by the occasional moan of the wind—as it pushed drifts of snow before his car—set Ryan's nerves on edge.

At the end of the driveway he had to take a couple of runs, reversing a few feet and gunning it forward to mow through a snow bank the plow had left behind. Skidding through on the fourth try, he maneuvered onto the road leading into town; its dingy white surface dusted with brown sand.

He drove at a crawl, not willing to test the road's reliability even with the sand. He could easily picture his car wrapped around a tree or in the middle of a field. Given Albertsville's tendency toward unexplained accidents, that might happen no matter how careful he was.

Something moved on the road ahead and he leaned over the wheel. The blowing snow made it difficult to see more than a couple of feet in front his headlights. Had Larry ventured out of the bush? As he drew closer, the dark figure ahead gathered substance with two legs, not four, and blond hair.

Millicent Douglas waved her arms.

Ryan pulled to the side. Her truck—the bottom of it any-way—lay a good five feet past the ditch.

Millicent's hands fell to her chest, fidgeting with the ends of a red scarf tied loosely at her neck.

Ryan switched on his four-ways and stepped out into the blizzard. He blinked, momentarily blinded.

Millicent rushed forward to hug him.

A strong scent of lavender drifted from her damp hair. Ryan tried not to curl his nose.

"Oh thank you for stopping. I thought I'd be stuck out here. The wolves have been coming closer to town this year and I did *not* want to be here after dark with them lurking in the bushes." She released him and her hands resumed worrying the ends of her scarf.

Ryan glanced to the bushes. They sounded closer each night but he'd hoped it was only his paranoia that made it seem that way. "You're okay?"

"Yes, I'm fine. I'm such an idiot. I dropped my phone, so I bent to pick it up. When I looked up again, I saw a stupid deer in the middle of the road. I don't know what I was thinking; I swerved, touched the brake, and hit the shoulder and that was it. The truck damn near flew. I might be a bit sore tomorrow, but I'm okay otherwise."

Ryan nodded and turned to the truck once more. She'd need a tow to get it out, something bigger than his car anyway. "Did you call anyone?"

Millicent laughed and shook her head. "That's the funniest part. I dropped my phone when the truck flipped and now I can't find it."

"Want a ride home then? I know you probably don't want to be seen with me, so we should get off the road."

She frowned. "Why wouldn't I want to be seen with you?"

"Come on. Carroll doesn't want me here. I don't really un-derstand why. It's not like I know anything about anything. But you're one of his right hand men... women. I'm sure he'd be less than impressed if you were seen too often in my company."

Millicent's eyes narrowed and she lowered her hands to her sides. "I don't care what that man says. I pick my own friends. I'd love a ride home, but not because I'm afraid to be seen with you. I hope you stay forever."

"Forever?"

"Yes." Millicent nodded and moved past him to his car.

Forever was a long time. Way too long to stay in this place. But if Ryan didn't stay the year, he'd never forgive himself. This was one battle Carroll would not win.

He climbed in next to Millicent.

She leaned forward in the passenger seat, to fix her snow-drenched hair in the rear view and paused when he shut his door. "I know. Hopeless."

Ryan didn't comment. He turned the key and pulled onto the road.

Millicent was silent for a couple of minutes.

Ryan waited. He'd mastered the comfort of silence. In his line of work, it was something you learned fast if you wanted to get the story. Most people talked to fill it, and needed little prompting to share things they wouldn't otherwise. Millicent didn't disappoint him.

"I want to say again how sorry I am about your grandparents. They were good people. So was your father."

She stared out the window, her hands back to her scarf.

"I didn't know any of them. But thanks."

"Your dad wasn't what they made him out to be. He was young and in love, and your mom was so beautiful. They had a future, but then she crossed Carroll and, well, you know how that turned out, right."

"Mmm," Ryan slowed as the sand ended and whiteness covered the road.

"I mean, sure she was young. Fifteen is a tender age, but he wasn't much older. No one thought anything of it, not even your grandparents, until Carroll got involved. Chad was just nineteen and was supposed to go off to university the year be-

93

fore. He met your mom, and I guess everything else disappeared for him. He took a job at the mill, the worst decision he could have made, and decided to wait for her."

"You remember all of this? You couldn't have been more than what—twelve?" Ryan didn't want to hint that she was too much older than her actual age, women got funny about that.

"I was fifteen. Your mother and I were classmates. She loved Chad more than anything and it wasn't your typical teenage first crush, nothing immature like that. They really cared about each other. Her parents had gone on some kind of trip, chartered a little plane. It crashed. She lost them just two months before she found out she was pregnant. She'd been staying with Melvin and Rachel while her parents were away, and they kept her afterward. Your mom probably told you all of this."

She paused. Ryan shook his head.

"Well, she was horrified. So embarrassed, and she didn't want to tell Chad because she knew he'd do the right thing and she wanted him to go to school."

"So she moved to avoid tying him down?"

The snow had eased a bit, enabling Ryan to see more of the road ahead. Darkness crept over the fields, elongating the shadows of the trees.

His mother had blamed people, not events, when she spoke of those days. She'd said ignorant people with dirty minds had forced her out, that she didn't have time for that kind of thing.

"No, she moved because she had no choice. She had a small inheritance, no friends, and someone planted drugs on her at school. Carroll made sure she knew her options. Leave or he'd make sure she never saw her child."

Ryan digested this as Millicent's mailbox came into view. He turned into the short driveway, pulling to a stop in front of a small cabin nestled among the trees. "This is nice."

"Thank you. It's all I have left. I had to sell the farm after Justin arrived, it was too expensive, and really, with just the two of us, I didn't need a big old house like that anyway."

She put her hand on the door and Ryan reached to touch

her arm.

She turned, raising a thin brow.

"No one stood up for my mother?"

"Your dad did. He tried to say the drugs were his, but Fred said he'd go to the proper authorities and have her declared unfit before you were even born. She couldn't bear that and they knew it."

"What happened to my dad? The truth, I mean. Not some half-truth wrapped in bullshit. Did he really find something at the mill?"

"Where did you hear that?" Millicent glanced to the end of her driveway and back to him.

"Nowhere, I'm grasping at straws. My grandparents hinted that the mill was the reason for all the trouble. What goes on there?"

"Just regular mill stuff. The mine is the real mystery."

"The mine?" Ryan needed to keep notes. So many clues but no way to decipher them.

"Forget I said anything. Please."

"I will, if you tell me what happened to my father. You must know."

"No one does, not really. Maybe Calvin and Farley, but they aren't going to tell the truth."

"Was it an accident?"

"No."

"Why don't you go to the police? I mean, you probably know more than everyone else. You can prove what they can't. Why do you let him get away with it?"

Millicent averted her gaze, staring out at the snow-covered deck of her house, her lips pressed together.

Ryan thought she might not answer. But then her shoulders slumped.

"Have you met our police? Fred is in Carroll's pocket. No matter what anyone reports, Fred makes it go away."

"Why not go higher than Fred?"

"Then I'll go away. That's how it works here. Only a handful of people went beyond Fred, and they're no longer with us.

One family made it out, or we thought they did. No one's heard from them since the day they drove out of town. Considering they said they were blowing the lid off Albertsville and we've yet to see anyone come by asking about it, I'd say that Carroll or someone working with him got to them before they made it out of town. You can't win against them."

"You can't cover up murder. Even the great Carroll Albert doesn't have that much power."

"Carroll controls everything, and that gives him all the power he needs. He makes sure he finds all of your secrets. If he can't dig anything up, he makes one for you. He could ruin this town. What little we have is valuable to us."

"Is your secret so terrible that it's worth keeping instead of being free of him?"

Millicent snorted. "It's more than just a secret."

She got out of the car and walked to her porch, mounting the snow-covered steps without turning back.

Ryan stared at the closed door. If only for the pain Carroll caused his mother, for the way these people turned their backs on a young girl when she needed them most, he'd find out what the hell was going on.

Sometimes, Carroll was certain that the good Lord tested him just to see if he was worthy of His favor. Ryan Cassidy had to be one of those tests. Slamming the laptop closed, he scowled. This snow would be another, slightly less catastrophic test. If the meteorologist that predicted a relatively dry winter lived in Albertsville he'd find himself on the wrong end of a chainsaw by nightfall.

It might not amount to much, early snowfall rarely did, but as Carroll stared out the window at the laden trees, the deck that resembled a large snow sculpture and the ominous clouds in the sky, he knew it was unlikely the snow would be a temporary nuisance. The forecast, according to the Weather Channel as of five minutes ago, called for several inches of the shit, followed by freezing rain and more snow before the temperature plummeted. They'd be stuck for a while if it froze. The roads out of town would be impassable until they could get the plows and sanders through. Such things were an unnecessary expense for Albertsville and Carroll stood by that decision, but sometimes he wished he didn't have to live at the mercy of the neighboring municipality to get the road cleared. Being stuck in town normally worked to his favor—but not when Cassidy was trapped here with him. Outsiders meant trouble.

Audrey wouldn't bother to find a reason to push him out. Carroll wasn't stupid. Until his last visit, she hadn't tried to force Ryan out at all. Now she had another reason to stall. Ryan couldn't leave with this damn snow.

The phone rang. Carroll tried to locate it among the mess in front of him. He rifled through the paperwork, damn responsibility. The small black phone vibrated on the edge of his desk. He picked it up and checked the number before putting it to his ear. "What did you find?"

Farley's voice crackled back, the weather making the connection sketchy. "Nothing. He had a girl, dated through college, kinda slowed down a couple years ago. Then his mom died and the girl moved away or something. Seems like a waste of time if you ask me."

"I didn't. Fred already told me this shit. Didn't you find anything new?"

"Let's see, he worked for some rinky-dink paper, then for the local news station, one of those freelance guys, sold his shit around to whoever would take it, and then Melvin and his old lady die and he quits that shit and hightails it up here."

"He has no criminal record? Not even a parking ticket? I find that hard to believe." Carroll looked to the ceiling, leaning back in the soft leather chair and propping his feet on top of the pile of paper that covered the rich brown oak of his desk. Cobwebs crept across the far corner of the ceiling, near the window. He frowned. What did he pay Calvin's idiot kid to do here all day? Did she think she was something so special she didn't have to actually clean to get paid?

Farley droned on about how deep he dug—blah, blah,

fucking incompetent excuses, blah. Carroll sighed, his mind on little Samantha Chambers. He'd paid Amelia for Sam's time and she'd been worth it at first. Now she thought he'd continue paying for nothing. He hadn't touched the little bitch since last summer; too chubby for his liking, took after her mother. Well, Sam would have to be reminded how things worked. If she couldn't slim down to proportions that he found attractive, she'd have to make herself useful in another way, or go.

"Well, in college he did get a possession charge but it didn't stick."

Farley's words filtered to Carroll's brain, dashing thoughts of the Chambers girl. "What kind of possession?"

"Weed. Nothing big. Got a slap on the wrist."

"Shit."

"Oh, and I froze my nuts off outside like you asked. He found some stuff."

"What stuff?"

"It's kinda hard to look in a window without being caught, especially in broad daylight."

Why did Farley think he cared about this shit? "What did you see?"

"He was looking in a container he took from the cupboard and he had some pictures. I watched for a bit, but he didn't do much."

"And?"

"He looked real pissed."

"That's all?" What had he found? Carroll had removed the file from the clock. They'd searched the cabinets, drawers, and under the beds. What else had Melvin stashed?

"Yeah, he put it all in his pocket and left."

"I want to know what he found. Damn it, what else could they have had? Did you cover your tracks?"

"With this snow? They'll be covered by now. Don't worry. I know what I'm doing."

"Sure you do. Go back and make sure he won't know you were there."

"Done. Then what do you want to do?"

"I'll get back to you. Just keep an eye out, he might give us something, you never know."

"Yeah, right."

Carroll shut the cell phone and set it down. He folded his fingers under his chin, and then leaned forward to rest his elbows on the desk.

His problem lay in Ryan's relative anonymity. Carroll didn't know anything about him, other than his connection to the Cassidys. Hell, the boy didn't even know them. What had his mother told him? Did she even mention Albertsville? Did she tell him what made her leave? He couldn't see that; Sara had far too much pride. She was loyal to Melvin and Rachel and her loyalty wouldn't have wavered for anything. That's how Carroll lost her. She'd thought herself above this town, and above Carroll's attentions. His gut burned at how she'd managed to evade him every time he thought he had her. Then Chad fucked everything up. He congratulated himself once more on eliminating that pain in the ass.

Really, Sara made it easier. When she'd left, the idiot moped about like a lovesick fool, too distracted by his broken heart to see the danger that lurked in the shadows. He'd been smart enough to find… Carroll scratched his chin, roughened by a day's growth of hair. He frowned, staring at the papers before him. Lovesick. Yes, that might be the answer. Perhaps Cassidy shared his father's tendency to be a pussy for anything in a skirt.

Audrey. There was something Audrey could do about Ryan Cassidy.

CHAPTER 11

Sage-green walls surrounded Ryan, and he wasn't sure he liked them. Audrey had marked the can "kitchen" so he'd trusted her judgment and slapped it on, reserving his opinion until he finished. To his eye, "sage" looked like dried up old snot.

No matter what she said, he was a black and white kind of guy and the color— though better than what had been on the walls—didn't relax him as promised. He tossed the brushes in the sink and ran warm water over them. Maybe once he'd added his own touches, got rid of the flowery canisters and seat covers, replaced the pink clock and the tea towels covered in azaleas, he'd change his mind.

"Knock, knock."

Ryan dropped the brush. Snot-colored water splashed up onto his shirt. He cursed.

Audrey laughed.

He turned. "Real funny. Where were you about an hour ago when the walls made me vomit?"

"You're kidding, this looks beautiful. So much better."

"You're brave, venturing out in that weather." He wiped his hand on the towel hanging over the stove.

"It's not too bad yet. Plus, I couldn't stay home. One of those days."

"You okay?"

She frowned. "What? Oh, yeah, I'm fine. So, you look like you're settling in for the long haul."

"Indeed, I am. Still going to try to scare me off? I thought we discussed this."

"I don't want you to leave, Ryan. Melvin and Rachel wanted you to have this place, and I think it would be a shame for it to revert to the town. It's been in your family for a long time, one of the few pieces of land Carroll and the others don't own. I just worry, that's all. Some people here are dangerous and I don't think proving a point is a valid reason to put your life in danger."

"A bit dramatic, don't you think?"

"No, I don't. But you'll do what you want. Men usually do. I'll try not to say I told you so when the shit hits the fan."

"What is this danger? Where is it? So far, Carroll has been quite pleasant. Sure he's a snake, but I know lots of those. You're treating me as though I'm retarded or something and I don't like it. What have I done so far that would cause this shit to hit the fan?"

Audrey's chin raised a notch.

Great, he'd pissed her off. Well he was sick of this cloak and dagger bullshit.

"That's just it! You don't have to do anything. People have disappeared because Carroll didn't trust them. Nothing more. They've got too much to risk to ever allow an outsider to stay in town. He's already threatened me about you. I doubt I'm the only one he's tried to shake down. Do you get what I'm saying?"

"He threatened you because I'm an outsider?"

"No." Audrey took a breath and looked to the window. "He's just really clear that he wants you out."

"What's up with the mill?"

"Pardon?"

"The mill. You know that place where they cut trees and make them into furniture or paper, or whatever it is they make. Is that the main industry here?"

"I guess so."

"How big is it?"

"I don't know. Big enough."

"I want to see it. One mill can't support an entire town."

"Just leave it alone. Please. Other things bring money into Albertsville. And you should stay away from those too."

He knelt to snap the lid on the nearly empty paint can, picked it up, and walked toward the hallway. He was getting nowhere fast. Should he ask about the letter?

Audrey wrung her fingers.

Not yet. As much as he liked her, he didn't know that he trusted Audrey. He'd tell her about the letter, she might tell Carroll and tomorrow he'd be no more than ash along with his tiny scrap of evidence.

"I picked Millicent up on the road earlier today," he said.

"Oh?" The chair scuffed across the floor. He paused to put the can into the closet that held his grandfather's outerwear.

Standing, he pushed the door closed and returned to the kitchen. He scanned the room. Maybe he could like the green. If he went blind. "Yeah, she flipped her truck. I'm surprised you didn't see it on the way here."

"Nope. It's probably gone now. The town cleans that sort of thing up fast. Was she okay?"

"A bit shaken. But she'll live. She is an odd character, nice though. I like her." He pulled a chair out and sat. Picking up the rose-colored placemat in front of him he folded it into a small square.

"She is nice, but way too far up Carroll's ass for my liking. Be careful."

"She said the same thing. I mean, she said to be careful. She told me what happened to my mother, but when I pushed for more, she clammed up." He toyed with the edges of the placemat.

"Well good. You don't need to be worrying about this town."

"Maybe." He turned the small square of fabric in his hands.

"You look like you're plotting something terrible."

Ryan caught her mock grimace and laughed. "No, just thinking. Millicent seemed to sit on the edge. Really, if Carroll is this huge menace you say he is I think it would take one person to take a stand against him and the rest would follow."

"She won't do it. Millicent likes what she has and she loves this town."

"I guess someone needs to make her see that nothing is worth living under someone's thumb."

"Don't look at me." Audrey held her arms up.

"Maybe someone else needs to see the same thing."

"Maybe someone else should just go back where he came from. Too bad that *someone* is just as greedy as the rest of us. We're all just backward rednecks bending over for Carroll. So stupid we can't see how easy the solution to our problems is. How nice that you can judge all of us from your glass castle."

Ryan stood and made for the den, leaving her at the table.

Audrey stared after Ryan. Her stomach twisted at his stiff shoulders beneath the black t-shirt. She hated herself for it, but she was already attached to his crooked smile, the way his cheek dimpled and his eyes sparked when he teased her. If he asked, she'd fall into bed with him in a heartbeat, completely unlike her. The image of his body over hers haunted her every time he looked her way. Maybe she should go see Dr. Reid.

She worried that Melvin's strength beneath the surface and Rachel's brashness made a dangerous combination for Ryan. He made a worthy opponent, but his stubborn impulsive nature refused to see the danger in front of him. Audrey bit her lip. How did he come to mean so much to her so fast?

Ryan would find the fields; he'd see the mine and he'd know the mill was just a front. How long would he keep that information silent? Who would get hurt if he didn't? Ryan didn't strike her as someone who'd stay quiet if he knew about the drugs. He'd never do something that made him guilty in any way. A healthy sense of right and wrong wouldn't be a good thing for a person living in Albertsville.

She'd seen how following one's feelings could turn to shit in this town. Rachel did everything with her heart: every word, decision and mistake had been motivated by the woman's feelings. She'd never forgiven the town for taking Chad from her and Audrey suspected that the reason Carroll smelled a rat was Rachel's inability to pretend she'd let the whole matter go. Hell, she nearly spit fire every time Carroll's name was mentioned.

Audrey stood, peeking around the kitchen door to the hall. The door to Melvin's den was closed, a dim light glowing underneath. So, Ryan was through with her. She shouldn't have said what she did. But if not for the money, would he have stayed? Would he have cared what was going on with Carroll or the mill? He didn't even know half of what Carroll had done.

If he dug deep enough, Ryan might uncover more than he bargained for. Audrey toyed with the idea of warning Carroll that Melvin knew more than he let on. She'd seen his files, and he'd been so close. One or two more clues and he'd have found the bones—if they existed. By now, they could be a pile of dust. Ryan might risk his life for something that wasn't there.

Ryan knocked and waited. The night before he'd remained in the den until Audrey's truck roared down the lane. Then he'd emerged and finished cleaning up the snot-colored kitchen. He hated admitting, even to himself, that he'd hid from her. He wasn't here just for the money, and even if he was, they were his family. That money was his birthright.

Hell, he didn't know what he was doing but he had to do something. His mother lived in fear for years. As a boy he hadn't realized that, but now, in light of what he'd learned, the constant moving, the way she never made friends, it all made sense. How long did Carroll terrorize her?

How long would he last in this town without understanding what was really going on? So far, people talked in circles, warning him but telling absolutely nothing. His gut told him Millicent wanted to let him in on the secret. She just needed a good reason to do so.

After another knock, shuffling sounded behind the door.

"Coming," Millicent called.

Her blurred features materialized in the glass panel alongside the door. She opened the door and forced a polite smile to her lips. "Ryan, what a nice surprise."

"Is it?"

She stepped back, waving him inside.

The snow hadn't stopped, except to turn to ice pellets overnight. In the morning, he'd awakened to blustering wind and huge sweeping gales of snow and ice battering his windows. After shoveling his car out, Ryan called Audrey to see about getting the rest of the lane plowed, but she hadn't sounded too optimistic. He'd loaded tools in the car and spent the morning shoveling himself out of his driveway. He had no idea what he'd do about the ice beneath.

Ryan stepped through the door, careful to pause and kick as much snow off his boots as he could before passing Millicent into the short hallway.

"Um…well I am surprised to see you."

Ryan unzipped his coat; it had soaked through. "Why?"

"Because your driveway must have been a nightmare. I figured you'd stay in and work on the house or something."

"It definitely wasn't fun to shovel that much snow. That's why I'm here. I need some help around the place, and I thought you'd be able to steer me to the right person."

"Like what kind of help?" Millicent took his coat and hung it on the tree at the base of the stairs before leading him into a clean, but shabby kitchen.

A black granite countertop, chipped at a corner near the double sink, ran the length of the far wall. Several jars, a coffee maker, and a breadbox took up most of the space on the left side. Old appliances filled the other side of the room. Their tan color had been more popular a decade ago than it was now. Cream-colored linoleum, marbled with shades of black and grey, although nice, had started to pull up and crack in spots. Her place needed more work than his grandparents' farm.

"I've been painting up a storm, but I'm only one man." he said. "Every room needs a fresh coat of paint, then the outbuildings need cleaning up, and the addition needs some major work. If I want to sell next year, I can't do it on my own. It wouldn't hurt to have an extra pair of shoveling hands either."

"I'd shovel for you," a young voice startled them, spinning Millicent around, one hand to her chest.

"Justin! Stop sneaking up on people like that."

The boy—who bore a striking resemblance to Carroll—rolled his eyes and shoved on an old pair of work gloves. "Relax, I was going to plow Merle out. I wasn't eavesdropping."

Millicent's cheeks reddened. "Sorry, this is my son Justin."

"You've got a plow?" Ryan asked.

"Yeah, Mom let me put one on the four-wheeler. It's not great, but it works well enough to make me a few bucks now and then."

"How much do you charge to clear a driveway?"

"Yours? That's a pretty long patch of road you've got up there."

"Justin—" Millicent warned.

"Joking, Ma. Christ, don't get your panties in a bunch."

Millicent's blush heightened to a brilliant pink and she turned to the counter. Pulling the red coffee maker from its position against the wall she flipped the lid. She reached to the far corner of the counter and dragged a jar forward.

"I'd pay you well. If you're looking for work I've got lots. That is, if your mom is okay with that." Ryan glanced to Millicent.

She closed the lid and punched a button on the front of the machine before turning around. "He's got school."

"Shoot, I could go to that shithole once a week and still pass. Come on, Ma," Justin groaned.

Millicent stood rigid, arms crossed over her ample chest.

She avoided looking her son in the eye.

Ryan scuffed his foot at a crack in the linoleum and turned. "I was thinking weekends, maybe after school some nights if he doesn't have any homework."

"Homework?" Justin rolled his eyes.

"I don't know how much help he'd be really, he's fourteen. He's never done much more than plow a driveway or two. He can't even pick up his socks." Millicent's tone brought color to the boy's face.

Ryan stifled the grin that tickled his lips.

The boy's features hardened, his blue eyes cool and angry as he glared at his mother. His angular jaw, full mouth and tall, athletic body screamed the mighty Reeve of Albertsville. Had Millicent and Carroll been more than friends? Is this why she seemed not to care whether she got on his bad side? Was Justin her insurance?

"I guess if he wants to do it…" Millicent sighed, bringing Ryan's attention back to her face. She frowned, her lips pressed into a thin line, her arms still folded tight across her chest.

"How much?" Justin asked.

Millicent gasped.

Ryan chuckled. "We'll decide on that after I see what you can do. Deal?"

"Sounds good to me." Justin shrugged and disappeared around the corner into the living room. The door opened, letting in a gust of frigid air before it slammed shut.

"If you don't want him to, I understand." Ryan said.

"No, it's fine. I'll be surprised if you can get him to do anything but bitch and moan."

"I'm sure he reserves that for you. Kids usually do."

Millicent turned away, reaching into the glossy oak cupboard and bringing down two cups. "I wish he'd direct it to his father."

Justin showed up two days later, bright and early, although he didn't look impressed about the fact.

Ryan stepped back and let the sullen boy pass him into the hallway. "Wow, I didn't expect you this early, especially on a Saturday." Ryan held his hand out for the boy's blue bomber jacket.

"Ma said I had to go early. Probably so no one would know I'm here."

"Why?"

Justin made a strange sound, like a grunt, and followed Ryan down the hall.

Ryan hung his jacket in the small closet before Justin answered.

"No one wants to be seen with you. Don't you know that? It's all stupid shit, really. Oh, sorry. Sometimes I forget about swearing when I'm in front of adults. Drives my mom crazy."

"That's fine. Doesn't bother me a bit."

"You'd be the first. I don't see how it's fair for them to swear around us and expect us not to do it too. Ma drops f-bombs at least a dozen times every morning. Then acts like it's the first time she heard the damn word when I say it."

Ryan laughed, leading Justin away from the kitchen to the double doors of the addition. He wasn't sure what to call the three rooms on the side of the house. They had little furniture. Someone had hung drywall and laid ceramic tile in an intricate mosaic pattern that Ryan assumed was meant to look like a garden. The same pattern repeated in each room, but the rest remained unfinished. He pushed the large set of pine doors open and stood back, so Justin could enter.

The boy shivered and rubbed his arms. "Shit, it's cold in here. Where's the heater?"

"Good question. I don't know."

The barren room rounded in the far right corner, where a window seat nestled beneath a wide ledge and a stained glass monstrosity that Ryan assumed was also a garden scene, although this one contained an angelic figure in the center. The opposite end of the room opened onto a smaller area, with only one bay window along the wall; the floor was unfinished and capped pipes poked up through the plywood on the left side. Off that area—which he figured must be a bathroom or perhaps a kitchen of some kind—was a duplicate of the first room, without the stained glass.

"This must be what Mrs. Cassidy was talking about last summer."

"Care to explain?"

"Oh, she wanted to build his and hers libraries or something like that. This one was Mrs. Cassidy's. She had that ugly window special ordered from the States. Melvin didn't like it; he was pretty clear on that."

"For a library, it's lacking in a few things, like shelves, furniture, heating... books." At the other end of the room, Ryan peeked into the middle area and gestured for Justin to join him.

"They just finished building when they—before the accident. I don't know what this is supposed to be though. Any guesses?"

Ryan laughed and straightened. "No. I hoped maybe they mentioned this. There are some pipes roughed in over there, so I thought a bathroom or a kitchen. I assumed this might have been an apartment or something."

"Good idea."

"Yeah, it is actually. I know they wanted a library, but an apartment, like an in-law suite, would make the house more appealing to prospective buyers." Ryan rubbed his scruffy chin. He hadn't shaved in a few days. This country life would turn him into one of the locals if he wasn't careful, although he didn't see himself wearing camouflage or plaid. Not ever.

"You could do that easily enough. Open up the wall over there, make this middle room the bathroom, but smaller, run the pipes out here to make a little kitchen, living room area and that far section, the part that was Melvin's, could be made into a bedroom. You could do it all pretty cheap too," Justin suggested.

"How would you know? Done a lot of renovations in your many years?"

Justin met his gaze, and Ryan regretted the joke. The boy looked pissed. "I know enough. I've worked with Merle

Jamieson every summer since I was six. He doesn't care if you're just a kid either, works you like a slave. I learned how to frame, plumb and run electrical before I was nine."

"Sorry, I didn't mean—"

"Nah, it's all right. I know what you thought. I'm just a stupid kid who knows nothing but computer games and action heroes. But that's what I want the rest of them to think, so I'd appreciate it if you didn't say nothing. When I blow this shithole out of the water, they won't know what hit them. My father will be the first to come toppling down when I do it too."

"Your father?" Ryan stepped back to lean against the wall and dropped his arms to his sides, stuffing his hands into the pockets of his jeans.

He wanted the boy to talk, but kids were different, you had to be careful how you held your body, your face, the tone in your voice; they picked up on all the small stuff. Adults were so wrapped up in themselves and their lives they never paid attention to the subtleties. But teenagers watched everything. If you wanted a kid to talk, it was like walking a tightrope of emotion. The more controlled you thought you were, the more they sensed.

Justin eyed him for a moment, the heat of his dark blue gaze penetrating right to Ryan's soul. Whatever he saw, it must have met with his approval. Relaxing his shoulders, Justin looked away and shrugged. "You didn't figure it out yet?"

"I have my suspicions, but I try not to make assumptions if I can avoid it."

"Huh. Makes you the first in my experience." Justin leaned against the wall on the opposite side of the doorway, looking down at his hands, picking an imaginary hangnail. "So, Carroll is my dad. Lucky me. See, he gives Mom money every month and I've heard them talking a bunch of times. When I was little they didn't even try to hide, like because I was small so was my brain. But now they're more secretive. I know she's not my real mom; she made sure of that. I don't know who my mom is. My birth certificate said her name was Mary, and no age."

"You've seen your birth certificate?"

"Yeah, Mom's not good at hiding stuff. She tries, but everything goes into her underwear drawer: money, letters, and my records. Kind of gross picking through that stuff, but I had to know. You know?" he raised his head.

Ryan's heart constricted at the need in his eyes. Poor kid just wanted to belong, to have a family and neither one of his parents really acknowledged him. Even Millicent, in her own way, rejected him when she revealed his parentage. "I do, sort of. I didn't know my dad, didn't even know his name. But my mom loved me and I was lucky to have a great step dad. Still, I had questions, wondered who I was, even though I didn't need him to make me who I am. I still felt... like something was missing. Part of me."

"Yeah, I wish I knew who my mom really was. I mean Mom—Millicent—she does her best. I know she loves me in her way, but she wasn't meant to have a kid. I think he made her take me. That kind of sucks, but it's worse knowing that he was like forty and made some girl, probably a kid if he was anything like he is now, pregnant. Then he forced her to give her baby away. I don't know if she's even alive."

"What do you think happened to her?" Ryan turned, hands deep in his pockets, and faced the boy.

He'd never been crazy about kids, but the sadness, the anger in Justin's voice made him want to hug the boy, to offer something he'd never gotten from anyone in his life; acknowledgement of his feelings, of his place in the world. The urge unsettled Ryan, setting off warning bells in his head. Getting too close to the kid could hurt them both in the long run. Carroll wouldn't like his blood—bastard or not—mixing with Ryan.

"If she's alive she doesn't know about me. Either they told her I died or gave me away. Something stupid like that. Or... he got rid of her."

"How does he get away with it?"

Justin shrugged. He rubbed a dark smudge on the bare drywall. "If I tell you something, you'll keep it quiet? I mean, you didn't hear it from me?"

"Of course," What now?

"Okay, so you've probably gathered that most of the people here, they've lived in Albertsville forever. The town started with a bunch of families. The council is always made up of those families. No newcomers, and definitely no nobodies." Justin moved along the wall, pressing a seam here, rubbing off a chunk of loose drywall mud there. "So there was this incident like at least fifty years ago. I'd say more than that. The town is about a hundred years old or something. Anyway, there was this escape. Some murderers or something escaped from prison. Took one of the families hostage."

"Wow, that's some history." Ryan couldn't begin to imagine the fear that family must have felt.

"That's not all of it. You see, the fugitives wanted to have a fair trial or something; I'm not sure what. I haven't pieced everything together yet, but the remaining families had a meeting. Wanted to decide whether or not to call the authorities about the situation."

"Why wouldn't they?"

"This is where it gets foggy. I know that there are some… less than legal things going on in the old mine. It's not shut down at all. To the outside world it is, but a bunch of buildings went up and only certain people can get in there. Kids at school all say he's got some kind of counterfeit thing going on. Some say it's a meth lab. I saw a truck go in once, the guys that came out were… scary. I think they make weapons in there. Carroll owns the property. He took control of it after Mom's dad died. But if you were here in the spring, you'd notice some other stuff too, out in the fields."

"Like what?"

Justin shrugged. "Plants and stuff. Look, people here don't survive with what they make at the stores or the mill. This town keeps going because of what's in those fields and what's at that mine. In Mom's drawer, there were bank statements. I asked Merle about them and he said that the ones that work for Carroll get a cut. Carroll transfers it into their bank accounts as payroll or something. The mill has like two hundred employees on paper, but in reality, there's only like twenty guys there full time. According to Merle, anyhow. I don't know if he's right. Anyway, something happened at that meeting way back when, and ever since then, the Albert's have controlled this place. Even renamed the town, but I can't remember what the real name was. That's the key, I think, to bringing my dad down. I think they killed that family instead of letting anyone else come into their town to see what was going on."

"That's crazy."

"Think about what you know about this town so far. Is it really that crazy?"

CHAPTER 12

Ryan wandered Audrey's store and tossed items into his basket. The roads were closed until further notice. This according to the only clear radio station he could find, which played ten in a row of your favorite country oldies from yesterday and today every weekday morning. Not a thrilling prospect.

Justin said he would come to the farm after school when he had no homework and on Saturdays, reserving Sundays to help Merle.

"What are you doing exactly?" Audrey's voice startled him.

He spun around.

Her mouth curved into a smile.

He stepped back. The way his stomach flip-flopped at those lips meant too many complications. "Fixing up the addition."

"The libraries?"

"Yeah, but I won't finish it the way my grandmother planned. An apartment would be great, and maybe convert another room into a library at some point. It makes no sense to have two."

"Good thing Rachel isn't alive to hear you say that. She thought it was brilliant."

Ryan laughed. "Well, I need practical, not brilliant."

"You're going to heat that with baseboard heaters. The whole thing?" She took the list from his hands.

"Yes?"

"Shit, that's going to send your electricity bill through the roof."

"Any other suggestions?"

"Why not use a woodstove or a fireplace in the main area? That would be more efficient and cost a lot less."

"That would mean a chimney, an opened wall, chopping wood, and a pain in my ass." Ryan grumbled.

"Suit yourself. I suppose you need at least three: one heater in each of the main rooms and another in the bathroom. Let me check the back." Audrey straightened.

As she walked away, Ryan wished he'd met her under different circumstances.

Not that the conditions of his inheritance or the strange mystery of this town was so important that he should put his life on hold. There was something about Audrey; a little part she held back. She might not be lying, but she definitely hid something.

The cowbell clanged. Ryan turned to Calvin Chambers' brooding stare. The coldness of his dark eyes sent a chill over Ryan's skin. Setting a box of nails into his red basket, Ryan looked away first, feigning great interest in the assortment of screws on the wall.

"So it's like that in the city, is it?" Calvin's gravelly voice was quiet.

"I'm sorry?" Ryan turned, raising an eyebrow.

Calvin stood at the end of the aisle, just a few feet away, hands stuffed into the pockets of his brown overalls. "People don't say hello?"

"I'm sorry, just distracted I guess." Ryan took a step forward, extending his free hand. "I'm Ryan Cassidy, but I'm sure you knew that."

"Yep. Calvin Chambers, but I'm sure *you* knew that." Calvin took his hand in a firm grip. Calluses roughened his palm. He squeezed a little harder than necessary before dropping his arm.

Ryan struggled to find something to say to this monster of a man. Massive shoulders, wet with snow that melted from wiry black hair that was a bit too long in the back, blocked Ryan's path to the door. His face, smudged here and there with grease and dirt, remained stony. Not even a hint of a smile. It would be unwise to allow silence to build for too long with Calvin. The urge to fill it with silly chatter overwhelmed him. "So, I heard you work at the mill?" He managed not to stutter.

"Why? What did you hear about me?"

"Nothing really. Audrey says you're a nice man, hard worker, and that's about it. I saw you at Sal's the other night and asked about you."

"Why?"

"Why did I ask? You didn't look too happy, your wife had lots to say to me, and so I was curious."

"Anita's a fool. Not a fucking lick of sense in her head. Don't know why I even married her. It's not like she's pretty. Her attitude stinks too."

"We all make mistakes, I guess." Ryan didn't know what to say. The man hated his wife; lots of men hated their wives. Lots of men also divorced them and moved on.

"Bitch keeps getting pregnant. Can't leave a pregnant woman you know, people talk. Shit, people talk no matter what a man does. The last one I don't think is mine, but what can you do about that?"

Ryan shrugged, uncomfortable with the conversation, uncomfortable with Calvin in general.

"You met Kim too." Calvin's dark gaze narrowed. His cheeks, already ruddy, colored even more.

"I did. Very nice man. He runs the mill?"

"Supposed to, but Farley calls the shots. Carroll and Kim, they own the mill, though I don't know how that works. Douglas sold Kim his share before he died, but Carroll still holds the most interest. Farley does what he pleases, forces us all to do the same. Kim, he's too soft to argue. Just does his job and goes home."

"If he owns part of it, then why doesn't he fire Farley?" He regretted the question as soon as it was out. He didn't want to know, he didn't need to know, and he certainly didn't like the way Calvin's jaw clenched or how his shoulders stiffened.

"You don't know nothing about how this town works. Fire Farley? Fuck, right. Your dad talked like you, and where's the great Chad Cassidy now?"

"You're right. I don't understand any of it. I'm sorry. I'm trying. I thought my father's death was an accident, he fell on the belt—"

"Fell on the belt? Yeah, that's what he did. Fell on the belt. There ain't no belt on the chipper, boy. Cassidy fell *into* a wood chipper. No surviving that. Listen, you're better off getting out of this place. Soon as that road clears, pack your shit, move back to where you came from. Things happen to nosy shits like you, bad things. Chad got nosy. He thought he could fuck everyone over just to get at Carroll."

"I see." Ryan turned to the items in his basket.

If Calvin jumped him, he had a box of nails, sandpaper, and several rolls of painter's tape as weapons. He could put up a good fight, but a man the size of Calvin, with the anger that radiated out of his pores, would make burger meat out of him in seconds.

"I'm not telling you this to scare you, or because I don't like you. I don't know you, and I don't plan on us getting too familiar either. I'm telling you because I think everyone should get a fair shot. Sort of my good deed for the year. Plus, you stay around poking your nose where it doesn't belong, you make work for me. Keep messing around with good folks and the odds that someone else will get hurt cause of your big mouth gets higher. Carroll will find a way to get rid of you permanently. The longer you stay, the more opportunity he has to sling his noose over your neck. Then, he tightens it so you can't do nothing but kiss his ass and hope to God he doesn't change his mind about keeping you alive."

Ryan stared.

Calvin shook, his face as red as the countertop behind him.

"Why do you work for him then?"

"None of your business."

"I'd think that if all of you got together he'd have nothing. Why not turn on him?"

Calvin shook his head, pulling his hand from his pocket to shake a dirty finger at Ryan. A bitter smile played on his lips. "That, Mr. Cassidy, is what's going to hang you. Big mouths tend to get shut real fast, and real permanent here. Albert could ruin us, all of us, and I'm not talking about a little rumor and shit like that. He could take away everything we have. We got a good thing here. Our children, our jobs, our lives revolve around this town. Notice there ain't nothing here except what we built? We could have had a Wal-Mart or a Foodland instead of the dinky little Grocery, but we said no thanks. We don't want outsiders here. Besides, they find out what your dad was gonna tell them, it would be a shit show and the only one who gives up nothing if that happens is Carroll. I've got too much to lose if you go mouthing off, and so does everyone else."

"You give him too much credit. He's just a man."

"Is he?" Calvin turned, marched to the door and pushed out.

Whatever he'd come in for hadn't been very important. Ryan stood holding his basket, Calvin's desperate gaze still clear in his mind.

"Ryan, that was a mistake," Audrey's voice brought him around.

He turned to her frowning face. She carried four long boxes.

"What?"

"Don't go around talking like that, please. It's going to get you into trouble like you've never experienced, and anyone around you at the time is going to get sucked into the vortex."

"You scared to be around me?"

"Yes. I am. Calvin is unpredictable. Farley is scary enough, but Calvin is worse. You never know which side of him you're on. No one fucks with him. And if he warns you about something, you listen. Please, be careful who you talk to and how you talk to them. Everything goes back to Carroll. Everything."

"Really? Everything? Hmm. Well, at least he'll be prepared if Karma feels the need to bite him in the ass."

"Holy snappers, that's a big mess." Ryan stood in the doorway of the addition and whistled.

The wall had come down, sort of. The left side of the room lay under a heap of drywall chunks and dust. Justin checked the studs he'd set in place, tape measure out and a well-chewed pencil between his teeth. The table saw that terrified him when Justin told him to buy it sat in the corner to the right of the door, covered in sawdust instead of the blood Ryan feared.

Justin laughed. "Knocking down walls is a messy business."

He had never encountered anyone who worked as Justin did. He arrived early, listened to Ryan's plans, and after determining that the wall was load-bearing, convinced Ryan that opening the door way up would suffice. They went straight to work after that. After a few hours, he forgot that Justin was just a kid, until he flat out refused to tackle plumbing.

"I can do this stuff well enough, but Merle never let me work with wires or pipes by myself. He said maybe in a year or two."

Ryan wasn't a handyman at all, although playing with his new tools had felt manly. Maybe testosterone and power tools really did have a connection. No matter how much fun the tools were, he couldn't tackle the work on his own. The only person in town willing to help with the plumbing was Merle Jamieson, who'd retired from contracting several years ago. How much could a seventy-year-old man really do? Hopefully enough to fix up these rooms, because Albertsville's two official plumbers hung up on him.

"When did Merle say he'd be here?" Justin picked the air nailer from the pile of debris and shot a couple of nails along the studs that framed the new doorway.

"After dinner, whatever that means."

"Normally dinner at Merle's is around six every night. My

mom wanted me home by seven. Shit." He tossed the nailer down on the pile again and reached around Ryan to shut off the compressor.

Did the kid understand how much the damn thing cost? He paid more for that than he did for his Blackberry. "That's okay. He can let me know if I can run the pipes out here or not. We can start another day."

"Yeah, but I don't want to put up the new drywall if we don't know where the pipes will go. That's just adding to our work."

They had to get lights in as well. He was on his own for that, since Justin refused to touch the wiring. Looking to the window, he berated himself for getting carried away in the den writing his tale of Albertsville instead of installing the lights. The sun lowered, casting a grey pall over the house and the rooms filled with shadows.

"Anybody home?" a high raspy voice called.

"Hey Merle, you're early." Justin wiped his hands on his battered jeans and walked toward a little man standing hunched in the doorway.

Merle Jamieson raised a skinny arm to look at the leather-banded watch that hung loosely at his bony wrist. "Meh, I ate earlier today. Figured you guys needed as much help as you could get."

"Thanks, I appreciate it." Ryan extended his hand.

Merle shook it in a strong but clammy hand. Although it was cold outside, Merle wore only a battered blue t-shirt with his name embroidered in white over the breast pocket. Maybe he left his coat in the hallway.

"Folks in this town are just damn stupid." Merle clucked his tongue. "We got plumbers, electricians and carpenters, all crying for work and they turn you down cause that uppity Carroll don't like you. Shameful."

"Ma says Carroll is dangerous, Merle. Wouldn't hurt to be careful what you say, you know? Especially to someone you just met." Justin pulled off his work gloves and looked pointedly at the old man.

Merle waved the boy away. "Your mother needs to wake up and smell the damn bullshit piling in her backyard. She shouldn't be afraid of nothing. She could tell more stories than enough to—" Merle glanced at Ryan. "Millie ain't got no backbone, that's the problem."

"What about you?" Ryan asked.

Merle turned his glassy blue eyes to meet his gaze. "I got plenty of backbone. Problem is I got nothing to tell. Just hearsay, you get me? I got no proof, but I'd sure as hell sing to the heavens if I did have it. Don't care what it means for this town. Nope, don't matter no more how I spend my final days. I've got nothing anyway."

"Merle—"

"Boy, I told you about this already. Don't go getting all prissy and emotional. I'm dying. Plain and simple. Just a fact of life. Old people die."

Justin's face reddened.

Merle hobbled into the room, a hand on his back as though the simple effort of walking pained him greatly. Maybe he shouldn't have called him to look at the pipes. The poor man should be resting, not bending over messing around with something he could learn to do himself.

"I better call my mom," Justin muttered before disappearing into the dark hallway beyond.

"So, ask me what you want to know before the kid comes back. I ain't going to tell him too much. Kids got big mouths and don't know when it's wise to keep them shut." Merle knelt down to inspect the studs Justin had just secured in the new doorway.

"I'm not sure I know what you mean," Ryan hedged.

"Don't try to give me that horseshit, boy. You're the new guy asking all kinds of questions. Pissed Calvin off, according to Kim. Not the smartest thing to do, but I guess you gotta make mistakes to learn from them. Kim also said Farley told Calvin to shoot anything that looks suspicious at the mill. That tells me Carroll is worried about something you've said. I figured you'd want to ask me a few things. If you didn't, you're stupid. So ask."

"Since you're offering, I might have a thing or two I'm curious about. But just so we're clear, I haven't been asking anyone anything really."

Merle snorted.

Ryan fought to hold his temper. "Okay, why do they hate me so much? They don't even know me."

"Ach, they don't hate you. Everyone's worried Carroll will think they're in with you if they act too friendly. Even poor little Aud is scared. She's trying her best to hide it, but I saw that bastard's truck outside her house the other morning. He stayed a while, left with quite a grin on his face and walking kinda stiff. Know what I mean? He's got her terrified, and for good reason."

Ryan's hands clenched into fists at the picture Merle's words painted in his mind. Carroll, easily twice Audrey's size, forcing himself—he took a breath. No, that's not what happened. She would have said something, acted differently. Wouldn't she? "So if they won't talk to me and I can't find out what's going on, then I should just quietly put in my year. Too bad claiming my inheritance isn't enough anymore. If my grandparents and father were murdered, someone will pay. I won't turn back and leave until I know what happened to my family. And I couldn't give a shit about the rest; they need to fix their own mistakes. No one else can do it for them."

"Just like I've been telling them. Listen, I don't know what happened to Chad or your grandparents, but Millie does. I think she knows a lot more than she lets on. She hates Carroll, though she hides it real well. You know the saying about a woman scorned?"

Ryan nodded

Merle pointed a crooked finger at him. "She used to love that man. Disgusting if you ask me, but I never claim to understand a woman's mind. Hell, women don't know why they do what they do. But Carroll fucked up on that one, treated her like shit, used her, abused her, and now she despises him. Just the right amount of pressure would open the floodgates, if you know what I mean."

"So, you think I should talk to her?" Ryan already tried Millicent and she'd given him nothing.

"Not saying you should or shouldn't. Just thinking she might be willing to point you to a few interesting places."

"Why aren't you scared?"

"Me? Like I said, I've got nothing to lose. Used to think I did when I lost my Emily. I thought what I had was more important than what was right or wrong. Emily passed away and I realized that we were all fools. That reeve of ours latched onto my grief, my doubt, and told me if I didn't shut my mouth and toe the line, I'd be to blame for the town going under. I believed that my friends hating me would be worse than anything he told me to do. I was wrong. Now, I got a few months, a year tops, and I don't care where I spend those days."

"Cancer?"

"Yep. Too far gone to do anything about it now. They offered, but I don't want to spend my last days so drugged I can't even move. Best let nature take its course."

Ryan nodded and they shared a moment of silence.

Merle fiddled with Justin's work, tugging a board here and there, running his hand over a piece of drywall. His shaking hands and stiff back betrayed him. His illness did bother him. How could it not? Dying was pretty worrisome.

"So, you really think Millicent knows about my family?" Ryan asked. Millicent had Justin to consider. Whether or not she had given birth to him, she'd raised Justin on her own. She wouldn't do anything to jeopardize his safety.

"Not just her." Merle winked and grinned, exposing a mouth missing more teeth than it held.

"How many?"

"I never really counted. Sometimes people share things. Problem is I can't do much about stories. If we can convince one or two that this town would be better without all that other shit, we might have ourselves a mutiny."

"What other shit? The mill?" Here it was again. Ryan wanted to scream. Everyone talked and talked but said nothing.

"Well, see I can't really say. Not because I'm scared or nothing, but because it's not for me to share. I'm not going to out anyone who's not wanting to be outed."

"No one here says much of anything. They talk and talk but it all adds up to bullshit."

"They're sheep. They need a leader. That's how Carroll has kept this place all these years. These people want to stop. They don't want to do what they're doing. They ain't proud of themselves, but they don't know nothing else. They're also scared. What if they mess it up and get screwed over? If they see a scapegoat they'll be more talkative."

"I'm the scapegoat?"

"You rather be a sheep?"

"No, I suppose not."

CHAPTER 13

The old black truck—in pretty good shape except for a slight dent in the hood—turned onto the slushy road. Intent on their conversation the two occupants didn't look to the side, where another black vehicle idled, its lights off.

Carroll lit a cigarette and shook his head. Millicent's tail-lights faded into the half-light of the evening.

He looked back to Cassidy's lane and frowned. Millicent should have known better. Letting Justin hang around Ryan was unacceptable. The kid had a big mouth. God knew what he told Cassidy already. He tapped the ash of his smoke in the brimming ashtray. Good thing Calvin called him when he'd seen Merle's old rust bucket turn into the lane.

If the illiterate loser wasn't so well liked in town, Carroll would have rid himself of the issue a long time ago. But Merle had seemed intent on not making waves, and Carroll couldn't afford to rile his town up too much. He could handle a couple of loose lips, but an entire town?

He turned the key in the ignition and butted his cigarette. Justin would not be allowed to fraternize with Ryan Cassidy. Merle? He'd deal with him very soon.

Shivering in her thin nightgown, Millicent checked the thermostat. If Carroll replaced the damn windows, then the house might actually warm to a balmy seventy degrees, and the furnace wouldn't keep putting off heat that escaped through the drafty glass panes. She turned the thermostat down five degrees and flipped the switch next to the doorway of the kitchen. Turning to the living room, she switched off the lamp next to a battered recliner.

Her back ached from her stupidity, and her truck still didn't run quite right but she couldn't afford to let Ferris go ahead and repair the damage. He'd already charged the new tires and windshield and set her up with a payment plan. She'd never pay for the rest. The steering column was fucked according to the mechanic, and he didn't want to let her take it out of the shop. "Not safe to drive," he'd said.

Sometimes, having Carroll behind you worked to your advantage. She'd got her truck back, but it cost a small fortune. He could be a little more generous considering she did more for him than the rest of them. Christ, he could spare a couple hundred extra each month, although he claimed Julia would find out if he did. Right. That woman didn't have a clue.

Feeling her way through the darkened hallway, Millicent mounted the stairs, her body sagging, eager to lie down and forget another day. Snow crunched and she paused. From the stairs she looked down at the door. The small ovals of frosted glass shimmered as headlights filled her driveway, big head-lights.

"Shit."

Sighing, she stepped back down and made for the door. Before she could wrap her hand around the tarnished brass knob, he knocked.

"You going to let me in or what? It's cold enough to freeze a polar bear's balls out here."

"It's kind of late, don't you think?" She flipped the lock and pushed the screen door open. He didn't fool her. It was close to midnight, and Carroll did not come calling this late without a reason.

Pushing past her, he strode inside and to the kitchen at the end of the small entryway. Apparently, he didn't need to see her. He stood in the darkness, his silhouette eerie in the moonlit window.

At the edge of the hall she stopped, her feet just inside the room.

Carroll turned, removing black leather gloves before loosening his coat. "So? How's the boy?"

"Fine."

"Any trouble at school lately?" Leaning against the counter, he tapped his gloves against his leg with his left hand, running the other through his hair to brush the snow off.

"No, he's doing well. What do you want?"

A smile.

Dread crept through her, lodging into her chest, cold and hard.

"I'm checking on the boy. I always come to see how he's getting along, don't I? I do care, wouldn't want to see something bad happen to him. I know how boys can be at this age, have two others at home, you'll remember. They get sullen and lazy, run with the wrong crowd…"

Millicent's cheeks warmed. He knew. She shrugged, hoping to appear unconcerned. "There isn't much of a crowd here to begin with."

"Hmm. No, there isn't. But there is a bad element that has recently moved to town. Certain folks I think it's best he stayed away from. Never know what they'll talk him into."

"Look, I let him help Ryan fix up the house for some extra money. That's all. He barely talks to him. Justin plows the driveway and helped him drywall today. Ryan is not interested in a kid, especially a kid that knows nothing."

"I don't care. He already knows too much. Just the other day he asked Calvin about the mill and his dad's death. Before that, you heard him at the meeting and he was asking you about the mill. You want him knowing about the crops? One phone call is all it would take. The cops come in to look at that, they're going to see it all. Not many people in this town will avoid jail. My son will not be responsible for ruining what we've got here. He doesn't go back there. Got me?" Carroll raised a black brow, his eyes losing the warmth they held when she met him at the door.

She recognized this look, had seen it too often not to know what he was telling her. She trembled inside, but forced her hands to be still at her sides, feeling suddenly naked in her thin cotton gown. "I can't do that to Justin. He's all excited about earning extra money. I can't afford to give him an allowance and I already said he could do it. He's got the money spent. What do I tell him?"

"Tell him whatever you want. He goes back there, you and I will have a disagreement, and you don't want to have a disagreement, do you, Millie? You tell him he can't work for Cassidy. Period." His voice held an edge of danger, of promise.

She took a shaky breath. If she backed down again, when would it end? Ryan was right. There was nothing wrong with Justin helping out, and Carroll couldn't tell her what to do with her son, not when he never bothered with him. She had paperwork that said the boy was hers, and that was something he couldn't make disappear.

"No." Soft, no more than a whisper, but it felt good to say it.

"What?" Carroll straightened, his head cocked to the side as though she had lost her mind.

"I said no."

"Oh, Millie. You say no, but that's not what you mean. I know you're shaken up. I think rolling your truck the other day must have bumped your head. Then there's this house…. I've been remiss looking after it. You need new windows, maybe a couple other repairs. Justin should have an allowance. I'll see to that. You're right to be angry with my ignorance over that, but you didn't mean to say no to me."

"I said no and I meant it. Ryan doesn't care about him and Justin said Ryan takes off as soon as he gets there. He's wrapped up in Audrey and barely notices anything else. I doubt he even cares about you as much as you think he does. He'll go away after the estate is settled and you'll never see him again."

"Is that what you think?"

"Why do you think he's remodeling? He's making an apartment so the property will be more attractive to buyers. Don't you see you're making a problem where there doesn't have to be one? If I were you, I'd be focusing on Audrey and what she could do for you. Ryan is quite taken with her." Millicent's conscience twisted uncomfortably at throwing Audrey at Carroll's mercy, but she had no options. She couldn't back down. Distracting him was the only way.

Carroll advanced.

Millicent took a step back, but he reached out grasping the front of her nightgown anyway, pulling her to him. The moisture from his coat soaked the front of her body and she shivered.

"It's not just Audrey who's hot for Cassidy. I can smell it on you. Fuck, are you mental? See a lot of Chad in him? You never got over him. Too bad he didn't want you, but that's life isn't it? Now you're soft on his kid. A little old for that nonsense I'd think."

"I do like him, but not like that. He's not trouble. I'd tell you if he was."

"Would you?" Carroll released her and brushed her shoulder with his as he walked to the door. "I catch the boy there again and we'll have words. I mean it. I'd hate to see anything happen to you... or Justin." He walked out without a backward glance.

Millicent fell to her knees, her body shaking. She couldn't keep doing this. Unable to look at the woman in the mirror anymore, ashamed of her cowardice, her dishonesty, she couldn't go on.

"God, help me," she murmured. Although, she suspected there was no real God in Albertsville.

———

Justin tiptoed back to his room and closed the door softly. He shook, fury burning in his gut so that he thought he might throw up. He paced the dark room, kicking clothes out of his path and chewing his thumbnail. There had to be something he could do about that asshole, something that would take him down.

"Fuck." Taking a deep breath, he sat on the edge of his bed, eyeing the phone. Merle would be asleep and with him so sick... But he had to talk to someone.

He picked up the phone and turned it over in his hands. The full moon shone through the window. He hadn't closed the heavy curtain as his mother told him, and a cool draft reached the bare skin of his back, forcing a shiver. Carroll threatened them, plain as day. His helplessness made Justin angrier. He wished he were big enough, old enough to do something. Who would listen to a kid though? The rest of this town never did a damn thing. They kissed his father's ass, groveled at his feet, all hoping they could keep him happy so he'd keep sharing the wealth. When would they see that as a group they were stronger? Why didn't they do the math? What would he do against a whole town? Blame everyone else? Fuck, people were stupid. It was like that thing they'd studied in history. What was it? Stockholm syndrome? Something like that. They worshipped their captor, their tormentor, and ended up so they'd try to protect him. That's what this town acted like. Captives. Carroll had held them hostage for so long that they had grown used to the status quo, believing he actually gave a shit.

His mother's footsteps on the stairs paused as she approached his door. He held his breath, praying she didn't come in. When she moved away, down to the end of the hall, he let the breath out. Turning the phone over, he pressed "talk" and punched in Ryan's number.

"Yeah?"

"It's Justin."

"You okay?" The genuine concern in his voice brought a lump of emotion to Justin's throat, momentarily choking him. He wouldn't identify it, didn't want to. He just liked hearing someone cared.

"Yeah—well no. I'm not. I think it's time to get my mom to do something about my dad. I can't do it myself."

"Can you come over tomorrow?"

"Uh, I don't know. I'll try. I can't give you a time. I might have to sneak away."

Silence and then Ryan took a breath. "Just don't do anything that could get you in trouble. This can wait."

"No, it can't. I don't know how long Mom and I will be around."

From Millie's driveway Carroll headed toward town. She couldn't win this one. She just had to be reminded who was in charge. Running a tired hand through his hair, Carroll jumped at the warbling of his phone. What now?

"Speak."

"Just intercepted a call from Millicent's house," Fred reported.

As Fred played the call, Carroll's blood boiled. Fucking little bastard.

"So?" Fred asked. He flicked the switch on the machine, dousing the static that followed the call.

"Let's show them what happens to traitors. You know who to call?"

"Yep."

"Do it."

CHAPTER 14

Millicent rushed down the stairs, wrapping a battered pink housecoat around her wet body. "Justin!"

The door rattled on its hinges. She rounded the bottom of the stairway to an empty living room. Up in his room playing those stupid games.

The pounding grew louder, more insistent. "I'm coming, hold on."

Probably Carroll again. She should have just told Justin he couldn't go to Ryan's, and then she'd have some peace. It's not like it would have devastated him forever. Millicent turned the lock. The door flew open in her face. Her bare feet slipped on the hardwood floor. She went down.

A man stood over her. A full ski mask revealed only his dark eyes, but she knew he came from Carroll. "Justin!"

The grandfather clock chimed its sickly tune. Noon. Ryan spent half of Sunday waiting for Justin. Maybe Merle would know where the kid was.

He switched off the computer screen and searched the scarred top of his grandfather's desk for the note pad where he'd scribbled Mel's phone number. It lay on the edge near the window, under the phone. An interesting scar on the desk near the keyboard caught his eye. He ran his finger over the grooves of a zigzag line. "M," for Melvin? Why would an old man carve his initial into a perfectly good piece of furniture?

Ryan moved the keyboard and his breath hitched in his chest. "ENI" hid beneath the keyboard. Mine spelled backward? He frowned, tracing the new letters. *Mine.* What did that have to do with anything? On his first day in the house, he'd found the pattern of the dust strange. The detail now leapt to his mind. So the computer hadn't been moved and forgotten. Why not take the whole desk? *Because it was on the list, stupid.*

From the drawer, he picked up the neatly typed lists of items. *Mine.*

Before solving any riddles, he had to check on Justin. He punched in Merle's number.

"This better be an emergency," the old man grumbled.

"I think it might be."

"Ryan? What is it?"

"Justin called me last night and said he needed help. But he didn't know if he could get here, said he'd have to sneak over. I'm not sure what's going on."

A ragged breath traveled down the line, but Merle didn't speak. Ryan turned to look out the window. Outside, Larry moved along the tree line, sniffing the air and glancing toward the house. The gangly-looking animal moved gracefully through the deep snow. For Larry, it might have been fresh grass and the day as warm as a spring morning.

"Do you have a cell phone?" Merle asked.

"Yeah, why?"

"Phones aren't secure. Call me on my cell, with yours."

Merle's order shattered his moose gazing.

"Okay…"

Merle rattled off a number and the line went dead. He retrieved the phone from his coat in the hallway and punched in the number while he returned to the den.

Merle spoke at once. "Look, if Carroll was there, then we're probably too late anyway. Carroll doesn't let problems sit long enough to multiply. Know what I mean? So we park way up the road, I know a spot that the guys use when they hunt. Just a small clearing off the ditch, but it's hidden by a bunch of trees. We park there and follow the tree line to Millie's. We can't be seen, no matter what. If she is alive and unharmed, then I don't want to bring her more trouble by showing up there in the open. If she's not unharmed…"

"Then what do we do?"

"Nothing. We turn around and go home."

"But if we catch him—"

"What? We catch him and snowshoe out of town? You lost your mind, boy?" Merle barked.

"Oh. I forgot about the road."

"I didn't."

"Okay, I'll be there in under an hour."

"Faster." Merle ended the call.

The phone slipped from Ryan's hand and clattered to the desk.

He was living in a fictional world. People didn't get away with this shit in real life. They just didn't. He'd wake up in his apartment, his alarm clock would be blaring and his grandparents would be alive and still unknown to him. "I wish."

The air rushed from Ryan's lungs when Millicent opened the door. Under the dim light of the porch, her face showed a myriad of bruises, her lips swollen so that they no longer looked like lips. She limped away, wrapping her bloodied pink robe tighter to her body.

Merle charged through the door, shoving Ryan aside. "What the hell happened? Where's Justin?"

"Right here," the boy called from a dark corner of the living room.

Millicent had vanished to the kitchen and Ryan faltered. Should he go see to her? What the hell was going on?

"Carroll sent some guys," Justin said. "They locked me in my room or I'd have helped her. I would have. I couldn't do nothing but sit there and listen to her scream. I tried to get out."

Justin hung his head and his shoulders shook. Merle leaned forward and touched the boy's knee. "Nothing you could have done either way. You're one man against experienced goons."

"Why are you here?" Millicent stood in the archway that separated the living room from the rest of the house.

"Justin called and I—"

"Justin!"

"I knew he'd do something, Ma. I was right too. If you'd listened to me…"

"Even *I* didn't expect Carroll to take it this far." Merle said. "Who did he send?"

Millicent shrugged. "They wore masks, so I can't say for sure. They didn't even speak. Just came in, locked Justin in his room and started hitting me. I know Carroll sent them."

Millicent paced the floor of her living room, running unsteady hands through her blond hair.

Justin sat in an old brown recliner staring at his hands. Next to Ryan, Merle remained silent on the uncomfortable couch.

"Justin, I told you about eavesdropping. Christ, I warned you about the phones too." She sighed, shaking her head.

"But Ma, he's not going to stop. It's not eavesdropping when it's about me. He threatened me too. Don't you remember?"

"I remember. He wasn't serious about hurting you. Carroll talks like that but he never means it. That was to scare me. I should have listened."

Ryan fought the urge to shake Millicent. "I think that Justin's eavesdropping is irrelevant. What matters is that you two are in real danger."

Millicent spun to face him. The dim light that shone through the large bay window behind him, emphasized the bruising around her eyes and mouth. "Don't you think I know Carroll enough to judge how much danger we're in? It's not the first time he's tossed around threats, or sent messages like he did today. It definitely won't be the last. This is how he keeps us in line. Another week, two at most, he'll move on to someone else. It's how things work here."

"What do you plan to do during that week or two? Is Justin no longer allowed at the farm? Are you going to avoid me? I recall you saying you wouldn't do that, but under the circumstances, I don't see that you have any other choice. You'll give him exactly what he wants."

"What do you suggest I do? I said no and look where it got me. It's not like I just go along with everything he says. I try, but there's no fighting him on some things. In this town you have to pick your battles."

Merle cleared his throat legs stretched in front of him. He wore the same pants the day Ryan had met him, with brown stains on the knees and a tear in the pocket. Did he ever change his clothes? Judging by his smell, not very often.

"You can stop him," Merle said.

"How?" Millicent crossed her arms over her chest and stared down at the old man.

"Tell."

Millicent snorted. "Tell who? How? What am I supposed to tell them? The Reeve is a miserable prick? I didn't know they arrested people for being assholes. I've got no proof he sent those men. You're forgetting that several people have tried to tell. It never works."

"But you're not alone this time, Millie. It's always been one person, alone. He can manage that. But more than one… don't you get it?"

"That's not it and you know it."

"What is it then? He does nothing to help you, Ma," Justin said.

"Never mind."

"Millie, come on." Merle stood.

"No. Christ, I've worked and suffered for fifteen years to get where I am. Do you think I'm going to share what I've done to people who won't understand? Do you think I want Carroll to really mess me up next time or to ruin what I've fought so hard to salvage from my fucked up life?"

RENÉE MILLER

Merle reached for her shoulders, but she shrank from him.

He dropped his arms to his sides and sighed. "We've all kept quiet, and for what? This place is a delusion. Don't you see that? This security is false. We have nothing. It would take one person to come in and see what's going on and we'd be sunk. I kept quiet because Emily loved this town. I thought I did. I used to be proud to say where I was from. Didn't you?"

"I can't do it. Everyone will hate me."

Her anguish lodged in Ryan's throat, a burning, painful lump.

Merle shrugged. "How about we work together? Between us, we could gather enough information to make some big changes."

"I can't—"

"Just listen. Then decide what you want to do."

Millicent nodded.

Merle sat down again, shifting painfully on the old floral couch. Ryan knew his back hurt him constantly. Justin had told him not to draw attention to his illness so he said nothing.

The room brightened. Justin had switched on a floor lamp next to his chair.

"When Emily got sick, I tried everything I could to make her better. Everything. I took her to doctors, herbalists, and priests. Remember we spent that week in Toronto even. Christ that cost a pretty penny. But that doctor said there was nothing anyone could do. Took me a good six months to agree with him though. She took a bad turn shortly after that and I knew she wasn't long for this world." Merle paused, to run a dirty hand over his face punctuated by a long rasping breath. "The night she died, Carroll came in to offer his "support," telling me he'd pray for her and that the town was behind me. He also said something that made me pause. He told me I had to take over her legacy, cause she had no more kin.

"Emily heard him, though I didn't understand what he meant. She waited till Carroll left and apologized. I asked what for. Go look in the back field, she said, the one she sold before we got married. Then she told me to look in the box where she kept her papers under the bed."

"What did you find?" Ryan's imagination conjured all sorts of things. Any one of them would change his view of the old man.

"Pot. Three acres of the shit. Next to it, a drying shed. It's not much but enough to send me to jail for a good while. In her papers, I found bank statements showing money transferred to Emily's savings account from the mill. She never worked a day at the mill. So that meant the money came from the drugs. I was so pissed I burned the whole fucking thing the day she passed."

"Pot? Really? This is the big secret?"

"No, not the *big* secret, just one reason the people here toe the line. You know how much cash that shit brings? It's all over the place. Shit, most of the wealthier people here would be in jail if anyone knew."

"So, you've kept silent because you don't want people to know your wife grew pot?"

"Shit, no. I don't care if they know that. Hell, it's gone and she's gone, makes no difference to me now. I had to give the land over to Albert anyhow, because I wouldn't work it like he asked. Christ, I couldn't do it even if I had been willing. This old back's been waging a steady revolt since that shaft collapsed at the mine when I was a kid. I felt so guilty when I signed the papers that gave up everything Emily's family worked to keep. Emily's great grandfather fell on hard times soon after Emily was born. So, Carroll's grandfather offered him a solution. He would take the land off his hands—a big expense lifted from his shoulders—if he farmed the back field. They signed a contract. As long as Emily's family farmed what the Alberts told them to farm, they could stay. If not, they left."

"They had pot back then?" Justin asked.

Ryan laughed. "I'm pretty sure pot has been around for a very long time."

"To tell you the truth, I don't know if they grew that here way back then," Merle said. "I just know that when Emily's folks died, they ordered her to just do what she was told and to keep her mouth shut. I can't find those bank statements now."

"A judge would find them very interesting." Ryan said.

"I think someone took care of them, if you know what I mean."

"So how can you do anything? You burned the pot and the papers are gone," Ryan couldn't believe they hadn't taken at least a picture before ruining all of that evidence.

"Ah, he's still growing it out there but that's not really the worst of it. Look at what he does to people who don't toe the line. He's done worse too. What about the next visit, Millie?"

"Why can't you do this on your own?" Millicent's eyes pleaded with the old man. For what, Ryan wasn't sure.

"Like I said, no one can do it alone. He's too good. But together, we stand a chance. I'm tired, Millie. Aren't you tired?"

She turned to face Ryan. He offered her a smile, but she turned from him, from all of them, and padded to the kitchen.

Justin moved to stand but Merle's placed a hand on his arm. "Let her be. She needs time."

Millicent clattered around in the kitchen while they waited in the silent living room, each avoiding the others' gaze. A shadow fell over the room and Ryan looked up.

Arms at her sides—shoulders slumped in resignation—Millicent faced them. "I'll do it. I'll make up something about seeing him outside, maybe even hint about the mine. I don't know what's in there, but I'm sure Carroll won't like cops snooping around."

"Are you sure? Once we go ahead, you can't back out," Merle reminded her.

"I won't back out. What do we do? Where do we go?"

"Nowhere yet," Ryan said. "But I know someone who I think you should go to first. That way, if Carroll's reach extends beyond Albertsville we have insurance. Someone else, someone impartial, will be able to make the information public and no one can ignore it."

"Can we talk to someone now?"

"Think about that for a minute. First, we need to know

there really is something in the mine. They won't come just because *you think* there is. Once we're sure, we'll go to my friend. If he runs the story before you can get out of here—and I can't control that—then you're at risk. Think Carroll won't find out? You need to be safe, out of Albertsville, and far away from his influence before the shit hits the fan. I know another guy, an RCMP officer, but we need solid proof before I go to him. They can't come searching without a reason."

"That could take months."

Merle stood, rubbing his lower back as he straightened. "No. I think with all of us working together, we can find out what he's hiding soon enough. Just pack your shit and be ready. You and me are out of here as soon as we got enough to raise suspicion, whether you figure out what's at the mine or not."

"What about Justin?" Millicent waved toward the boy who sat on the edge of the chair.

"He'll come too. For now, he can stay with me. We'll tell everyone I'm getting real sick and need help around the house. I don't want him around here, just in case they come back. But both of you need to be ready to go."

"Okay. In the meantime no one says anything." Millicent looked pointedly at Justin.

He reddened. "I can keep a secret. Thanks for the vote of confidence though."

"It's not that. I know how that hot head of yours can explode. Don't let Carroll get to you. No matter what happens, you keep your mouth shut."

Ryan stood and picked his coat off the arm of the couch. "Don't worry about him. He's the one who convinced us to act. He'll do fine."

Justin nodded. "I want to see that bastard pay. Don't worry about me messing this up."

A chill ran up Ryan's spine at the resemblance to Carroll in the boy's expression.

"Oh and stay off the land lines, obviously they're listening. Cell phones only. You got one?" Ryan asked.

"Yeah, but it costs so much I never use it."
"You'll have to use it now."

CHAPTER 15

The bell over the door clanged. Audrey climbed over boxes—and the snow blower that Ryan had asked her to set aside—to the doorway of the stockroom. When she made it to the aisle, she was short of breath. Jesus, she needed to work out or something.

She scowled at the bits of foam and cardboard dust covering her black pants, and brushed her hands over the worst of it as she emerged from the narrow aisles.

"Hard at it?" Carroll asked.

She stopped mid-step.

He leaned against the counter—practically sitting on top—arms crossed over his chest. If Audrey didn't know what an asshole Carroll Albert was, she might have felt a flutter of attraction. His hair, a touch of grey showing at the temples, curled away from his forehead and his long body, still in excellent shape, appeared relaxed, yet strong. He looked as though he could take on anything *and win*. A shiver crept over her spine.

Bracing herself, she straightened her shoulders. "Aren't I always hard at it?"

"You don't have to. I offered you help once, but you refused. Pride isn't such an attractive trait when it only serves to make your life harder."

"It has nothing to do with pride."

He smiled.

Goosebumps rose on her arms. That smile, where his lips lifted just slightly while his eyes stared right through to her soul, meant nothing good. She waited. He'd spill his venom eventually. She'd regretted more than once already agreeing to look after Mel and Rachel's estate. To think, if she had nothing to do with it, she wouldn't know or care about Ryan, and Carroll would have continued to ignore her existence.

"You haven't been to see your friend in a few days. Did you two break up?"

"We had nothing to break up, but he's been busy with renovations and I have to pay my bills."

His smile vanished. "You're supposed to be keeping an eye, pushing him out of town."

Audrey's hands curled into fists. Wasn't she better than this? Certainly, she was better than him. She forced a smile. "It's hard to push him out of a town no one can leave at the moment."

"True, but while you've been paying your bills, he's been making mischief. I don't want him doing that. It bothers me."

"What kind of mischief?"

"Talk. The worst kind. He's been hanging around Merle and just the other day he had Justin over at his place. I know Millie's too smart to be swayed, but her son... he's young and impressionable. He'd believe anything from a city boy. And Merle, well he's just miserable enough to go along out of spite with whatever Cassidy asks him to do."

"Merle has always done what's right for this town. Ryan won't convince him to do anything he doesn't want to do." Audrey silently cursed Ryan. She'd warned him to keep his nose clean. Why would he make himself so damn obvious? What happened to just putting in his year?

"I want you to keep him busy for a while. Think you can do that?"

"Why?"

Carroll raised a thin brow.

They were so perfectly arched that nature couldn't have created them. Did he wax or pluck?

He advanced.

She did not move away, that had been her first mistake the last time. Audrey lifted her chin, determined to stand firm.

"It's not for you to question why, just do it. I have to clean up his mess and I can't do that with him constantly underfoot. I need him away from the farm and away from Millie for a few hours. Clear?"

"Sure. Whatever." Audrey smiled. Did he feel the hate oozing through her pores? He should.

"Good. I don't want to have to put pressure on you, but I will. Remember that."

Her chest burned from holding her breath. Slowly she let it out, as he turned to leave.

He pushed through the door and strolled out onto the street as though he hadn't a care in the world.

When he disappeared from sight, Audrey slumped. Her legs shook as she moved to the counter to sit on the stool she hid beneath it.

Ryan had to see reason. If he wouldn't, she'd wash her hands of him. Couldn't she just call that lawyer and tell him she quit? Audrey pressed a finger to her head, against the pain that throbbed between her eyes. Ryan could not go around stirring people up the way that he was. He probably didn't even realize he'd done that, but Carroll didn't care if it was intentional. She had to make Ryan understand that he needed to put in his year quietly, disturbing the status quo as little as possible. Christ, next fall he'd be gone and the rest of them would have to deal with the fallout.

Beneath the cash register, a green light flashed "ready" on the phone. She punched in the number to the Cassidy farm, her stomach tightening when his smooth, quiet voice lodged a flutter in her chest. She hated lying to him. Every time he smiled Audrey longed to confess everything; how she'd let Carroll force her into his web, so tangled that she wasn't sure how to free herself.

"Hello?" Ryan repeated.

"Sorry." Audrey took a breath. "What's on the agenda to-day?"

"Not much. I'll do what I can with this addition. Merle's coming out on the weekend to help me run the pipes so I can put a little sink and a small bathroom in. Actually, I planned to come into town to see what you had. You busy?"

"No, quiet as usual. I hoped maybe we could meet for dinner or something. You should take a break... rent a movie. I'm kind of going stir crazy with this weather." She sounded lame. Good thing she had no real hopes of a relationship with him. The rate she was going, it wouldn't happen anyway.

"I don't do chick flicks."

His deadpan voice made her chuckle. She didn't do chick flicks either. "No, I thought maybe some oldies, comedy preferably, but if you need blood and car crashes, I don't mind."

"Your place or mine?"

His question, his tone of voice, though innocent sounding, did stupid things to her. "Uh... mine I guess... yours is liable to tempt us both to work rather than relax."

"Sounds good. Dinner at six?"

"Six it is. Meet me at the store."

"Deal. Don't work too hard. I don't want you falling asleep and drooling on me while I'm trying to watch the movie."

Audrey gripped the phone tighter. Ryan was a good guy, in every way. What kind of person manipulated someone like him? She did, by playing Carroll's game and following his orders. Something she'd vowed would never happen. *Pull yourself together.* Right. "Okay, see you later."

"You bet."

Before replacing it on the base, Audrey held the phone for a few moments more. What if she told him everything? Would he hate her? Pity her? She didn't know which would be worse, and didn't care to find out. After this, Carroll would leave her alone.

Merle drove out of the Douglas driveway and turned right, toward his old ramshackle place. Carroll flicked his cigarette out of the window and rubbed his jaw. Christ, he'd been so busy that he'd forgotten to shave. Damn that little prick and his troublesome family. Every time he turned, a fucking Cassidy lurked behind him messing around in his business.

Justin often stayed at Merle's so seeing him in the cab next to the old man hadn't surprised him, but the bags in the bed of the truck sent bells ringing in his head. They were up to something. He wanted Justin out of the way for a while, but not if meantime Millicent plotted away with Ryan. That didn't suit his plans. Not at all. Just what did Ryan tell Millie to do? What did Millie tell Ryan? Too many possibilities led to places Carroll didn't want to go.

Farley slouched in the passenger seat. "That's a lot of luggage for a sleepover. The kid moving in with Jamieson?"

Carroll glanced to the thermos of coffee on Farley's lap. The man lived on that shit, despite warnings about what the vile fluid did to a man's insides. "I don't know. Justin can stay with Merle. I'm not concerned about that. I'll deal with that old fucker later if I have to. You said they stayed here for a while?"

"Yeah, couple of hours. Then Cassidy hightailed home and sat in that office for a really long time. Thought you said we couldn't get no Internet out here? He's got one of those dialing things and everything."

"Why? You want to surf the digital highway? Like you could operate a computer. Can you even read?"

Farley stared and chewed his lip. "Well, let's get this show on the road then. I want to get home to bed. Big day at the mill tomorrow."

"Big day? What, you got a date with Kim? Calvin won't like that much." Carroll chuckled at the other's scowl.

Farley's hands tightened around the black thermos. "Fuck you. I ain't no faggot. Christ, that's not funny. Closing a mill ain't as simple as closing up a store, you know? The machines need prepping and things have to be cleaned up. Fucking Kim… you really are on a roll tonight."

Carroll turned the key and pulled out of the ditch. He couldn't imagine a man wanting another man in a sexual way. It made him sick. But he didn't let on to anyone how he felt. You catch more flies with honey, and the sweeter the honey, the bigger the flies. By allowing Calvin and his lover to believe that he thought everyone should do what made them happy, Carroll had insurance. Sometimes money wasn't enough incentive. They believed him to be an ally if not a friend. But really, they deserved to go straight to hell. What they did was unnatural and wrong. God would punish them as they deserved to be punished. Carroll didn't need to worry himself with judgment.

The afternoon's fading light licked the roof of Millicent's cabin, shadows emphasizing the spots where the brown shingles pulled away. She'd nagged him time and again to get the roof fixed. Carroll promised now and then to see about it, but it was low on his priority list. The place didn't leak and as long as the current roof did its job, why would he waste money on it? "You know the drill?"

Farley nodded as they stopped behind Millicent's truck. "Yep. You talk. I stand by. Don't know why you need me anyhow if I'm just there to look pretty."

"If she gets uppity, we'll have to force her to see reason. I can't get my hands too dirty and that's what I pay you for. You up to it?"

Farley grunted an inaudible reply as they got out of the Hummer. The frigid air whipped powdery gusts of snow. Carroll shivered. Fucking winter. Everything got cold and wet and his problems mounted. People didn't mind this town when they could come and go as they pleased, but give them a few days stuck within a few kilometers of space and they all go fucking batshit. His responsibilities became endless.

Eyeing the house, Carroll bit his lip. Every window glowed, lit up like a damn Christmas tree and eating away his money. Carroll stepped to the door and opened it. No need to knock on his own door.

He held the screen door for Farley before walking down the narrow hall to the kitchen. As his eyes adjusted to the brighter light, his gut boiled in fury. Boxes everywhere, some empty and some half full of items told an interesting story. Carroll kicked the closest one out of his path, the sound of dishes clattering and breaking soothing his rage.

"Carroll, I—"

"Save it, Millie."

She stood by the breakfast nook, her back to the window. The lavender sunset that filled the lower panes framed her face, giving her a softer appearance, reminding Carroll of when she was younger and easier to control. Age seemed to have altered her ability to reason and make sane decisions. Well, he would re-teach her that skill.

"Going somewhere?" Farley asked.

Carroll didn't silence him, although he recalled telling the idiot to stay quiet. Millie ignored him anyway, turning to face Carroll.

"No, I told you the place needed renovations. You continuously ignore me so I'm doing them myself, starting with the kitchen."

She lied. It was obvious in the way her hands tugged at her grey sweater. Although she looked him in the eye, her mouth trembled and her head tilted to one side. Just a fraction. Not enough for anyone else to notice, but Carroll knew Millie well enough to detect the little things that gave her away.

"Is that why Justin is staying with Merle?" His gaze on Millicent's, Carroll lifted the flap of a box containing Justin's video console and games.

Her cheeks bloomed. Another sign.

"No. He—they... Merle isn't well and Justin wanted to help him out. I don't see any reason for him not to go. It teaches him to be responsible. Are we worried about Merle now too? Really, Carroll, you'll have to start making lists. I can't keep track."

Carroll sighed and moved to the sink. He picked up a piece

of newspaper from the counter and opened the cupboard. Bare shelves. Lowering his gaze, he reached for the toaster, the only thing remaining on her once cluttered countertop. "You forgot to pack the toaster."

"I don't need to. I'm fixing the cupboards so it can stay where it is. I can't afford to replace the counter."

"Why do you keep lying to me? Haven't I at least earned the right to hear the truth? We're friends. I care about you, and you care about me. Your insistence on making shit up makes me wonder if you're plotting against me. Why else would you be planning to run away, Millie?"

She stopped tugging at the sweater, arms at her sides. Straightening her shoulders, she lifted her chin.

This should be interesting.

"Bullshit. If you gave a damn, you'd care that I can barely make ends meet. You'd care that this place is falling apart and that I'm at my limit with your son because I can't afford to raise him like you told me to. You wouldn't have sent someone to beat me up the other night either. I'm fine, by the way, thanks for asking. If you really cared about me, you'd give a shit about things like that. But you don't. All you worry about is what's good for Carroll and nothing else."

Farley shifted behind him. No one, not even Farley, knew about Justin's birth. She'd pay for that and deal with Farley's new knowledge later. "I don't know what you're talking about. Someone beat you up? That's awful. We talked about Justin a long time ago. I told you I'd see that you had what you needed. I always do. You're usually so patient. Why are you doing this now? What's got you all fired up? I bet it's Cassidy."

Millicent bit her lip, her gaze flicking briefly to Farley. Carroll didn't have to turn. He would be leaning against the doorframe, arms crossed, as he always did when they visited someone. It was his attempt at being intimidating.

"Well?" he prompted.

"I'm done with this bullshit. Done," she muttered.

"What bullshit?"

"Yours, his, this town… I can't do this anymore. We

shouldn't suffer for what someone else did. You can't keep controlling us."

A bubble burst in Carroll's chest, sparking a burning sensation that scalded his throat. Millicent never defied him. She never plotted against him. She wouldn't have considered it without Cassidy's encouragement. "So, you think you're just going to leave? You can't do that."

"I can do what I want. You aren't my father and despite what you believe, you don't own me. You don't own anyone. If I want to leave, I can."

"Interesting."

Carroll linked both hands behind his back and lowered his gaze. He moved slowly, scuffing a toe on the cracked linoleum as he stepped toward her. It really was in bad shape, but a cracked floor didn't warrant this betrayal. His control slipped, just a fraction, but the feeling of his grip loosening produced an uncomfortable flutter in Carroll's chest.

He'd taken Millicent for granted, or at least her loyalty. He should have seen the signs. His warning had given Ryan the perfect opportunity. Millicent had always been unstable. He'd selected her years ago because of that slight imbalance in her personality. Unstable meant weak, malleable, but he'd manipulated her for so long that he'd forgotten a soft mind was easy prey to anyone bold enough to take control. By God, he hated admitting fault but he was only one man, subject to the frailties of lesser men if he wasn't careful. He'd learn from this.

Ryan had moved in on Millie fast, probably fucked her for good measure, and now she'd allowed him to use her. What had she told him? How much more did he know now? Time to correct his negligence. Millie just needed to be reminded of who really had control. It was not Ryan Cassidy.

Pausing when his feet met hers, his expensive steel-toed boots touching her gray wool socks, Carroll raised his head and met her eyes.

She shivered.

He smiled, and reached to tuck a piece of blond hair behind her ear. She'd always been a little on the heavy side for his taste, but not unattractive. The lines around her eyes and mouth didn't detract from the perfectness of her face. Heart-shaped—with a full mouth and luminous green eyes—Millie had been a beauty and could still be described as such. He could imagine Ryan managing to get it up for the old girl, had even been tempted himself a time or two just for old time's sake. Carroll was too smart to muddy the waters of their current relationship though. "I don't want to fight with you. I think you're blowing the situation out of proportion. You can't look after yourself. You need me."

"No. I'm not blowing anything out of proportion and I definitely don't need you. I'm leaving and Justin is coming with me."

"Really? Millie, come now. Let's think about this. Where will you go? The roads have barely been cleared. Do you know what they're like further out? I don't think so. You'd risk Justin's safety?"

"The roads are fine."

"I don't think you understood me the other day. I warned you what would happen."

She wavered. He saw it in the way her eyes moved to his mouth, away from his gaze. So close. If she couldn't be swayed....

"I understood you. That's why I'm going. You're no longer in charge, Carroll. You can threaten all you want. What are you going to do when the whole town turns on you? What if everyone decides that they have their own minds? Going to kill everyone?"

Millicent's gaze met his once more in a silent dare.

Eager to meet her challenge, Carroll stepped forward. If she couldn't be swayed she was no longer of any use to him. "Not everyone, Millie. Just you."

CHAPTER 16

Her chest burned, it would soon burst if it didn't get air. The steely grip around her neck tightened, bruising the windpipe and straining her eyes against their sockets. Millicent gagged.

Carroll grinned.

"Please…" she tried, but it came out a garbled grunt.

Carroll cocked his head to the side, frowning. "What's that? I'm sorry Millie, you're not making sense. Tighter? Anything to please my lady. You always did like it rough."

His fingers dug in her tender flesh. She clawed at his arms, kicked at his body. Laughter, Farley's, reached her ears and fury mingled with the fear that grew in intensity as she struggled to take in air. He'd kill her this time. Why didn't she keep her mouth shut? She'd done just what she'd warned Justin against doing.

"No," she choked.

"Carroll, she's getting a little grey. You want me to handle this?" Farley's voice sounded far away.

Millicent tried to turn toward him, but she couldn't move under Carroll's grip. After squeezing a short, painful breath, spots danced before her eyes. Her limbs grew heavy. She struggled to raise them, pushing feebly at Carroll's chest.

"No, I think I want this one." Carroll leaned in, putting his weight into her and crushing her airway.

She swatted feebly, her arms as useful as Jell-O. Their eyes locked and Millicent knew she was going to die.

"Carroll, come on. You can't—" Farley said.

"Shut up."

Millicent convulsed, unable to fight any longer. Brilliant colored lights sparked and whirled before her eyes before darkness took her.

"So? What's the plan for tonight?" Ryan pushed his dinner around the paper-lined basket.

"Are you going to eat that or play with it?" Audrey asked.

"I'm not sure."

"I can't believe you call yourself a Canadian and you've never tried poutine." She shook her head.

Ryan stared down at the gelatinous blob of French fries, gravy and cheese curds, his stomach revolting at the thought of shoving the brown mess into his mouth. He'd heard of poutine before, but he'd never seen it or even pondered what it was. He shouldn't have told Audrey to order for him when they'd arrived, but he'd had to use the washroom and she'd seemed so on edge. He thought he'd make it easy on her. Well, he succeeded in making himself nauseous.

"It just seems so wrong." He lifted his fork, dripping with stringy cheese and globs of gravy to his mouth.

Audrey waited, grinning while he chewed. "Well?"

He smiled back. "Fucking awesome."

"Wow, the f-bomb. I knew you'd love it."

Ryan dug in, amazed at how the unsavory combination tasted like a chunk of artery-clogging heaven. Audrey listed their movie options. Ryan curled his nose up at a few suggestions but never stopped shoveling his dinner into his mouth.

She laughed. "Are you going to breathe?"

He looked up.

People sat at the bar, their eyes fixed on Ryan. Most of them wore knowing smiles. A couple snarled at his rather unattractive display. Though their table sat nestled in the far corner and the lights were low, Ryan's cheeks warmed just a little.

"Sorry, this is good shit." He set his fork down and resisted the urge to lick the empty basket. But it was a struggle.

"I told you it was good. Hey, how about westerns? Clint Eastwood is my hero." Audrey batted her eyes and fanned her face dramatically.

"Sure."

"Wow that was easy. Saves time too. We don't have to go to the video store. I've got every movie Clint ever made sitting in my living room."

"You need to get out more."

She set aside her fork, her dinner barely touched.

He glanced at it. Why was she acting so strange? First telling him that she'd rather they had dinner and watch movies at her house than go out. He'd joked and teased, and eventually persuaded her to go to Sal's for something quick to eat. Then, when he'd returned from the washroom, Carroll had passed their table, Farley tagging behind like a good dog. He'd nodded at Audrey. She'd stiffened in her seat but waved back. Her cheeks had colored but she made no comment. Added to that, Audrey's usual slow, easy air vanished. She rarely used unnecessary words or movement, just comfortable in her skin. Tonight she'd chattered incessantly, as though trying to fill the air... or distract him.

He pulled out his wallet and laid some bills on the table. "That should cover it, right?"

"Oh no, I'll pay for my half."

"No. Where I come from, I pay. I let you have your way the first time, but I have some pride, you know. Nothing Neanderthal about it, so don't even go there. Besides, you're supplying the beer and movies later. Right?"

"Beer? Sorry, I forgot to pick it up. I have wine."

"Wine it will have to be." He sighed and stood. "Does it come in paper or plastic?"

Audrey stood as well, almost toppling the chair in her haste.

She righted it, shaking her head and led him to the doors. "I have some class, Mr. Cassidy. It comes in cardboard."

The credits rolled. Audrey eyed the remote laying on the coffee table next to her feet, but she couldn't force herself to sit up. Her gaze fell on the empty bottles of wine at the other end of the table and she moved her cheek against the soft cotton of Ryan's shirt.

"Another?" his voice rumbled against her ear.

"I couldn't drink another drop. One more and I'll be mumbling incoherently and crying about every wrong ever done to me in junior high."

"I meant another movie."

Feeling silly but unable to care, she slid her hand down his chest to the waist of his jeans. He stiffened and a bubble of excitement formed in her belly. She'd told herself he wasn't attractive, not her type, but the more she knew about him the deeper her attraction grew. Would he push her away if she kissed him? She was so stupid about this stuff.

Audrey moved to look up at him and her breath caught when their eyes locked. Ryan's eyes had darkened, the pale blue lined by a deeper shade. A muscle twitched in his jaw.

"What?" She reached up to brush a strand of hair off his brow. He needed to have it cut. It curled around his face, always falling over his eyes. But he didn't seem to notice.

"I should probably go home."

"Are you okay to drive?"

"No."

His gaze shifted to her mouth and she licked her lips self-consciously. Ryan's cheeks flushed and a strangled sound escaped his throat. He lowered his mouth to hers. Audrey wound a hand in his hair. Soft, just as she thought it would be. She pressed against him, looping a leg over his thighs. His arms came around her until his hand gripped her bottom, pulling her closer.

"Stay?" she asked against his mouth. He slipped his tongue

past her lips, and deepened the kiss. Audrey tasted the sweetness of wine on his tongue, but then he pulled away.

"Should we do this? I mean, with all that's going on..." he looked away, one hand stroking her leg.

"If you don't want to, I understand." Her throat stung with humiliation and she tried to pull her leg back.

Ryan tightened his hand on her thigh.

She risked a look at his face, knowing that her eyes were moist, probably red-rimmed from wine and misery.

"Of course I want to." He drew her hand to the front of his jeans.

Her cheeks warmed but rather than pull away as she always had, she curled her fingers around the hardened muscle beneath the worn denim. Ryan drew a ragged breath. His other hand snaked around the back of her neck pulling so that she was forced to lay back. He followed, covering her body with his.

"No regrets, okay?" he asked.

"And no strings," she replied.

He smiled and ran his hand up her body, slipping under her sweater to trace a pattern over the sensitive skin just below her breasts. "Just tonight. Then... whatever? You think I'm that kind of guy?"

She smiled. *No, you're not.*

Ryan lowered his head to fasten his mouth to her neck. Then his tongue traced a warm line to her ear where his teeth tugged playfully on her earlobe. She shifted to lay fully beneath him, her legs free to wrap around his middle.

"This couch is too small," Ryan grumbled.

He slipped one hand under her back and fiddled with the clasp on her bra. She lifted herself, allowing him more room until the taut lace gave.

"We could go to the bedroom," she gasped. Sparks of pleasure streaked through her body as his fingers teased a nipple.

"We could."

"Now?"

Urgent fingers moved to the bottom of her shirt and tugged it up. "Sure," he murmured, lowering his head once more to trail his tongue over her stomach.

Ryan's head swam, and it wasn't just the wine. Her scent filled his nostrils, lingering on his tongue even before he'd tasted her skin. Soft, like vanilla but not quite, mingled with something earthy; deeper, more intoxicating than any bottled scent could produce. She moaned as his mouth closed over her breast, dragging his teeth lightly over her nipple.

Audrey's hands roamed his back, pushing at his pants and then his shirt. Ryan raised his body, tugging the t-shirt over his head before moving long fingers to his jeans. Green eyes followed him as he stood. He lowered the denim, taking his boxers with it.

Her cheeks colored, and her breath quickened into soft pants. "Here?" she asked.

Ryan shrugged. He didn't want to risk stopping now and move to the bedroom "Anywhere." He knelt down, so their bodies barely touched and traced her lips with his tongue.

She lifted her head from the soft brown suede of the armrest.

He pulled back.

Suddenly she pushed herself up, wrapping her legs around him so that he almost toppled over. The couch really wasn't ideal. His long legs hung over the end when he stretched out and there wasn't enough room for their bodies to lay on it, let alone roll around.

Ryan gave into common sense and tried to stand. He opened his mouth to suggest they move, but Audrey clung to him, nipping at his neck. Fed up with wrestling like a pair of kids on the too small couch, he lifted her with him and turned his head so that their mouths met. Her tongue joined his. He skirted around the couch, the room spinning He swayed. "Where's the bedroom?"

"Straight down the hall. The right. Third door." Her voice

had deepened, no longer a soft caress.

The raspy sound did wonderful things to Ryan's body. He moved as fast as he could with her mouth exploring his face, his neck, her nails scraping over his back.

Counting the doors, Ryan pushed through the third on the right, and his foot struck something hard. White-hot pain exploded through his shin and Audrey squealed as they fell in a tangle of arms and legs.

"Sorry." He tried to move off her but she pulled him back.

A giggle escaped her lips.

"Beds are overrated anyway. They creak don't they?"

She lowered her hands to her pants and squirmed beneath him, shoving the soft corduroy down until Ryan finally came back to reality and realized she couldn't kick them off with his legs covering hers.

"Let me." He pressed his mouth to her face, moving down over her breasts then flicking her belly with his tongue.

Audrey arched her back, and wound her hands in his hair.

He bit into the soft skin of her hip, drawing a low moan from her. As he moved lower, Audrey gasped. Encouraged, he slipped the pants over her knees parting them as he knelt to kiss the inside of her thighs.

Ryan breathed her in, his hands trembling as he gripped her hips.

Audrey tensed when his mouth found her. She arched into him.

A low growl escaped his chest as he licked.

Her hands found his hair once more, pushing his face further against her. "I—you don't have to do that," Audrey breathed.

Ryan frowned, but thrust his tongue inside her. He forgot the strange comment as her body tightened around him. She squirmed and he moved his mouth to thrust his tongue into her once more.

"I've never—shit that feels so good," she said.

She'd never what? Ryan lifted his head.

Audrey's eyes were wary. She bit her lip and released his

hair, lowering her arms to her sides. Sensing her discomfort, he slid up her body until he lay over her, his face inches from hers.

She met his eyes, before brushing her mouth over his, biting his lower lip and drawing it into her mouth. Her hand moved between them and she wrapped her fingers around him, squeezing gently.

"God, don't do that," his voice sounded ragged even to his ears.

Audrey jerked her hand away.

He laughed.

"What?" she asked.

"Nothing. You're so… jumpy. It's like you've never done this before."

"Sorry."

"Don't be sorry. If you want to stop—"

"Not on your life."

"Shit, I don't have a condom or anything. We shouldn't—"

"It's okay. I mean I—God, this is so awkward. I'm on the pill. I mean, I haven't been taking it long but it's not like I've been sleeping with the town, if that's what you're worried about. Of course you have to take my word for it, and that's okay if you'd rather wait until you have a c—uh, protection. I'm ruining this, aren't I?"

Ryan smiled. "No." He shifted so that he pressed against her. The moist heat of her body burned his skin as he pushed into it. Unable to breathe, he looked down at her face when he sensed something odd. Audrey gripped his shoulders. Her pale face flushed. Then she pushed her hips against him, crying out as the resistance gave way.

No, this wasn't right. Jesus, what had he just done? "Why didn't you tell me?"

"Would you be here if I had?"

He stared at her, the answer clear. No. He wouldn't have touched her. To know she'd gone thirty years without—and then to just give it to him with no promises of anything, humbled him more than he could ever express. A small voice at the back of his brain questioned why she'd waited.

Audrey moved beneath, her body clenched around him. He couldn't stop now. It was done. Covering her mouth with his, he kissed her maybe a little too roughly, tasting blood as his teeth—or hers—tore his lip. A sound, more of a whimper filled his mouth as he pushed against her.

"I can't." He didn't finish the thought, his body taking over as he thrust repeatedly until her face blurred and his ears filled with the roaring of his blood.

Audrey bucked against his hips, meeting him. She cried out again as a violent shudder wracked her body.

Ryan collapsed, careful not to crush her small frame beneath him and pressed his mouth to her cheek. Her skin was damp, and he licked salty tears away from his lips. "You're crying. Audrey, I'm so sorry. If I'd known…"

"I'm not crying because you hurt me. Well, it hurt a bit, but that's not why I'm crying."

"Why?"

"I can't believe I wasted so much time being afraid of this."

"Oh. Afraid?"

"I thought it was something scary, demoralizing… just silly childish things. It's not like I was saving it for marriage, I was just… too scared. Can we just lay here? I don't want to talk." She shifted so that they lay next to each other, the cool wood of the floor pressed against Ryan's hip as she nestled her face against his chest.

"You have to be the only woman on the planet to ever say that."

Audrey chuckled.

"I hope you know that you can get pregnant the first time. Jesus, this was so irresponsible of me."

"Relax, I told you I'm on the pill. I'm not an idiot."

Ryan caressed the top of her head, the riotous curls damp with sweat. He relaxed and drew her closer. As he floated in the twilight between sleep and wakefulness, a muted call filtered through the window. Low and mournful, it sent the fine hairs of his neck on end. An omen?

RENÉE MILLER

CHAPTER 17

"Well, well, would you look at that?" Carroll slowed the SUV as they passed Audrey's cottage. Cassidy's car sat at the curb, a good covering of snow blanketing its roof and windshield.

"Jesus, it's past midnight, you think they—?" Farley left the idea unspoken.

Carroll gripped the steering wheel and pressed the accelerator. Fucking right they did. She took her orders a little too seriously. Bile rose to Carroll's throat as he pictured Ryan getting what he should have taken a long time ago. Fuck, this was *his* town, not Cassidy's. Audrey belonged to him.

"Carroll?" Farley's voice drifted through his haze of fury.

Shit, he'd missed Farley's turn. "I'm just taking a little drive. We need to get our stories straight,"

"We don't need stories."

"We don't? You have to plan for every eventuality, Farley. How many times do I have to explain this?"

"Right, I didn't think of that. So, what's our story?"

Carroll stared at the snow-covered road ahead, tapping the steering wheel in thought. "Whatever fucks Cassidy the hardest."

Audrey lay with her cheek on Ryan's chest, listening to his deep even breaths. A slight snore now and then disturbed the early morning silence. She stared at the window next to her bed. The frilly lace curtain her mother made turned the pale light into a dappled pattern on the blue comforter that covered them.

Carroll would know. The thought sickened her. That she'd allowed him to control her made it worse.

He'd said to keep Ryan distracted for a few hours. She only meant to keep him late enough so Carroll could search for whatever he thought Ryan hid at the farm. Oh, who was she kidding? She hoped this would happen and sought Doctor Reid about birth control because she wanted to make sure nothing prevented her from doing just what they'd done. Guilt burned against her ribs, forcing a heavy lump down at the bottom of her stomach. She hadn't used Ryan. What they shared, while it worked to Carroll's advantage, wasn't meaningless. She wanted him because she'd never felt this way about anyone before. It was special. Ryan was special. If he knew....

"You awake?" his voice startled her.

She blinked away the tears that stung her eyes. "Sort of."

"Regrets?"

"Of course not. You?"

"Do you have to ask?" His fingers tickled her back.

Audrey shifted to tilt her face.

He brushed his mouth over hers briefly before pulling away. "Should I go home?"

"Do you want to?"

"Well I thought maybe you'd want me to before... well, before anyone was up and around."

"This is not the eighteenth century. A woman can have a man stay the night and escape the scorn of her neighbors, you know?"

Ryan laughed and kissed the top of her nose. "Good point. But I don't want certain people using this against you."

"Don't worry about me."

"Someone has to."

166

The fist of guilt that gripped her stomach tightened, clenching her insides painfully. She turned so he couldn't see her misery. She didn't use him. This was real. She shouldn't feel so terrible about it.

His hand roamed over her hip, tracing circles up her side before his fingers closed over her breast. "We've got at least an hour before it's officially morning."

Smiling Audrey turned.

He pulled her on top of him, linking his arms around her back.

"What can you teach me in an hour, city boy?"

"Let me show you, little girl."

"Weird." Audrey shifted her truck into park. Ryan's house was dark, the curtains drawn against the brilliant morning sunshine. Getting out of the truck, she moved toward the barn. A chill crept along her neck at the sight of open doors and tire tracks.

Why? Had Ryan noticed? Those tracks were too big to be from his car. They looked as if a truck or an SUV had driven through the snow. A Hummer? *Maybe.* Her breath, sharp and painful, caught in her chest and lodged there.

Torn between checking the barn and making sure Ryan was okay, Audrey stood immobile for a moment. If she went to the barn and someone was still there…. No, find Ryan first.

Turning toward the steps, Audrey scolded herself for letting her imagination get carried away. The door may have blown open, despite her certainty that she'd locked it before Ryan even arrived in Albertsville. Maybe he'd removed the padlock. Maybe he'd explored and hadn't locked it back up.

But the tire tracks….

The door opened before she reached the top step.

"You're early." Ryan's hair was mussed, his eyes red-rimmed.

Her chest tightened at his scowl. Maybe last night meant nothing to him, despite the tender kisses he'd shared before the sun rose. "Sorry?"

"Nah, I just—I need coffee. Couldn't sleep." He disappeared inside the house, leaving the door open.

"It's all right. No need to invite me in, I'll just follow you. Coffee sounds good," she muttered to his retreating form.

After stomping her boots on the mat, Audrey stepped inside and closed the door. Shadows loomed over the hall, and in the living room grew longer, stretched by the scarce furniture in what used to be her favorite room. He'd taken nearly everything out. Men had no clue.

Ryan moved about the kitchen.

She watched him run water into the coffeepot and smiled when he almost dropped it in the sink. Cursing, he shuffled to the left, disappearing from her view. Someone felt the wine. She shouldn't have doubted him. He wouldn't treat her so callously.

She took a breath and joined him. "Headache?"

"Giant." He nodded and turned from the counter. He didn't look at her as he shuffled to the chair and sank down.

"Sorry?"

Ryan smiled and raised tired eyes. "Stop apologizing. I know I can't drink wine. I figured after this morning—well, after we did what we did—never mind. I thought I'd escaped the headache. It just lurked there waiting to attack when I was alone and defenseless."

"It should go once you've eaten. That's what I've heard anyway."

"Great. I forgot about breakfast."

Audrey's gaze moved to the large windows behind him. He'd drawn the shades to cover half, but the barn was still visible... and the tracks. "Hey, did you go out to the barn over the last couple of days?"

Ryan frowned. "No. Why?"

"When I pulled up I saw tire tracks. The door is open."

Silence.

Ryan's face paled. He turned to the window. The muscles in his shoulders stiffened. "Let's go check it out."

Ryan stood and strode from the room. The closet creaked

open.

Audrey scrambled to her feet. "Ryan?"

His footsteps sounded down the hallway and when she rounded the corner, he'd already slipped his boots on and opened the door. He paused, raising a brow.

"Do you have any thoughts on why it might be open?"

Something in his voice, a coolness that she hadn't heard before, sent her defenses up. "Why would I?"

"I don't know. Just a thought. Don't mind me. I'm seeing conspiracies everywhere I guess."

"Maybe we should take something. A gun maybe."

She didn't want to go out there at all. If it was Carroll, they would be defenseless and she knew he would do what he felt necessary to save his own ass.

"I don't own a gun. Normal people don't feel the need for one. People who live in a civilized fucking town do not carry weapons. They don't let people get away with murder, extortion or drug trafficking. They definitely don't become a part of it out of some fucked up belief that some big secret could hurt their pathetic little lives. Is everyone getting a cut from the pot? Is that it?"

She shook her head.

"Well, whatever it is, you do the crime, you do the time. Cliché I know, but true. Jesus, I've had it with the cowardice that's so thick around here, I can smell it no matter where I go. Know what it smells like?"

Ryan's tirade forced a lump to Audrey's throat, making it impossible for her to speak. She shook her head again. A guilty blush warmed her cheeks and she looked away.

"I'll tell you. It smells bitter and rotten. Like spoiled food, or a shitty diaper left out in the heat to attract flies and cook the shit until it's ripe enough to peel the damn paint off the wall."

He turned and stomped out the door leaving Audrey with a choice. Follow, or run away. She swallowed the panic that rose and followed, jogging to catch up with him.

Up close, the tracks showed big tires, like Carroll's SUV.

Two sets of footprints began where the tracks ended. Audrey's heart fluttered in her chest as they approached the open door. He paused a few feet from the barn.

"You didn't see the light this morning?" she asked.

"No. I didn't know there was a light out here. I was tired. I think I slept most of the drive home to be honest."

Audrey caught the twitch of his lips and relief flooded through her body. He wasn't angry with her, which meant maybe he didn't suspect what she had been up to when she invited him out. God, she wished she could take back her promise, that what she'd found with Ryan wasn't clouded by Carroll's ever present shadow.

"Let's check it out. Whoever was here is long gone. They wouldn't come back on foot, and I don't see any other tracks." He waved an arm at the ground.

She nodded. "Just, be careful. We don't know what's in here. If it's Larry, he might be scared."

"Larry should know better than to leave my lights on." Ryan stepped slowly toward the door. He disappeared inside.

Audrey attempted to follow, but couldn't force her feet to cooperate.

"Son of a bitch," Ryan's tone was pissed and mixed with a trace of fear.

She froze at the threshold. "What?"

"Stay there. Don't come in."

It was enough to force Audrey forward. She turned the corner into the stalls, to a shadow that swayed under the glare of the bare bulb over the narrow aisle.

A cry escaped her lips.

"I told you to stay out Aud. Fuck, this is really bad."

"Millicent," Audrey had no more words.

Millicent's cold eyes bulged. A rope circled her neck and ran up over the rafters. Her hands hung at her sides, fingers curled into claws.

"Christ, we have to call the police."

"What? Are you crazy? They've done this to frame you. Please Ryan, don't call them. Just… just…"

"Just what? Let her hang there? Cut her down and bury her in the frozen fucking ground? What? Tell me, Audrey, what the hell do I do with a dead woman in my barn? I call the cops. That's what I do. They can't frame me anyway. I was with you all night. When you tell them—" his blue eyes darkened and he tilted his head.

"What?"

"You will tell them, won't you?"

"They won't believe me anyway." It was Carroll's plan all along. Audrey's stomach threatened to rebel. He'd just involved her in a murder. Not just any murder, but Millicent's. She never liked the woman, but she didn't deserve to die. "Jesus, why Millicent?"

"I don't know. A couple days ago, I went over there and those bruises you see on her face and arms were brand new. She had a fat lip too. Something tells me that little visit had something to do with this. Damn, if I'd known I wouldn't have pushed her." He ran a shaky hand through his hair.

Pushed her? Oh, what have you done, Ryan?

"We need to find Justin and whether they framed me or not, we must follow the proper procedure here and call Fred. A man who has nothing to hide doesn't run. I have nothing to hide." Ryan stood at Millicent's feet.

Audrey forced herself to look away from the tightly curled toes. "Do you think Justin's okay?"

"I think that Carroll isn't stupid. Two murders are much harder to cover up. Shit, one murder in normal circumstances is hard to hide."

"He might plan to make it look like a murder suicide. She kills Justin and takes her own life."

Ryan ran both hands through his hair this time, making it stick out at the back. Audrey looked at him with new eyes. The man standing before her, with his cold glare and the twitching muscle in his jaw, was not the laid back, passive guy she'd believed him to be. Carroll might regret taking on this particular Cassidy.

"Or he might be planning to fuck me. All he needs is one

dead body for that. Let's call Merle. Then I'm calling Fred. You'll stay, tell them that you followed me here for breakfast and we noticed the door was open. Or, if you aren't backing me up on this, go home. But don't bother coming back. No strings, like you said."

Ryan turned and brushed past her. Audrey stared at the empty space he occupied a moment before. The worn wood floor darkened where he'd stood, a puddle of slush rimmed a circular stain. The floorboards next to it heaved. She stepped closer.

Funny, all the boards but two were tightly nailed in place. Audrey knelt, forcing her thoughts away from the dead woman above her head and pulled at a board. It came free, revealing a small space between the floor and the earth. She reached, hating the tremor in her hand as she grasped a cookie tin nestled into the dirt. Three words covered the top, written in black marker. *Fuck you, Albert.*

CHAPTER 18

The contents of the cookie tin lay on the table. Ryan picked up a worn leather bound journal and flipped the pages. "What the hell is all of this?"

Audrey shrugged. "Clues?"

"To what?"

"To where the bones are hidden?"

A floor has no bottom, the wall is not solid, and an empty space is full. The riddle in his grandmother's letter suddenly made sense. The floor had no bottom. Not exact, but close. The floor held a box beneath it. So a wall is not solid? "I think it's time I knew what this damn secret is all about. How is Carroll holding all of you with one secret?"

"It's... complicated."

"I like a good puzzle."

"Look, I don't know the whole story, and even if I did, I don't know that it's wise to tell you. These people have a lot to lose. Don't you see?"

"What? What can be more valuable than freedom?"

She tangled a small hand in her hair and then lowered it to her lap. The curls bounced back into place. Ryan's hands itched to touch them again.

"Fine, you want to know? Carroll knows where his great

grandfather buried the Bakers. He also has the minutes from the meeting where the town decided to kill them."

"What?" So, Justin almost had the story right. Shit, he should start taking notes. This book was going to be a masterpiece if he lived to write it.

"Can we just call Merle and take care of the problem in the barn first?"

Ryan replaced the lid and carried the box to the den. He stared at the desk for a moment, his grandfather's vandalism screaming at him, but he couldn't make sense of it. How could a murder more than a century ago cause a town to be at one man's mercy? *Mine... the mine? The desk is mine? What the fuck did mine mean?*

"Jesus Christ," Merle drew a ragged breath. Muffled sounds filled the phone for a moment.

The silence stretched and Ryan grew restless. His cell beeped, warning that the battery was low. He'd taken enough pictures of Millicent's body, the tracks outside and every corner of the barn, to fill an album. He worried it had no power left at all, but they couldn't use the landlines and Audrey didn't carry a phone.

"So Justin's okay?" he prompted.

"He's pretty damn excited about getting the hell out of Dodge, but yeah, alive and kicking. Fuck, I don't wanna tell him about this. Who wants to tell a kid their mother is dead?"

"I know. If you want, you can wait. I'll talk to him." The thought of telling Justin about his mother brought a bitter taste to Ryan's mouth.

"Nah, he needs to be able to grieve if he wants to. If you're here he'll try to be a man about the whole thing. He's just a kid. Christ." Merle's voice broke. Ryan's throat tightened at the sound.

"If you're sure then, I'll call Fred. I'm sure he's waiting for my report."

"Yeah. Hey, should I go over to Millie's? You know, before

they come and hide the evidence?"

"I don't think they killed her there."

"Really? You know this? How?"

Ryan thought of Millicent hanging in the barn, barefoot, toes curled. He pictured her hands, clawed as though grasping something. *Her last hope.*

"Good point. Get over there fast, and get out faster. If they've left anything make sure you take it. Document any tracks, signs of a struggle, whatever you think might help our case against him. Maybe take a camera," Ryan chewed his nail, a habit he thought he'd left behind. "You know what? Don't tell Justin right away. You don't need him involved in that. I don't know how far Carroll will go, but something tells me that blood means nothing to him."

"Fuckers."

"Exactly. Do me one favor though."

"What's that?" Merle asked

"Be careful."

"I will. You too."

Ryan pushed end and tucked the phone in his pocket. Audrey stood next to the window, gazing out at the barn.

Seated at the table, he couldn't see the open door. Her body blocked it from his view. She'd been silent since they came back to the house. Her gaze never met his and she carried herself stiffly. Either she was hiding something, or she knew something, but for whatever reason she wasn't sharing it with him. Audrey was scared.

"You okay?" he asked.

She startled but didn't turn. "No."

"I'm calling Fred. You want to leave?"

"No."

He waited, but Audrey remained at the window, arms crossed on front of her, hugging herself. Her head lay against the glass.

"Is there something I should know?"

"Probably, but it's not important right now. Call them."

"What is it? I don't want to go into this thinking you're

keeping something from me."

She lowered her arms and stared at her feet.

How bad would it be? Was she going to tell him last night was a mistake? No, she'd been fine until they went to the barn. He'd attributed her strange behavior last night to nerve, anxious about the two of them being along, but now he wondered. Did she know what Carroll had planned? That didn't fit *his* Audrey. Hell, he didn't know what to think.

"You'll hate me," she said.

"I couldn't hate you. Never." He could think of a few scenarios that would make him angry, but he doubted anything could destroy the new feelings he'd discovered for her. Besides, Audrey couldn't be guilty of any of that. If she was, then he was a terrible judge of character… or she was a brilliant actress.

"I knew they were up to something."

No. "And?"

She released a shaky breath.

To think Audrey was involved in this somehow physically hurt. He'd trusted her.

"Carroll wanted me to keep you busy. To distract you. But what happened with us, I didn't plan that. That's not a part of this. Carroll told me that I had to start doing my share or…well let's s ay the options weren't great. I just—I don't know. I was scared. I knew he was up to something but I never imagined this. I thought he wanted to get in here again. I wouldn't have cooperated if I knew the truth."

"So last night was a set up?" Anger warmed his gut and Ryan clenched his fists.

"No. Well, not entirely. I only meant to keep you busy for a while. To keep him happy so he'd leave me alone. There's so much you don't know, that you can't understand." Her shoulders shook as she cried silently, pressing her face to the windowpane.

He wanted to hold her, but damn it, she'd helped Carroll set him up. Audrey may have been the key to him being framed for murder. Whether she knew or not, she still played her part. "You lied to me."

Audrey turned. Her eyes, moist with tears, showed a misery that he hadn't expected. It sent a shiver of ice through him. She hated herself. That much was plain. But she should. Damn it, she should feel guilty. What kind of person helps someone like Carroll Albert? What kind of person lies to someone they claim to care about?

Someone who is terrified of the alternative.

"I kept things from you, yes. That's just as bad as lying. I care about you, Ryan. Last night was real, not planned, not to trick you in any way. Real. I didn't think I'd feel this way about you, and when he kept pushing me, I got scared. I have no other excuse. Fear does strange things to a person. You wouldn't understand."

"No I don't. I can't, and I won't pretend to even try. Guilty is guilty. You people need to look at the bigger picture here. That's the problem. God, Audrey, if you'd all just come together, the man wouldn't stand a chance. He's one man, in a tiny shithole town. Not even a town. An outpost. It doesn't even get a fucking dot on a map. If you guys stood up to him, went to the cops about everything that's going on, he wouldn't stand a chance. He's just as guilty as you are."

"It's not about that. Most of them aren't guilty of anything. Don't you get it? He's got more than that. It's hard to explain. There's something going on at the mine. Just what that is, I don't know. No one but Albert, Farley and Fred are allowed in or out. The place is supposed to be closed, but at night, it's all lit up. Electric fences around the buildings, protecting whatever's going on in there. I do know we've benefited from whatever they're up to. Financially I mean. This town functions because of it and we turn the other way so that it continues to do so."

No matter what he argued, she kept on with the "it's complicated" bullshit. His thoughts turned to her guilt. She'd said he had nothing on her, so why did she follow his orders? "What did you do that you want to hide so much it's worth lying to someone who cares about you?"

"Nothing."

"If you lie to me one more time, you may as well walk out that fucking door and never come back. I can tolerate a lot of things, I can be pretty open-minded too, but the one thing I cannot stand is a liar."

"I haven't done anything. I haven't lied to you. It's not that I'll go to jail. It's what he'd do if I talk. It's what he'll do to this town, my friends, and yes, to me. Don't tell me he can't, because he's proven that he can. Millicent has always been at his side and now…"

"What's he done up till now? To you, I mean. What's he done to you personally?"

She turned back to the window and Ryan's chest burned. Did Carroll hurt her? Touch her? He didn't rape her. Last night proved that. But did rape have to include intercourse? Of course not, Ryan scolded himself. The man could have raped a young girl in many ways without actually having sex with her. How many girls had Carroll terrorized? A red haze filled his brain at the image of Carroll's hands on her.

Audrey grew up here, and if Carroll had noticed her as a young girl… there was at least fifteen years between them. The turn of his thoughts made him nauseous. Carroll could have worked on her for years. Trained her to fear him with no more than a look, a touch….

And still, she gave herself to Ryan without hesitation. She trusted him with something no one else ever had. How could he be angry?

He looked beyond her blind submission to Carroll, and saw the real person beneath her sunny exterior for the first time. She tugged at her sleeves, her gaze riveted to her hands. She seemed to have shrunk in a matter of minutes, from the giant, happy personality he first met to this quiet, uncertain and miserable woman who hated herself.

He closed his eyes and forced himself to see things from her perspective. Hell, she'd been so afraid of sex she had avoided it… until last night. Until him.

"Come here." He opened his arms.

Audrey cowered at the window, chewing her lip. "Ryan—"

"Fine, I'll come to you."

He closed the space between them and she crumpled into his arms. Her shoulders shook but she made no sound. *Fucking bastard.* Ryan kissed the top of her head. Audrey had given herself to him, not Carroll. She had no one to stand up for her. In murdering his grandparents, he'd taken the only protection she had left. Not anymore.

"Look, I don't care what he did or what you didn't do. You're a victim. Do you hear me? Whatever happened in the past is not your fault. He did it, not you."

"But I could have stopped him," her voice softened, edged with a tremor that threatened tears.

"How? When? You couldn't have stopped him, not by yourself. Honestly, Audrey, you have to stop letting him manipulate you. Now is the time to stand up and tell him you won't do it. You're not alone anymore."

"What about when your year is up? What then?" She turned and pinned him with a glare, her eyes a brighter shade of green with the moisture of unshed tears.

"I won't leave you. I owe him, not just for my grandparents, but for my mother, and for you. If it takes that long to see that he pays for that, if it takes ten times that long, I'll stay until it happens. No matter what."

She sniffed.

Audrey straightened, and walked to the table, taking the phone from his hand. "Let's call Fred and get this over with."

He took the phone, and met her gaze. She nodded. Ryan leaned down, pressing his lips against hers. A sob caught in her throat. Although he hated to hear it, the sound pushed his fury, his resolve to see Carroll held accountable for all the pain he caused. Carroll might have thought he gained the upper hand with Millicent hanging outside, but he'd just made his worst mistake.

Carroll paced as Fred mumbled into his phone. They'd waited hours for Ryan to discover Millicent, and he was tired. Why did the damn fool feel a need to perform? It's not as though they had to convince anyone of their innocence.

The plan, which had come to Carroll while his hands squeezed the life from the traitorous bitch, was perfect. Even if they couldn't pin it on Ryan, he'd ensured the suicide angle would work just as well, sending a warning to everyone involved. You don't fuck with Carroll Albert.

"Ready?" Fred interrupted his thoughts.

"I've been ready. What did he say?"

"It was Audrey. She said Ryan was too upset to talk. She noticed the barn door open and the tracks first. Gonna be hard to determine a suicide if I have to include that in the evidence. I told you we should have left the truck in the driveway and carried her. You could have covered your tracks on the way back."

"Yeah, you know it all. The tracks would have been there no matter what. You think people can't tell that someone's been through the snow just because they cover the footprints? Come on."

Carroll strode to the doorway, grabbing his coat from the chair on the way. He turned, pushing his arms into the sleeves, in time to spot Julia's worried frown; she'd heard more than she should have.

"Keep your fucking mouth shut," he warned.

She nodded, and took a step back.

Carroll didn't wait for Fred.

The slamming door shook the walls. Julia stood, her hands clenching the chair so tightly that her knuckles whitened.

He stayed in the shadows of the hallway, longing to comfort her but knowing she'd push him away. Why did they do this every time? He pulled the recorder from his pocket and pressed "stop." Would she listen to reason? Not likely. He'd tried years ago.

Julia's sniff drew his gaze to her rigid form. Here she goes. Put the armor back on, push the murder of an innocent woman from your mind. Back to being the good wife. The obedient wife. Hell, they were pathetic.

He backed down the hallway, slipping the recorder back into his pocket. When things looked a little more advantageous for them they'd make their move. He didn't want to leave her behind. Julia was the reason for most of his good memories. But he wouldn't wait forever. Some day they had to stand up and be counted. Though at present, pathetic and scared was better than dead.

CHAPTER 19

"Why is Carroll with him?"

Standing on the deck, Ryan followed the Hummer pulling in ahead of Fred's police cruiser. Audrey drew closer, her voice guarded; a whisper. "There is an election coming up. Perhaps as Reeve, he needs to show that crime merited his full attention. It's how he works. He's gotta be in the middle of everything."

Ryan nodded. Of course. Why would he change his habits over a mere murder? The two men exited their vehicles, frowned and walked toward the deck. Very serious. He almost laughed. Actors they were not. Fred kept glancing to the barn, one hand on the gun at his hip. Did he really think he'd need that? Did it matter? Ryan suddenly realized how vulnerable he was.

"Thanks for coming so fast." Ryan stepped forward.

Fred remained rooted to his spot, but Carroll continued to the bottom of the porch steps. "Fred called me and I just couldn't believe my ears. Are you sure she's—"

"Dead? Check it out. I'm sure you'll want to see for yourself either way."

Ryan led the way. Behind him, footsteps crunched in the snow. Later he'd compare the new prints with the old ones, if they hadn't already switched boots.

Before calling Fred, he and Audrey had taken pictures of the original tracks, but not to show him. Ryan had transferred the files from his cell onto the computer and then emailed them to himself before copying them to a memory stick, which burned a hole in his pocket.

Audrey's heart hammered painfully against her chest. Her breath fogged the glass.

Ryan stood stiff, proud, as though daring Carroll to accuse him. He should be more careful. It wasn't only flies that came to honey. Carroll Albert responded well to the sickeningly sweet stuff too. If he'd just act as though he'd been scared, or slightly affected by what happened, Carroll might have been fooled into letting up on him.

The three men walked toward the barn, Ryan leading the way, boldly turning his back on the other two. Audrey wouldn't have trusted them enough.

Carroll turned, as though sensing her presence. Their eyes met, pinning her in place. She bit her lip as his full mouth curved into a smirk. He winked, rubbing his neck before pointing toward her. Audrey stilled. She longed to run, to escape while they busied themselves with Millicent and setting Ryan up. But she couldn't do that to him. Her heart was mixed up in things and now she stood to lose more than she'd ever had.

Did Carroll hope that would happen? Did he really know her better than she knew herself? He claimed to and right now, as she watched him walking far too close to the man who held her heart, she believed he might be right. He knew how to manipulate people into a corner. He used her most obvious weakness and set the right circumstances so she could dive right in.

She turned from the window. Her heart wanted Ryan. Audrey needed him, needed his faith and his support. Carroll must have seen that need. Well he fucked up. Audrey straightened and glared out the window. She wouldn't betray Ryan again. Carroll might have pulled the strings up to this point, but Audrey wouldn't be played anymore. She'd do whatever to recover Ryan's trust. Even if it meant hanging next to Millicent.

The air had turned bitterly cold, burning his lungs. Lightheaded he blinked several times to clear his vision and wondered if it affected Carroll and Fred the same way. At the barn door he turned and stood back.

Fred neared the door. "You stay right here. I don't want you contaminating the scene any more than you already have. You didn't touch the body, did you?"

"No, I didn't touch *her*. I walked in; saw Millicent, then came back to the house and told Audrey. Then she called you."

"It's pretty wet over there," Farley pointed to the damp spot beneath Millicent's feet. "How long did that take?"

Carroll stood at the threshold behind Fred, hands deep in his pockets.

"I don't know. A couple of minutes? Maybe a little longer. I was staring at a fucking dead woman hanging in my barn. Time isn't something I was keeping track of."

"Audrey was here too?" Fred pulled out a battered notepad and a pen.

"Yes, she noticed the door was open and woke me up."

Carroll snorted. "Woke you up? She didn't spend the night?"

Ryan forced a tight smile, and met the older man's cold stare. "Actually, I spent the night at her place. Drank too much wine and I didn't think it was wise to drive last night. I left this early this morning, but I was more worried about sleeping off my hangover. I didn't even look toward the barn. Audrey came by a couple hours later. I promised to make her breakfast in exchange for putting up with me last night."

"What time did you get home?" Fred asked.

The light in his pale eyes sent a chill of warning through

Ryan. No, he wasn't going to be pinned down to a time. Millicent's time of death was likely to be pretty damn close to whatever time he gave them.

"I'm not really sure. I didn't check the clock."

Fred chewed his lip. "Okay. I'm going in. Carroll, you better stay out here too. Let me know when Tim gets here."

"Will do." Carroll leaned against the barn wall, opposite Ryan.

"I'm sorry. I'm not sure why you're here." Ryan smiled, keeping his tone even.

"This is my town, my people, and when someone dies, especially in such an awful way, I make it my business to make sure that there's nothing suspicious going on."

"Interesting."

"Is it? Don't other politicians care as much?"

"Not unless it's an election year. Oh, wait. It is an election year isn't it?"

"Well, I'm always involved." Carroll turned to the house, where Audrey stood at the kitchen window, watching them. "Is Audrey suddenly shy or too sore to walk out here?"

It took all the control he could muster to remain still, but Ryan didn't take the bait. Fucking pig. "Careful, Carroll. Your redneck is showing."

"What?"

Ryan smiled. "Audrey didn't come into the barn, so she knows very little. Just what I told her."

Audrey had worried she'd break under pressure. Although, they both knew what time he returned home, she consented to say she wasn't sure. Part of him wanted to shake her for being so afraid, the other part wanted to pack her up and take her away from Albertsville and Carroll's power.

Tires crunched through deep snow. An ambulance, sans lights or siren, pulled in behind Fred's cruiser. "And that is? We hardly need a paramedic. Unless he's a miracle worker."

Carroll shot him a glare. "That's our coroner, Tim Reid."

"Isn't he the doctor?"

"Yes, and he's also a coroner. It's quite common in rural areas, you know?"

"I suppose."

Doctor Reid, a tall thin man of about forty, stepped out of the ambulance, carrying a large black bag and a white box. His shoulders slumped just a little when Carroll waved, and although he was a distance away, Ryan thought he caught a muscle twitching in the man's face as though he clenched his teeth.

"Glad you could make it so fast, Tim." Carroll stepped forward when Tim reached them. Holding out his hand, he gripped Tim's thin fingers and clapped the frail-looking man on the back.

"Well, you said it was urgent," Tim mumbled.

His voice was soft, pleasant, as Ryan thought a doctor's should. The nervous energy that emanated from him though would have Ryan considering his options before allowing the man near him with a scalpel.

Fred emerged moments later, carrying his notepad and shaking his head. "She's all yours, Tim. Carroll, I think as long as you stay back, don't touch anything, you can go see her. I've taken what I need to."

Ryan frowned. Carroll would go in before the coroner had assessed the scene? He was no expert but he thought that no one went in before the coroner was finished. Of course, his experience was limited. Watching CSI did not make him any more knowledgeable than anyone else. Still, something smelled bad here.

Fred headed toward the house.

"Aren't you going to examine the tracks?" Ryan asked.

"Why? You guys messed them all up this morning. No point. There's yours and Audrey's and that's all I can determine for sure."

"And yours and Carroll's. Let's not forget the tire tracks. What about those? They seem almost identical to the ones you guys made coming in."

"Could be, but since Carroll wasn't here, and I wasn't here, we know they aren't the same. How about you don't try to tell me how to do my job, Mr. Cassidy? That might help. Oh, and don't go anywhere."

"Where would I go?"

"Just procedure. We don't know that Millie wasn't dead before she found herself hanging in there. I'm asking you to stick around, in case I have questions. Besides, running would make you look awful guilty."

"She hung herself. That's what it looks like to me. How can I be guilty of someone's suicide?"

"You think I'm stupid?" Fred turned back and advanced until they stood toe to toe.

Ryan gazed down his nose at the shorter man. "Of course not. I know you're far from stupid, or you wouldn't be Chief here, would you? Seems to me a smart man stays at Albert's right hand just as you are. Then that man doesn't have to hide anything, right? Since I don't have anything to hide either, I'll stay put. Happy?"

Fred tried to intimidate him, but Ryan didn't back down. He continued to smile, arms at his sides. Finally, Fred gave up and retreated to his car. Ryan let out the breath he'd held and glanced to the house.

Audrey stood at the window shaking her head, one hand covering her mouth.

❧❧

"Well?"

Tim didn't answer for a moment. Scraping under Millicent's nails, he tried to forget who it was that hung above him, and what he knew about how she got there. Christ, he just wanted out—away from this fucking town and this lunatic. "Well what?"

"How did she die?" Carroll's voice held an edge, the same edge it held when he made deals, as he had when he called Tim last night.

"Suicide?"

"You're not sure?"

Tim straightened, pocketing the small bag of scrapings. Suddenly he was tired and fed up with toeing the line. Carroll could play his games with someone else. He just wanted to go home and forget that the woman hanging above him shared his bed not long ago. Someone he had dared to hope he might know better. Another victim of Carroll Albert's obsession with power.

"Look, it's just you and me here. I don't know what you want me to say. I said I'd do whatever you wanted, just tell me. Suicide? Murder? What?"

"*Here* happens to be in a barn, where anyone can hear us, Doctor Reid. That means that we're professionals, and professionals follow procedure. They don't make shit up. Now, what do you think happened here?"

He squirmed under the heat of Carroll's stare. Fuck, he was good. "Looks like suicide to me, but I won't know until I examine the body."

"Time of death?"

Damn it, Carroll should have filled him in. Was he recording this? Hoping to have something new to hold over his head? Torn, Tim shrugged. "I don't like to speculate. I'll let you know."

"I'll see if Fred can get someone to help you cut the body down when you're through."

"Thanks." Tim muttered and turned back to his toolbox. He pulled out his camera and another collection bag.

"And Tim?"

Tim sighed and met Carroll's gaze. Carroll pointed to Millicent and then back to Tim. "Make sure that evidence gets to Fred's desk by tonight. Don't be late. Hear me?"

"Loud and clear."

"Good. I'll be back in a bit." Carroll nodded to the dead woman above him and shook his head. "Damn shame. She was a good lay."

Carroll left the barn, his chuckle lingering in the frigid air.

Tim stifled the rage that boiled in his chest and slammed a gloved fist into the wall. Hot tears spilled over his cheeks and he needed several deep breaths before he could turn back to his task.

He stared up at Millicent's face, into her bulging lifeless eyes. They seemed to plead with him to do something, to tell someone. "I can't, Millie. You know that. Why did you have to defy him?"

Realizing he'd spoken aloud, Tim checked the door. Ryan Cassidy stood there, his back to him. Did Carroll hope to frame Cassidy for this? It would make sense. Well, it was one thing to cover the murder, but he wouldn't allow someone else to pay for Carroll's crime. If push came to shove, he'd tell Carroll it was suicide or the truth, and that was his final decision.

Gathering his equipment, Tim sniffed, hating the tears he couldn't hold back. If only he had the balls to tell the truth. But he'd worked hard to earn his position as doctor, coroner, and an upstanding member of the community. His grandfather had opened the hospital and he'd carried on the tradition. He held the world—or at least a small part of it, in his hands as long as he did as he was told. If Millie had succeeded at whatever she'd done to piss Carroll off....

He opened another bag and knelt to her hands once more.

CHAPTER 20

The light felt too bright. Ryan blinked to clear his thoughts. Audrey sat across the table, Merle to his right and Justin on his left. He didn't want to discuss anything in front of the boy, but Merle insisted that Justin had a right to know. The tremor on the boy's hands as he lifted the cup of hot chocolate to his mouth, told Ryan he wasn't able to handle so much at one time.

"So, tell me about how things work here. Who's in charge, really?" Ryan expected Audrey to answer. Instead, Merle cleared his throat.

"Carroll is. After him comes Fred, obviously. Calvin and Farley are the muscle. They do the heavy work... or the dirty work, whatever you want to call it. Tim, the doctor, he's involved somehow. Your family used to have some pull around here. Your great grandfather kept Jarrod in check by appealing to his ego, but when Melvin took over the farm, he refused to take part in what Carroll and the others were doing. That's when shit started flying."

"What do you mean?"

"The field ain't empty cause your grandpa couldn't farm. Things started happening to his crops, his livestock, his equipment; he couldn't keep up with the accidents. Eventually, he threw his hands up and quit. After Chad died, they just stopped fighting."

Ryan imagined having an entire town working against him. His grandparents were beat before they'd even started the war. "They didn't quit. My grandfather found something."

"Yes, he found the spot," Audrey said.

"The spot?"

"What's left of the Baker family and those convicts."

Ryan thought about the shoebox that he'd put away without examining. "Are they at the mine?"

"We don't know. I doubt it." Merle tapped a dirty finger on the table. "I think they're at the mill. Chad went there on his own the night he died. It was closed. He was onto something and they caught him."

"A wall is not solid, an empty space is full. Does that mean anything to you?"

"No," Justin said.

"Where did you get that?" Merle asked.

"A letter from my grandmother. My grandfather left a clue too. Something about something being on display."

"It makes no sense." Merle scratched his ear, pausing to look at his finger before wiping whatever on his knee.

Ryan cringed. "Justin, you thought there was counterfeiting or something going on."

"Yeah, so?"

"What about the money? The evidence on display, hidden in plain sight. Maybe it's at the bank."

"Nah, too easy." Merle dismissed the idea. "Besides, ain't no counterfeiting going on at that mine. Weapons. Plain and simple."

"Know what's really scaring me?" Ryan asked.

They stared.

"This shit isn't sounding the least bit insane. It sounds sensible to hide a counterfeiting operation at the mine, and a weapons ring. Hell, I wouldn't be surprised to find a goddamn meth lab in there."

"No, they had to shut that down," Merle said.

"There *was* a meth lab? Jesus, I was only kidding."

"Just a small one, back in the late nineties, but every time Carroll assigned it to someone, the house caught fire. They had no clue what they were doing. Wasn't worth the trouble."

"Oh my fucking God." Ryan pressed both hands to his head. Bad dream. Bad movie. One or the other, it had to end soon.

Merle stood. "Well, Justin and I should get going. You let me know if those riddles start making sense."

"Yeah, and when they do, you can bring the straightjacket because that's a sure sign I've joined you in the insanity."

Merle chuckled, leading Justin out of the room. They shuffled down the hall.

The door opened. Closed.

"Why can't you just leave it alone?" Audrey asked.

"He killed someone and now he's trying to frame me for it. That's why I can't leave it."

"If he knew what we talked about—"

"Audrey, he is not a god. I know you all believe he is, but he's just a man. Like me. He has a weakness somewhere. You guys just need to believe it's possible."

"It's not that I think he's indestructible. I'm worried about how many people will go down with him."

"Are you one of them?"

She paused and turned toward the window. "No. I've told you that."

"What did he do to make you so afraid of him? To you, I mean. What has he done to you? Why can't you tell me?"

Audrey bit her lip, her eyes held fear and hopelessness so profound his chest ached.

"Nothing. He's done nothing. I've told you that too."

"Soon you'll have to stop lying. You're only hurting yourself." Ryan stood, unable to witness her pain, frustrated that he couldn't take it away.

"Where are you going?"

"I think I might be coming down with something. I need to see a doctor."

Leafing through a dog-eared copy of TIME would have helped pass the time, but for the chairs. The ugly orange plastic seats seemed designed for torture. To say Albertsville's hospital was small would be an understatement. It wasn't a hospital at all, but a clinic with an operating room.

"So, do you guys have just the one doctor?" he asked the woman behind the small desk in the corner.

She looked up, to peer at Ryan over small wire-framed glasses and smiled. "Doctor Reid is quite capable of handling most emergencies. There is a hospital less than an hour from here. We can get help if we need it."

"I guess I'm used to the city. Medical facilities on every corner."

"Well, don't worry. Doctor Reid is very competent. He's delivered every baby in this town for the past ten years or so and performed lots of surgeries as well. He's very capable."

"What about terminal patients?" Where would Merle go should he become too sick to stay in his own home? Would he be at the mercy of this place?

"Well, we do have six beds here. We can accommodate this town. Are you afraid you're terminal, Mr. Cassidy?" Her lips twitched.

Ryan smiled. "No. Not yet."

She lowered her grey head back to her paperwork.

Ryan went back to not reading his magazine, and shifted his ass for the umpteenth time.

Finally Tim Reid emerged from a small door next to the nurse's desk. "Mr. Cassidy?"

Ryan stood and walked to the desk, hand outstretched. "We met a couple days ago at my grandparents' farm."

"Yes, too bad we couldn't meet under better circumstances."

"I know."

"If you'd just follow me," Tim turned to the woman behind the desk. "Trudy, hold my calls. Okay?"

"Done." Trudy didn't look up from the papers.

Ryan followed Tim through the door to a surprisingly large office. On the right was an examination table, a curtain hung in the corner from a track on the ceiling extending around the bed. A small sink and cupboards lined the rest of the wall but for a stool tucked into the corner.

Tim motioned toward the left side of the room, where an old wood desk occupied most of the space before two comfortable-looking chairs. A bookcase flanked the far side.

Ryan took a seat and Tim joined him. The drawn blinds gave the room and Tim's face a grayish pallor. "So?"

"This is going to seem presumptuous, but I don't have time to beat around the bush or any of that shit."

"Okay."

"Reeve Albert. Are you and he close?"

"Close? No." Tim steepled his hands beneath his chin and gazed at Ryan thoughtfully.

"Friendly?"

"No."

"How did Millicent die?"

Tim stared, his face set. He then sucked in a breath, letting it out slowly before answering. "Suicide, but I really can't discuss it with you."

"Do you believe that?"

Tim tapped a finger against his chin and blinked.

Ryan waited.

"I shouldn't be talking to you, Mr. Cassidy. You do realize the spot I'm in, don't you? If Carroll even knew you were here…."

"I'm sick. Must have caught a cold while shoveling the driveway the other day. Maybe you found something interesting like a heart murmur, which required several visits. In any case, you can't discuss my case; confidentiality and stuff. But when pushed, you'll be willing to confide that I am a very sick man and should probably return to Calgary where I can receive proper medical care for my condition. Of course, I don't how long that will take, and I don't want to give up my inheritance so I'm hesitant. You've almost convinced me to just give up and go back to the city. For the sake of my health, of course. That's what we discussed in here should anyone ask."

Tim leaned back in his chair, fingering a blue tie that matched his shirt to perfection. He took another deep breath before glancing at the door and back to Ryan. "What do you want from me? I can't share information in an ongoing criminal investigation, especially when you're the prime suspect."

"If I can arrange for someone to help you, would you give up the real report on Millicent?"

"What is on file *is* the real report, Mr. Cassidy. I'm not sure what you mean."

"Let's stop playing games. Neither of us has the time for that. You're an intelligent man, wouldn't be here running this practice if you weren't. Millicent didn't hang herself. I know that. You know that. Everybody in this town knows that. She was leaving and Carroll caught wind of it."

Tim stared at a spot just beyond Ryan's shoulder. His hand ran over the silk tie, as though petting a cat. He chewed his lip for a moment, and then blinked before his dark eyes focused. "Did you know Millicent and I were intimate? Not exclusive, but we'd shared a few nights here and there. I felt a strong affection for her. She was a good person."

Ryan shifted. Maybe he'd made a mistake thinking this man had common sense. Who just shares something like that with a complete stranger? Tim's eyes welled with tears and Ryan leapt at the opportunity. "So? What are you going to do for her?"

"I scraped some skin from under her nails. It's gone now with a few other odds and ends. Mailed to a friend. Just out of curiosity."

"What does he have on you?"

"Does it matter?"

"Very much." Ryan's heart raced. He almost had him.

"I've considered this a lot lately. More than ever, I've pondered it over the past few days. How bad would it be for the world to know what goes on here? Not bad enough to make it worth living day to day wondering when the axe will drop. I'm tired. I could have had a job in Toronto working at Sick Kids. They offered it, and I had to refuse. Carroll didn't give me permission to go. You know what that's like? Being someone else's puppet, dancing to their tune because you're too afraid to do anything else? In Albertville you listen to Carroll. You don't, you end up dead."

"Have you done anything for him that would send you to jail?"

"Yes, *if* he can prove it. The things I've covered up for him just keep piling up. It started with an accident report years ago and just continued. But I've realized recently that he may not be able to do anything to prove I knew what really happened. I mean, I turned the evidence over to the police, as I should. He'll simply ruin my career with the ensuing speculation. I suppose one might wonder if this could be considered a career."

"Do you think he killed Millicent?"

Tim turned his chair toward the covered windows. He placed his arms behind his head and closed his eyes. "Yes," he whispered.

Ryan pulled his wallet from his pocket and leafed through the contents. The red and white card hid near the back. He turned it over.

Tim handed him a pen, eyeing the card as though it contained a virus or something.

Ryan scribbled a name and an email address on the card. "If you decide to do this, forward the results and any other information to this email. You know, if you ask them, they'll make sure you're safe."

"I'm afraid no one can do that."

RENÉE MILLER

CHAPTER 21

Ryan expected to see Audrey's truck in his driveway. Merle's truck parked in her place, casting a long shadow in the early evening light, was somewhat disappointing. He slowed, coming to a stop next to the old black Dodge and opened his door.

Merle eased out of the cab.

Ryan's gaze darted to a boy exiting the passenger side. Not Justin, although he looked like an older version of him.

"Hey, hear you haven't been feeling well," Merle said.

"Wow, news does travel fast. I did feel a little under the weather this morning, had to go see the doctor."

"Can we go in? It's not wise for Michael to be out here." Merle nodded to the young man who joined him, eyes downcast.

Leading the way to the house Ryan stepped aside to allow them in and scanned the driveway and the fields before following. So far, he saw nothing, but that meant little. Carroll probably had lookouts in the bushes or something. With any luck, Larry would trample them, or better yet, the wolves might catch their scent.

Merle stood in the narrow hallway, the boy near the kitchen doorway. "Boy wants to talk to you. Alone."

"Okay. Who is boy?"

"Michael, well we call him Mickey. He's Carroll's oldest boy."

"Oh. That's nice." Ryan didn't know what to say.

Mickey kicked a booted toe at the wood floor.

"I'll be back in an hour or so to take him home. If he wants to go that is."

Ryan didn't have the opportunity to refuse or accept as Merle shuffled past him and out the door. His old truck coughed to life and then snow crunched as he backed out of the driveway. Ryan looked again at Mickey.

"Kitchen?" he asked.

"Sure."

Ryan walked past the boy and flicked the switch. He'd grown used to the old booger color and even liked it somewhat. Audrey had been right. White would have looked awful in this room. He'd been too hard on her.

"Can you close the curtains?"

Mickey's voice startled him. He nodded and went to the big windows to pull the curtains closed, although the sheer fabric didn't conceal much. "Okay?"

"Yeah, I just don't want to get caught here. I don't think Dad would hurt me. I'm the heir to his vast dynasty after all. But I don't want to gamble on that and end up being wrong. There is my little brother after all, and a few others he thinks I don't know about. Know what I mean?"

"I do. So, what's going on?"

Ryan took the chair opposite Mickey and waited as the boy picked at a key ring he'd dug from his coat pocket, flipping it over and scratching the gold front, etched with an A.

"Guess it's best to just tell the whole story. I was dating this girl, Amy Thomlinson. Her dad owns the bar. You know Sal?"

"Yes. I like him very much."

"Yeah, well, anyway I was dating Amy. We've been going out for like three years, she's fifteen and I'm sixteen, in case you're wondering."

"I wasn't. But good to know. Does Amy have a mother too?"

"No. When Amy was two, her mom overdosed. Heroin. See, Sal got real funny when Amy turned fifteen. Said we should make plans to get out of here if we were serious about each other. I'm going to be seventeen next week and I'm graduating early. He asked me to take Amy with me when I went away to school."

"That's kind of odd." Ryan couldn't imagine a father wanting his daughter to run away with her boyfriend.

"Not really. I think Sal worried if she stayed too long here, she'd be stuck just like everyone else. So, we did it. We made our plans and were going to leave together in June. I even got an apartment for us. Well, Sal got it, but I'm paying for it. I called Amy to tell her about it the other day and she wouldn't take my call. Sal said she was sick and then told me not to call anymore. I was kind of freaked out. Sal's like a father to me, more than my dad is anyway. I didn't understand. I should have known better, should have been more careful. Don't know why I thought I was different."

"Most fathers want the best for their sons. You shouldn't have to be afraid of your parents. That's not normal. You don't try to control someone you love."

"My dad doesn't love anyone but himself." Mickey's mouth twisted in a bitter smile. He tapped the key ring on the table and looked up, his face red. "Anyway, Amy sent me a letter. I just got it today. She hasn't been at school or anything for at least a week. Probably longer. I don't go all the time so I'm not really sure. Anyway, her friend brought it to me. I don't even know where to begin."

"You don't have to share anything that's too personal." This wasn't going anywhere good. Knowing Carroll's penchant for young girls he suspected that Amy had been approached, and not in a fatherly way.

"It's not painful, it's disgusting. I'm pissed. My dad called her and told her I wanted her to meet me at the house. We'd planned a study date at the library and that's where I was, waiting for her. He said I was tied up with something, but I'd meet her and she bought it. She told me in the letter that she tried to leave but he wouldn't let her. He dragged her upstairs to my room. To *my* fucking room. Then he raped her. The son of a bitch raped her in my bed."

Ryan had no words, no breath in his lungs. He couldn't have been more shocked if he'd witnessed Larry the moose talking. Carroll was bad news, but to rape his son's girlfriend? And in his son's room? It was a double slap in the face and Ryan's heart ached for the boy who stifled a sob as he wiped his nose.

"That's not even the worst part."

"I'm sorry, Mickey. I don't know what to say. I don't know how it could possibly be worse than that. I'm just so sorry for both of you."

"It's okay, I don't know either. But she had more to tell. That happened a month ago. She was supposed to get her period last week, and she didn't. She went to Doctor Reid and he told her she was pregnant. It's not mine because we've never...."

Ryan let out a thin breath and rubbed his eyes. Holy shit, did the man have no boundaries? Then a thought occurred to him. He felt slightly guilty but maybe this was the opportunity they hoped for.

"Does Sal know?" Ryan asked.

"She told him it was mine. My dad told her if she told anyone what happened, he'd take the bar. Sal's been behind on the mortgage. Amy went to the police. Fred Smith, that useless sack of crap, told her the same thing my dad did. Except he told her that making up stories could get people hurt. People close to her. Then he said if she didn't want to see her dad ruined, she'd shut her mouth and quit telling lies. Fucking jerk."

"You believe her?" The wheels turned in Ryan's head faster than his thoughts could keep up. Jerk was an understatement. These men were sick bastards.

"Of course I do. She'd never lie about that. Amy liked my parents, wouldn't believe what I told her about my dad. Now, she's stuck. She says she can't go anywhere. Not with a baby. I haven't seen her but I'm not even sure I can look at her.

What's that say about me?" Mickey looked up, his blue eyes pleading.

Ryan shook his head. "Nothing. It says that your father betrayed both of you. If you love her, you'll figure it out. First we have to decide what to do about it."

"What do you mean?"

"Are you afraid of your dad?"

"Afraid of my dad?" Mickey's eyes widened. He laughed, but the color in his cheeks—and the tremor in his hand as he turned a key ring—spoke volumes.

"Carroll should pay for what he's done to Amy. He can't hurt you if you move before he does."

Mickey shook his head.

Ryan wanted to throttle the kid. What the hell was wrong with these people?

"She begged me not to tell anyone, because she's worried about Sal. I guess he and Amy have nothing without the bar. If I turn my dad in for this, he'll make Amy pay. I can't do that to her. There's no way she'd tell anyone."

"Come on, the bar is a thing; a place. It's nothing compared to a child. Sal would manage without it, and so would Amy."

"I can't do it, she'd hate me. I thought maybe you could do something with it, like maybe find more stuff on my dad. Amy's not the only girl he's raped. I know it but I can't prove it. I mean, I remember stuff with my babysitters, but no one would believe me. I was just a little kid and I don't remember anything in particular, just snapshots; like bits and pieces of a dream."

Ryan stood and paced length of the kitchen. Outside the wind blew against the windows, rattling the panes as snow pelted the glass. *Fucking snow.*

"What makes you think he won't blame Sal if I turn him in? He's going to figure Amy told me. So again, he'll retaliate," Ryan said.

"No. See, if you turn him in for other stuff, tell the cops you heard rumors or whatever, then my dad won't have a reason to hurt anyone else. They can't control what you do.

Right? You don't have to use any of this stuff about Amy. I only told you because I wanted you to know how awful my dad really is."

"Mickey, you don't understand. I can't just say your dad raped some anonymous girl or that I think this or that is going on. They'll want evidence."

"I might have something here." Mickey pulled a tape recorder from his pocket. "I started taping Dad a few years ago, after I found him with one of the Chamber's girls. Julia—my mom, told me to be quiet about what I saw. But she tore a strip off him later… and got knocked around for her trouble. I thought maybe if I had enough I could convince her to do what everyone else is too scared to do but she won't. I don't know what you can do with it. The one in there's what I taped yesterday."

Ryan took the recorder, almost afraid to press play and glanced at the boy.

Mickey rummaged inside his coat and pulled out a fistful of tiny tapes. He set them on the table.

Heart pounding, repressing his excitement Ryan pressed play.

"Ready?" Fred's voice sounded a little tinny, but was easy to recognize.

"I've been ready. What did he say?" Carroll.

"It was Audrey. She said Ryan was too upset to talk and she noticed the barn door and the tracks first. Gonna be hard to determine a suicide if I have to include that in the evidence. I told you we should have left the truck in the driveway and carried her. You could have covered your tracks on the way back."

"Yeah, you know it all. The tracks would have been there no matter what. You think people can't tell that someone's been through the snow just because they cover the footprints? Come on."

Shuffling sounds, a door opening and then Carroll's voice. *"Keep your fucking mouth shut."* The dull thud of a closing door.

Ryan pressed stop.

"How do I tell them I got these tapes? I'm not even sure we can use them. This gives away nothing. They didn't call each other by name. Jesus, Mickey, you were there. Why not just turn these in?"

"I can't."

"I can use this but it's going to take time for other things to fall into place. By then, your dad might catch on and we're still screwed. I need more, something solid. Do you have anything to prove Amy was raped? Pictures?"

"No. She didn't want Sal to know. Do you have any idea what that would do to him?"

Ryan closed his eyes, his head throbbed and he ignored the urge to pack his stuff and forget Albertsville. They were sick, all of them. What kind of man rapes his son's girlfriend? What man rapes any woman? Jesus, he's ruined a child's life—three children. Amy wasn't the first, and she wouldn't be the last victim of Carroll's perversion. How could everyone just stand by knowing what the man is capable of? These people needed a wakeup call. A big one.

RENÉE MILLER

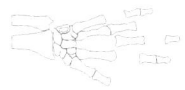

CHAPTER 22

In his grandfather's den, Ryan inspected the painted cookie tin Audrey found in the barn. Beneath a pile of paper lay a journal. Ryan suspected the paper, mostly unreadable notes, had been camouflage for the small book.

Mickey had left, angry and frustrated because Ryan couldn't promise him anything. What did he expect? A rape with no DNA evidence? He couldn't do anything about it. If only Amy would go to the police. She carried all the evidence they'd need. If she'd just tell them Carroll fathered her baby, they'd order a paternity test. Surely she and Mickey realized Carroll couldn't allow that baby to be born.

He listened to the rest of the tapes, but the quality was poor, and most of them were one-sided phone conversations. Sure, to someone who knew what was going on, they sounded incriminating, but to an outsider, they could mean many things, not one of them criminal.

Ryan sat back in his chair and opened the weathered book to the first page. *January 1950.* The sentences were stilted, the writing sloppy, as though done in haste, but he had little trouble recreating the scene they described.

The twelve of us sat in a room in the newly built mill. We were terrified, worried for our families, our livelihoods. After arguing and pleading with each other for hours, we had but one decision to make.

The Bakers had spent three days as hostages to that murderous bunch of convicts. Maximum-security prison they called it. No trouble for anyone, no way to get out. Yet somehow five of the bastards broke free. The radio guy said there was a reward, if one could collect it.

I can't say I liked Jack Baker. His grandfather might have stood next to mine and the other twelve men, when the town was founded, but he had a big mouth. Speaking against what we'd begun at the mine, quite openly in fact, warning us we'd all go to jail for it. Jarrod tried to explain the situation, using the smooth voice and charming smile that only the Alberts possessed, but Jack never seemed to get it. Those weapons bring this town a lot of money. So do the drugs. I'm not proud of what we've done to build this town, but it's not as if we make weapons or sell them. We simply hold them until the owners pick them up, for a fee of course. This mill will never amount to much of anything. If left to rely solely on the mill or the farms we'd all sink. But Baker, he threatened daily to go to the cops and to bring the whole operation to a close.

We'd all but given up on finding a solution that didn't bring the cops sniffing around. Jarrod stood and made our decision for us.

He said if we got rid of them, no one had to know anyone was here. No cops, no media, nothing changes, he said.

Ben Swift reminded Jarrod that these were our friends and we couldn't just let them die. But he didn't look so certain.

Jarrod just smiled, told us that Jack Baker would ruin us given the chance.

I don't know why it sounded good, but it did. All I can say is I was scared; we were all scared. Jarrod propped a long leg on the chair and cracked his knuckles. We should have known then we were in deep trouble.

He reminded us that no one knew those convicts came

here. He was right. The cops won't look for them here. Why would they come to this shithole? If we gave these men what they wanted: the guns, the money, a vehicle, and God knows what else, then the cops would find out. Giving into their demands was not an option.

We call for help, the feds are in town and oh, won't that be a wonderful thing? They see everything that's going on. Everyone goes down because of one family. A family that didn't even care about this town, according to Jarrod.

We eliminate the problem by burning the whole fucking thing down, two birds with one stone. Baker and his bullshit are gone, and the cops never need to know that those convicts came to this town. Jarrod laid it all out, and we had to agree, he made sense. What choice did we have?

We did it that night, surrounded the house while Chambers cut the phone lines. Then we dumped gas all over the ground outside, on the porch, splashed it on the windows. Surely we will rot in hell for this. I thought about backing out, truly I did, but then a match sparked, lighting up Jarrod's face. He smiled and tossed it on the porch. There was no going back then.

The next morning we discussed who would clean it up. Jarrod told us not to worry. He'd take care of everything. Told us there was an old shaft in the mine where he could dump the bodies, it would be a simple house fire. Tragic, but not unheard of. The Bakers had been sleeping, he said, and told us that we weren't to discuss it, even amongst ourselves. To be honest, I was glad never to speak of it again, but the flames swallowing that house, licking the windows where the children slept in their beds; that will haunt my soul until the day I die.

I don't know, maybe I could have forgiven myself in time. I mean, I only wanted to protect my family and my town. But Jarrod didn't return for nearly a week. When he did, he dropped a bombshell on us all. Said he hated long trips and asked us what happened while he was gone. Then he asked if we'd seen the convicts they mentioned on the radio.

The rest of us were confused at first, but he quickly cleared up all doubt.

We said that he knew what happened. Jarrod denied it. Said he wasn't here, then told Bill to look at the minutes. As soon as I realized that he took the fucking minutes from that meeting, I knew how things would be.

The record of the meeting, the only copy that Jarrod's wife signed, indicating she'd been there, showed that Jarrod was not present.

Jarrod asked us to imagine what would happen if the authorities found the bodies of Jack Baker and his family. Of course, he'd be horrified to know what we'd done, furious that we threatened his wife to ensure her silence. The authorities would certainly be right to send us all to jail for the rest of our lives if they believed his version of events.

I asked where he put them.

Jarrod grinned and wagged his damn finger at me. Called me a nosy boy and said as long as we all looked to the good of the town, he wouldn't reveal a thing, not to anyone. If we crossed him, he'd have to unearth some awful secrets. He also decided the town needed a new name. Albertsville, he decided. We agreed.

What were we going to do? He had us right where he wanted us. If I could take back what I did, I would. I'm ashamed to say it's not so much because I regret that family's death as much as I hate being under Jarrod's thumb.

—— ——

Ryan rubbed his eyes, burning from reading the faded ink. So the bodies weren't at the mine. A note in red ink lined the edge of the page.

"Under their feet."

Ryan ran his thumb over the paper. The black ink was smooth, the page softened with age and the ink with it. The red ink... he licked his thumb and pressed it over it. The red ink smudged. The black did not. A new entry? It made no sense. Under their feet?

Ryan leafed through the final pages, which revealed nothing more than a few entries about weather, births, and deaths. He held the book for a moment. Carroll was genetically inclined toward evil.

Where did that old bastard hide the bodies?

The snow came down in sweeping drifts. Wind caught the flakes and carried them in tiny whirls down the dark road. Ryan leaned over the steering wheel, as though that would make it easier to see through the white haze beyond.

He'd sat alone in his grandparents' kitchen, figuring out the right thing to do. Carroll had killed his father, or at least ordered someone to do it. He'd done the same to his grandparents. He couldn't offer proof of either of these, but he had no doubts. Carroll had also terrorized his mother for years. The sweetest, kindest woman Ryan had ever known, punished for what? Not doing what he expected? Falling in love? For that alone he hated Carroll Albert. For the murders, he expected him to pay. But should he be the only one sticking his neck out and snooping around? What about the rest of these people?

They'd grown so used to the status quo that the very idea of doing something different and standing up for themselves had become more terrifying than Carroll. Ryan suspected that they found a certain security in their hopelessness. If the situation was impossible, then they couldn't be held accountable. If they couldn't be held accountable, then they didn't have to make a moral choice. Their laziness and complacency is what allowed Carroll to manipulate them.

When the realization hit him, Ryan jumped from his chair and grabbed his keys off the counter. Before he could change his mind, he left to visit Sal.

Driving the main street—his car moving at a slow crawl—Ryan searched the darkness, hoping that Sal didn't close early. He didn't want to have the exchange with Amy present, which he'd have to do if he had to knock at Sal's home. A few feet ahead, lights blazed above the bar. Well, most of them blazed.

About every third or fourth bulb had blown giving the sign a Morse code look about it.

He paused to collect his thoughts and then climbed out of his car to face the weathered doors of Sal's Bar and Grill. The steps were slick and snow covered. If he were in the city, they'd have been cleared and salted. Lawsuits were something to avoid at all costs, but these didn't happen in Albertsville. He slipped, grabbing the handle of the door in time to right himself and glance around feeling a little silly.

Grumbling, Ryan walked inside the dim bar and yanked the door closed behind him.

"Hey, I was just going to lock up." Sal waved from the pool tables on the far side of the room.

"I didn't know the roads were so sloppy," Ryan lied. "Thought I'd come for a beer. That old house gets kind of quiet, and I'm not used to that."

Sal laughed and walked to the back, toward the bar.

Ryan followed, his determination faltering. The man would be devastated if he knew what Carroll had done to Amy. But if someone didn't do something….

"Coors, right?" Sal asked.

"What? Oh, yeah, Coors is fine."

Sal's smile wavered for a moment. He turned to get the bottle of beer from the cooler behind him.

"So what really brings you here?" Sal set the bottle in front of Ryan and waved away his offer of money. "Nah, it's on the house. Just don't tell anyone or I'll go broke."

"Thanks. I wanted to ask you about something I heard."

"Sure,"

"Uh, it's something I read in a book that belonged to my great grandfather. I don't know if you know any of what happened here sixty years ago, but it was worth a shot."

Sal raised a bushy brow.

"I know about the Bakers," Ryan said.

"What do you know?" Sal straightened, picking a stained rag off the counter and shaking it out.

"I heard that something happened a long time ago, something that the founding families decided, and Carroll is using it to blackmail everyone."

"And? What if it's true?"

Ryan picked at the label of his bottle, trying to form the words in his head to minimize the impact. "What happened that night was years ago. It can't hurt anyone now. I don't understand how Carroll uses it to hold everyone in line. Is protecting the town's image worth risking your child's safety? Do you want to stick around so that Albert has time to hurt your children and their children too?"

Sal folded the rag and set it back on the counter, then rubbed a scruffy chin before turning to Ryan. "Listen, you're new here so I'm going to explain something to you that most of the others would just know. It doesn't matter about what happened back then. That's not the issue. If word of those bodies gets out, this whole town will be crawling with RCMP. The drugs, the shit going on at the mine, the way everyone has turned a blind eye to Carroll's bullshit, taken money we know came from that stuff, all of it would be known. People here would be arrested, tried, and although most of them might get off, the damage would be done. They'd lose everything. I'd lose this bar. The only reason I still have it is because Carroll let a few payments slide. If this bullshit is exposed, I lose it all. Amy loses it all. She's everything to me, and I'm all she's got. You know? I have no family, few friends, and no one outside of this town. Where would she go if I went to jail?"

"The government would—"

"The government? Fuck, you are not that naïve, are you Mr. Cassidy? Our good Reeve would likely slip off without a dent. You can be damn straight he'd never go to jail for anything. The fucker is slippery. Nothing sticks to him. The rest of us? We have more than just ourselves to think about."

"But if you've done nothing wrong, you could get out and start fresh, out from under his thumb."

Sal snorted and looked up to the ceiling. He shook his head. "Okay, you're right. I could leave, but I haven't been exactly guiltless. I've been selling liquor illegally. You know what that means? I have no liquor license. There are laws in Canada, things you have to abide by when you sell booze, and I don't do that. Why? Cause if I did it legally, I'd be sunk. Carroll provides me with what I need. I pay almost nothing for it. In the grand scheme of things, turning myself in to fuck him isn't a terrible idea, and with good behavior, I'd probably do a few years for my stupidity. But the issue here isn't how much time I'd do. I don't give a damn about that. The issue is Amy. She'd be alone. Would you leave your child at the mercy of this town?"

CHAPTER 23

Carroll leaned back in his seat, waiting for Audrey to arrive home. After thinking it over, he realized she'd fooled him. While she did keep Cassidy occupied as he asked, he suspected that she agreed to do it as part of a plan she'd concocted with Ryan. She'd been awfully willing to fall into bed with the little prick. They wanted to hang him, but he was too smart for that. Did they really think he wouldn't catch on? He'd caught the intimate gesture when Fred questioned her. The way Ryan's hand touched her hip as she leaned into him, the look that passed between them. Cassidy had beaten him to the punch and nailed the little slut the very night she was supposed to be following orders. Instead they'd laughed behind his back.

A shuffling from across the road caught his gaze. Audrey's small form huddled into a bulky jacket as she trudged through the deepening snow toward her house. She fished in her purse, probably for a key, head bent, paying no attention to the space behind her. He opened the door and jumped down, shivering at the frigid wind that blew through the air. Curse them both for forcing him out in this shit. God, he hated winter.

Careful not to make a sound, Carroll pushed the door just until it closed and then crossed the street. Audrey still hadn't noticed him and fumbled with keys, finally inserting the right one and pushing the door open, before flicking on the light inside.

"My, you do work late," Carroll held the door.

Audrey backed away, scowling. "What do you want?"

"What do I want? Oh, so many things. You know, it seems you've forgotten that I always tend to have my way."

"I haven't forgotten. It's because you're a liar and a cheat, and let's not forget a murderer." Audrey raised her chin.

How cute. She thought he gave a damn that she knew about Millicent. Like she could prove anything. Tim and Fred had swept that away nicely and he and Farley had taken care of the body. Millicent no longer existed.

"I know what you're up to with Cassidy, and this is my friendly warning to you. Stay away from him. You'll never pin anything on me. I'm too smart and you don't have the imagination to do it anyway."

Audrey's face reddened. She stepped toward him.

He enjoyed her anger, the way it made her green eyes darken and her body tremble, it was almost as pleasant as watching her fear. *Almost.*

"You told me to distract him. Did you forget that? So now you don't like that I succeeded? Tough shit. You can't control these people forever. They're going to get tired of it someday and then what? You can't take on the whole town."

"Ah, Cassidy's been doing more than fucking you I see. Not the wisest move on his part. See, I'd have gotten my pleasure from you and left it at that. But then, I know how big a woman's mouth tends to be. He doesn't. The bottom line is I can't have you conspiring against me. So that leaves me with a problem. What do I do with you?"

She retreated, her gaze shifting to the door for a moment before turning back to him. Carroll watched her shoulders slump. This was better.

She shook her head. "I'm sorry, okay? I'm tired and just not in the mood to argue. I haven't been plotting anything with Ryan. I've been trying to get him to leave, just like you asked."

"Why is he still in my town then? He should've left before

the snow came. Are you that good in bed? I have had a hard time believing that. Been taking lessons since I last checked?"

Audrey bit her lip, rewarding him with a pretty blush that crept up her face. "No. My personal life is none of your business."

Carroll stepped inside, forcing her into the hallway. Slowly, he ran a gloved finger down her face.

She flinched, and closed her eyes.

He could easily prove how little power she possessed. But he didn't have time for that. A quick warning, for now. "I can make it my business any time I want, Audrey. There's nothing you can do about it. Are you going to cry to your new boyfriend? Tell him I fucked you? Do you think he really gives a shit about you or this town? He's a city boy, and he'll leave as soon as that house and the money are his. As for you, you'd be used goods. Tainted. He can do a lot better than you and he knows it. He's using you."

"You're wrong. I don't need Ryan to do anything. If you touch me, I'll kill you. I'm not afraid to use a gun."

Carroll laughed at the fire in her eyes. Damn, she believed she could do just that. Precious. "You haven't killed me yet."

The wind rattled the windows. Audrey listened as snow and ice assaulted the small cottage. She lay on her side, her head on the edge of the pillow, unable to sleep. Each time she closed her eyes, Carroll's face floated before her, and the feel of his hands on her body brought waves of nausea.

His threats echoed through her head. Audrey struggled to hold the familiar fear at bay. Ryan would be there if she asked. Carroll was wrong, Ryan wasn't using her. But as she'd stood in the hallway, with Carroll's shadow towering over, that certainty wavered. For a brief second, her heart remembered the disgust in Ryan's eyes when she told him what she'd done. He might not understand her fear, but he did care.

Rolling over, Audrey blinked the tears back. Frustration with herself, the situation and with Carroll's arrogance burned in her chest. If only she could guarantee he would go away, that the police would believe them and someone would put the lying bastard behind bars forever. If only they'd promised that no one else here would get hurt in the process. But no one could give her assurances, and Carroll could charm anyone when he set his mind to it. He'd be sure to turn it up full blast for the police.

Somewhere outside a door closed and her heart skipped a beat. Who would be out? Feet crunched in the snow, moving closer to her window. The temptation to get up and open the blinds was strong, but not as strong as the fear that paralyzed her. She listened. Silence.

Stop being silly. Someone might be out late, probably drinking at Sal's. Kim lived on the street behind her, and often cut through her yard rather than go the long way around when he'd had too much to drink. Still, she listened, her breath coming in short gasps as her heart pounded against her chest. But if it were Kim walking through her yard, why the slamming door?

A thump. She sat up.

A door closed. *Her* door. *Please be Ryan.*

But she'd locked up before going to bed and Ryan didn't have a key. The only other person with a key was… Millicent.

Audrey reached for the phone next to the bed. Fumbling, she knocked the lamp off the nightstand. Her fingers finally closed around the receiver and she pressed talk. The phone beeped as she punched Ryan's number in. She hoped the sound would scare the intruder off, though deep in her heart she knew it wasn't likely to scare him one bit.

Footsteps in the hall moved closer to her door. A sob caught in her throat as she brought the phone to her ear. The knob turned and she watched, terrified, the bedroom door opening and a dark figure framed in the gloom. He smiled, and Audrey realized the phone was dead.

"And who would you be calling at this time of night?" Carroll asked. He slipped off his coat and tossed it over her dresser next to the door.

He left his gloves on. God, why did he leave his gloves on?

Audrey shivered at the cold light in his gaze as he neared the bed. She scrambled back, but wrapped in the blankets, she was too slow, barely making it to the edge before he reached and tangled one gloved hand in her hair to drag her forward.

"No, I prefer you on the bed."

Audrey screamed and the back of his hand whipped across her chin. Her teeth sank painfully into her tongue and she tasted blood.

No. This wasn't happening. Carroll only wanted to scare her. She glared up at him. "Get out."

"Oh, now that's no way to treat an old friend. You gave it to Cassidy. I think it's only fair I get to sample what you've been dangling in front of me for years."

"No. Stop this. I swear, Carroll, I'll go to the police. The real police, not that fuck up Fred."

She pushed at him but he pulled on her hair, forcing her face up and so she had to stare into his eyes.

His head bent to hers, he ran his tongue over her lips before chuckling softly. "You will? I don't think so. It's just you and me here now. No need to pretend you don't want me. You've wanted me since that night in my room. Remember that night? I do. If not for Kelly dying on me…."

Audrey gasped and kicked at him. "No. I'll scream so loud, someone will come."

He pinned her easily with his body. "Please do. I love it when they scream."

Ryan dreamt of summer, of the empty fields next to the house full of corn and some other plant he imagined might be hay. Larry the moose grazed as Ryan sat atop the old tractor, bumping through the cornfield doing whatever it was that farmers did on tractors. It didn't matter, in his dream he knew what he was doing and he did it well. The tractor thumped and Larry made that mournful sound. The tracker thumped again and again. His dream faded and he woke in his bed, staring at the wall. The thumping continued, and then a voice. *Audrey?*

Ryan leapt from the bed and ran down the stairs, stumbling as his foot missed a step, he skidded down the last couple of steps, catching himself at the bottom, but crashing into the door.

Audrey pounded again. "Ryan, wake up!"

Ryan turned the deadbolt and fumbled with the knob. The pounding stopped, replaced with a sniffle and a strange choking sound. Finally, he yanked the door open. His breath caught in his throat. "Audrey? What happened?"

He switched on the light. The breath left his lungs as he took in a purplish bruise on her jaw and swollen lips; the lower one split and scabbed over. Through a haze, his brain registered marks further down, deep reddish teeth imprints on her neck.

Her chin trembled and she lowered her head, her shoulders shaking.

Ryan pulled her inside and held her close. "Was it Carroll?"

Audrey continued to cry silently. Her body shuddered. She rubbed her cheek on his chest.

He pushed her gently so that he could see her face. "Did Carroll send someone to do this?"

"He came in when I was in bed."

"Son of a bitch. I'll kill him."

"Can we sit somewhere?" Audrey stumbled away from him, down the hallway and toward the kitchen.

Ryan closed the door and followed. If Carroll had sent someone to do this, he'd kill them with his bare hands. Then he'd pay a visit to Carroll. Liquid heat, unlike anything he'd experienced before boiled in his gut, a tremor surging through his body. As Ryan entered the kitchen, Audrey slumped in a chair, her back to the window.

"Was it Carroll?"

"He wanted to scare me."

"And that means?"

Audrey shook her head and stared at her hands. She wouldn't meet his gaze.

His heart ached at the defeated slope of her shoulders. "Audrey, you have to trust me."

"I do trust you. That's why I'm here. But I love you, and I don't want anything to happen to you because of me. I don't want you to hate me for letting him—"

"Don't ever say that again. You hear me? You didn't do anything. I'd never hate you for what he did. Come on, Aud. Have a little faith."

She lifted her head and the mess Carroll made of her delicate features sucker-punched him in the stomach. "Promise me you won't do anything stupid and I'll tell you."

"Did he rape you?"

"Does it make a difference?"

"Yes, damn it! I can't promise you I won't kill the fucker given the opportunity. I just can't let him get away with this."

"Ryan, don't you see?" Audrey took his hands and pulled him to the chair next to her.

His leg shook, the need to see Carroll pay for hurting her so strong he wanted to crawl out of his skin.

"He wants you to lose it. He wants you to come after him in a rage. You do that, and he has a reason to get rid of you. Self-defense, he'll say."

Helpless rage burned in his throat, desperate to break free. "I'm not stupid. He won't have a chance."

"He's planning for this. I bet he and Fred are at his place right now, laughing over how clever they are."

"But he can't get away with this."

Audrey nodded and wiped a shaking hand over her face.

God, she looked like she'd been in a car wreck. The teeth marks on her pale skin taunted him, dared him to turn the other cheek. He'd be a coward like the rest of this town if he didn't do something.

"What did he do? I want to know everything" He lowered his voice.

"He ripped the phone out and then he came in and beat me up. He didn't rape me, okay. I thought he might, but he did other things. It could have been a lot worse."

Ryan jumped off the chair and strode to the door.

Audrey grasped at his shirt.

He struggled to shrug her off. "No. Enough is enough. He can't just do these things, especially not to you."

"If you go, he's gotten what he wanted. You'll get yourself killed. I'll never forgive you if you go out that door."

Ryan stopped before the edge of anger in her tone. Fuck, why be angry at him? He wanted to make things right.

He turned.

She flinched and something snapped deep within him. "God, I want to hurt him until he begs for mercy and then I want to keep punching the shit out of him until he's so fucked up, he can't even speak much less give that cocky little grin."

"I know. I do too, but not this way" Audrey took his hands in hers. "How far are you really willing to go to see that Carroll gets what he deserves?"

"As far as we have to, I promise."

"Let's see that he pays, but not by playing his game. Not anymore."

CHAPTER 24

They spent the remainder of the night planning. After taking pictures of Audrey's injuries Ryan called the police in Timmins, who suggested they report the crime to their local police. Frustrated and angry at his helplessness, Ryan had finally hung up. For the moment, they would postpone trying to nail Carroll for Audrey's assault.

She'd tried to downplay what Carroll had done. In her opinion, it would have been far worse had he raped her. Ryan disagreed. Carroll didn't *only* beat her up. He'd gone into her home and stolen her sense of safety and security. He'd threatened her and made her believe he could do worse. Hell, Ryan believed he'd do worse too. Carroll had violated Audrey. He didn't have to mix sex into it for it to be just as traumatic.

Assault wouldn't send Carroll away for good. He'd probably get a slap on the wrist at best. They needed something bigger, something that would implicate Fred, Farley, and Calvin as well, so that legally and physically, Carroll wouldn't have the upper hand anymore.

Audrey stared at her hands the soft light of dawn illuminating her face and the evidence left there by Carroll. "What are we going to do now? No one will talk. I will, but not to Fred. I'd rather die than have to tell him what happened."

Ryan shook his head, not sure what they would do. The key was finding the Baker's. Ryan's heart raced. "We have to find those bones."

"What?"

"Don't play dumb, Audrey. I've already been told the story in its many versions. Now I know the truth. My great grandfather kept a journal and Melvin put it in that shoebox. It detailed everything: the fire, the fugitives, the Bakers; all of it."

"And how do we find them? Sixty years is a long time. They're long gone. Why do you want to find them anyway? What good will that do?"

"I want Carroll to think I've found them and that I plan to go to the press. I want Carroll so mad that he comes after me. I want him seeing red. If he's that pissed, there's a good chance he'll slip up. There's a town meeting tonight, isn't there? Let's call Merle. Let's rock Carroll's world a bit for a change."

At the back of the room, Ryan and Audrey waited on their seats for the council meeting to run down. Merle said they'd go through regular business and at the end Carroll would announce the candidates for council. Did Carroll tear up his paperwork? Nah, Carroll wouldn't have even looked at the forms filed, believing that his control was total and no one but those who had his blessing would dare run.

"Okay, now to the matter of this year's elections, which I know is what you've all come for tonight." Carroll held out one hand.

Farley placed a thin folder in it.

Carroll opened the file, scanning the first document. "I will read the names of the candidates and to make it official, each candidate must have someone to second the motion. Clear? Good. Now, let's see…"

Carroll read off the expected names: Farley, Fred, Reverend Ira, and Doctor Reid. Ryan turned to the right side of the room, where Tim sat stone-faced. He blinked, but didn't turn to look at anyone. Then Ryan stifled a laugh when Carroll spotted the last form, his face reddening.

"Well, it appears we have a new contender. Ryan Cassidy wishes to run for….reeve? Is this true?" Carroll pinned Ryan with a warning look.

Ryan stood. "Yes, I'd like to run. There isn't any law that says I can't, is there?"

"I—you don't even really live here. That house isn't in your name yet."

"Well, the bills are in my name. I just paid the taxes for the second half of the year, a bill that came to my mailbox with my name on it. I do believe the property is essentially mine. At the very least, because I pay taxes I am a resident. Isn't my great grandfather one of the town's founders? I believe I fit all the prerequisites for running."

The room fell silent. A cough echoed from the front, following an uncomfortable shuffling of feet to his left.

Ryan smiled.

Carroll leaned to his right, whispered to Fred and paled at his reply. The form in his hands shook, rippling the paper.

Check, Mr. Albert.

Carroll whispered something back to Fred who nodded, then stood and cleared his throat. "Come on, Cassidy. This is stupid. No one in their right mind would second your motion to run. Would they?"

Fred's cool gaze scanned the crowd.

Ryan didn't have to look around him to know they avoided his eyes.

"Well? Why don't we ask? Make it official." Carroll looked around the room, a confident smile on his face. "Would anyone like to second Ryan Cassidy's motion to run for council? Would anyone like to support an outsider? Of course, I know no one here would go against their friends, their kin, and vote for a city boy hell bent on ruining our little town. He probably wants to clear out that property for a strip mall or some other nonsense. Would any of you support that? After all that this town has done for you?"

Ryan figured he'd pull out all the stops, but hadn't imagined

RENÉE MILLER

a speech like that. What the hell was he doing? He couldn't threaten these people like this. It was on the record. If—his gaze went to the secretary, who examined her nails—anyone took notes.

The room fell silent as Carroll met each person's gaze. He shrugged and opened his mouth to speak when Merle's scratchy voice cut him off. "I'll second it."

"What?"

"I'd vote for Ryan any day if it means you bastards are knocked off your high horses. Anyone else with a lick of sense would do the same. It's time for a change. Time to let someone else take charge. Someone who will put a stop to this non-sense."

Merle didn't turn to look at him, but resumed his seat, skinny arms crossed over his chest.

Ryan couldn't stop the grin that spread over his face. Audrey elbowed him. He reached for her hand and squeezing it reassuringly. He hadn't wanted her to come, but Carroll would expect her to. Thankfully, Carroll didn't seem to notice her.

"Are you drunk, Merle? I'm sorry, but we can't accept your second to Ryan's motion." Farley dismissed him with a wave of his hand.

"Fucking uppity little pricks," Merle stood. "You know damn well I ain't drunk. My vote counts."

"You haven't been sober since your wife passed you useless old shit. I've watched you. I know. Sorry, Ryan's motion is de-nied."

Merle turned to the crowd, his face red. Ryan worried with his poor health he'd have a heart attack any moment and shook his head. But Merle's lips set into a thin line and Ryan knew nothing would stop the man now.

"Are you all going to let them away with this? Chrissakes, stand up for yourselves. Ain't never going to be a change if you don't make it happen. They don't want Ryan in because they're afraid. He won't toe the line and that scares the shit out of them. Wouldn't it be nice to have someone running this town

226

that believes in honesty and actually wanted to do good? Fucking cowards, every last one of you."

"All right, Merle. That's enough. Out with you." Fred stepped around the table and advanced but Merle refused to be silenced.

"You think you can manhandle me like you do your woman, *asshole*? I don't think so. I might be older than dirt but I can kick your sorry ass any day."

Farley grabbed Merle's collar and the older man threw a punch. Fred deftly avoided it and yanked the old man's arm behind his back.

Ryan winced and stood but Audrey tugged him back.

The room stilled, not even a murmur against Fred dragging a screaming Merle outside.

"I'm not backing down." Ryan said.

No one replied. Carroll shuffled papers and looked at the other members of council.

"I'll second his motion. And I'm not drunk." Audrey's voice trembled but she stood next to Ryan. Her hand crept into his.

He smiled.

Carroll glared, biting his lip.

Audrey stiffened but remained standing, her gaze steady on the Reeve.

"So, Ryan is officially in the running," she said.

"Fine. Mr. Cassidy is also on the ballot," Carroll muttered.

A faint applause rippled through the room.

Carroll's face reddened but he said nothing.

Chairs scraped the floor as more residents stood, clapping.

Ryan smiled, a little embarrassed. Then a gunshot blast shook him away from his victory.

Audrey's mouth formed *NO!*

Ryan dragged Audrey from the room, vaguely aware of the people pushing behind him to get through the doors as well. Cries rippled through the crowd as they emerged on the steps of the town hall, and stopped as one at the scene before them.

Fred smirked and holstered his gun. At his feet lay Merle,

his head torn open, blood pooling on the ground around it.

"What the hell did you do?" Ryan stumbled down the steps, toward Merle.

"Stay where you are, Mr. Cassidy or I'll be forced to draw my weapon again."

Fred's words froze Ryan in place.

"I'm afraid Merle assaulted a police officer and pulled a weapon. I had no other choice."

Ryan's gaze fell to Merle's limp hand. Indeed, it held a knife. A small, relatively harmless pocket knife. No fiercer than the one Ryan carried as a kid. "You shot him? Couldn't you manage to restrain him? Fuck, he's a seventy year old man suffering with cancer. You could have easily taken the knife from him."

"My life was in jeopardy. I believed that and I acted. See folks, this is what happens when we let outsiders in. When you allow some slick city boy brainwash you into believing there's something wrong with our town, then you get crazy and irrational. This is sad. If not for Mr. Cassidy, Merle would still be here. I loved the man, but he left me no choice."

Fred pulled out his phone and turned from the crowd.

Someone muttered behind him, a few whispers followed, but no one said a word against Fred. "This is a fucking joke. It has to be a joke."

"I wish it was," Audrey's voice sounded small.

Murmurs met Ryan's ears.

This is too much.

What are we gonna do? He'd kill us.

He'd destroy us.

Proves that we can't do a damn thing, Reeve's got us by the balls.

Wish Merle'd had a gun. Maybe things would have been different.

"Let's go home," he said and walked to Audrey's truck, parked just beyond Merle's body.

CHAPTER 25

Ryan sat alone in his grandfather's den. Through the window, the snow blanketing the ground reflected the moonlight, illuminating the darkened room as he searched desperately on the Internet for something, anything they could do to act against Fred's blatant act of murder. He'd thought Merle might have been a bit senile over the phone issue, but he'd been right. They weren't secure, and neither was good old Canada Post, not with Albertsville's finest running it. Besides, it would also be too slow.

Any communication he sent would have to be e-mail: instant, and not managed by Carroll. It sounded paranoid and crazy even to himself, but Ryan believed Carroll had the power to do all this town said he could. Hell, he probably wouldn't even have a phone connection much longer.

He'd stared for several minutes at the first email he'd written, edited, deleted half of it, twice added the words he'd previously removed, and then deleted it again. They didn't have time to wait. While the authorities in Timmins read his email and decided whether it warranted their intervention, Fred had time to gather witnesses to support his claims. How many people would lie and say they watched the entire thing? How many would refute them?

Running the fingers of one hand through his hair, Ryan resisted the urge to punch the computer screen. It would do no good, other than possibly making him feel a little better, and it would wake Audrey, who needed to rest. She'd picked up Justin after the meeting. The poor kid raged and vowed revenge before dissolving into the tears he'd held back since his mother's death. Now he slept upstairs in the spare room.

After Justin fell into a troubled sleep, Ryan had lain with Audrey, holding her in his arms and stroking her hair in silence. He wanted to sleep, but his mind refused to be still. When Audrey's breathing slowed and her lips parted, Ryan gave up on doing the same and crept out of bed.

Counting to ten, Ryan forced his rage down, and focused on doing something productive; another email to a group that moved faster than the legal system. Opening his mailbox, he began a letter to his editor at the newspaper.

"Hey, you have Internet?" Ryan nearly jumped over the desk at Justin's voice.

"Yeah, but it's just dial-up."

"Can you show me?"

"You've never used it?" Ryan wasn't surprised. Carroll wouldn't let them have Internet. They might speak to real people.

"Nah, Mom said we couldn't get Internet way out here. I'd like to know how it works."

Ryan waved Justin over. "My password is Dennis, my middle name. Can you remember that?"

"Sure."

"Okay, actually, I have an idea. If anything happens that you can't get into this one, there's a laptop upstairs under my bed. There's a cord with it. I have a modem connected to the phone line here, the router allows me to use the laptop, but the laptop has to be plugged into a phone line. You with me so far?"

"Yeah, I think so." Justin watched as the dial-up powered through its connection. "Slow, isn't it?"

"Dial up is always slow, but it's worse here at night for

some reason. Anyway, you have to plug the cord that I'll leave attached to the laptop into a phone jack. You can't use the phone; if someone's online, you'll bump them off. Same if you're on the phone and someone tries to log onto the Internet. The person on the phone will get an unpleasant screech. Okay?"

"Yeah, the thing is basically like calling someone through the computer, right?"

"Right. Once you're online, if you go into my email here, there's an address book. I've got two names in this one here." Ryan clicked on his emergency list. "This guy, Jacob, is an RCMP officer, but this is his personal email. He handled a case that I covered for the paper. That's how we met. He was transferred a year ago to this area. I emailed him the other day about your mom. I'm just waiting to hear back. Tonight, I sent an email to the RCMP's General Complaints address on their site about Merle. They should reply because Fred is a police officer involved in a shooting. They like to investigate those things. Anyway, if anything happens to me before I hear back from them, I want you to e-mail this guy first, tell him what happened, mention me, and instruct him to bring help. Make something up if you have to. Got it?"

"So, why don't you do that now?"

"And tell them what? We've got nothing to tell them when they get here. But if I can find where those bones are, Carroll will freak out. He'll do something extreme to shut me up. I want you to get them here if that happens."

"Am I waiting till he kills you?"

"I'm hoping they get here before that."

Ryan hadn't thought that far. It would give them something to arrest Carroll for, but what if Ryan disappeared along with the others? Dying didn't really appeal to him, not for this shithole. A thought tickled his brain, pushing its way through until he couldn't ignore it. "There was no funeral for your mom."

"No, I didn't expect there'd be one. Why?"

"If he took her where his grandfather took the others…"

"We'd have him for her murder. Do you think he, you know, cleaned up the body?" Justin shuddered.

"Sorry, I know it's hard."

"No, I'm okay. I just had a thought of those remains and the nasty that would be with them. I'd hate to be the one to find them."

"Tim has evidence. If he does the right thing, they'll have pictures, scrapings and whatever else he got. With the marks around her neck, which I'm pretty sure will match Carroll's hands. There might be enough to convince them he's worth investigating. There might be hair, fibers, who knows what else, but I want more."

"The bribery, threats, and ass kickings aren't enough?"

Ryan pushed the chair back. "We don't have proof of that stuff. Sure, if they could get the bank records.... But they need warrants I'd imagine, and to get a warrant, they'd need evidence to back their suspicions. Have a seat, mess around a bit. Remember, if anything happens, contact Jacob. Actually, from now on when I go out, I'll call you every hour. If I don't call, contact everyone in that emergency list. Got it?"

"I will. What if I can't get to the computer?"

Shit, that would probably be what happened too. "I'll get a list of phone numbers together for you too. I carry my Blackberry with me, but there's a spare cell phone in the car that has those numbers programmed in it too. I guess we should have it charged just in case."

"What are you going to do?"

"First I want to piece together some clues, and then I have to get into the mill."

The lights outside Sal's bar went out. Moments later the door opened and Sal emerged, keys in hand. He turned, bending slightly to lock up.

Carroll got out of his vehicle.

Sal looked up as soon as Carroll's feet crunched in the snow. He wasn't a fool and always kept an eye over his shoulder. Slouching, he hung his head low, pocketing the keys and shoving his hands in his pockets.

So he expected my visit. Guilty conscience?

"I don't know what you want Albert, but I won't say nothing to no one. So just leave me alone."

Carroll chuckled and crossed the road.

Sal backed up a step.

"I noticed Mr. Cassidy's car outside last night." Carroll stopped just before the curb and tucked his hands into his coat pockets.

"Yeah? So, people can't have a beer anymore? That's a shame, seeing how people drinking beer is what pays my bills and your mortgage."

"Don't get smart with me. You know what I'm saying. Cassidy's been snooping and I doubt he missed an opportunity to ferret out whatever information he could from you. What did he ask?"

"Like I said: nothing. He had a beer, we talked about the shitty weather and he went home." Sal shrugged.

When Sal lied he couldn't look a man in the eye and he'd yet to meet his. Ryan had gotten something out of him.

"You're a terrible liar, Sal. What did you tell him?"

Sal opened his mouth then closed it and ran a hand through his grey hair. He took a deep breath that shook his entire frame before finally meeting Carroll's gaze. "Look, he asked about the Baker's and that fire. That's all. Shit, I didn't think you'd care. I mean, you don't keep it a secret or anything."

Melvin Cassidy had gathered enough information that the right person might figure out where they were. If Ryan found duplicates of what Carroll took from the clock, then he'd certainly be able to put the pieces together. If he found the Baker's.... "The difference is that it is our information, not Cassidy's. He's an outsider. Did he tell you he could help you? That's what he's been telling everyone else, so why should I be surprised?"

"No, you've got it wrong. He was just making conversation." Again Sal's gaze met Carroll's forehead rather than his eyes.

Amy hadn't shared what happened with her father. Otherwise Sal might have been a little more hostile, or at least angry enough to tell him to fuck off. Perhaps it was time to remind Sal how much control he didn't have and where his association with Cassidy would take him and his pretty little daughter.

Snow had begun to fall once more and Carroll pulled a hand out of his pocket to dust it off his shoulders before smiling. "Okay, I'll give you the benefit of the doubt here and believe that you haven't told him anything. After all, the booze is your crime, not mine. But just in case you feel tempted by the boy's charming façade, let me remind you what will happen."

Sal opened his mouth to speak.

Carroll raised a gloved hand to silence him. "No, I don't give a damn about our deal. What I want you to remember is that sweet young thing you've got at home. Amy, is it? Of course it is. I know that. Amy and I get along quite well. She even confided in me not long ago. Seems she's gone and broke off with Mickey because of our conversation. I hate to see the boy hurt, but I could tell that your girl prefers men, not kids, and I thought it best that things were brought into the open before my boy got hurt. She's quite the mature woman, you know. You've done a fine job raising her. I'd hate to see anything happen to her, or her baby."

Sal's eyes narrowed and Carroll glanced down, amused at the way the man's hands clenched into fists that he'd never have the balls to use.

"What do you know about Amy? Your boy will pay for that kid. His last name doesn't relieve him of responsibility."

"Oh Sal, do you really think it's Mickey's kid? That boy can't wipe his own ass without his daddy holding his hand. Sex? Please. Daddy had to take care of that for him too."

⌒ ⌒

Sal let himself back into the bar and walked to the cooler. He took a beer, twisted off the cap, and set it on the bar. He pulled out a stool. What the hell did he mean? Daddy took care of what? "Fucking bastard."

"Dad?" the front door banged shut and Sal met Amy's worried frown as she walked toward him. "I heard the door slam. What's going on? You coming upstairs soon?"

"Who got you pregnant?"

Amy's face paled and he knew Mickey hadn't been the one.

"Who, Amy?"

"Dad, it—"

"Tell me."

Amy's chin trembled and she strode to the bar. Her blue eyes filled with tears before she crumpled onto a stool.

Sal reached around and pulled her into his chest as huge sobs wracked her body.

"I said no and he didn't listen."

"Who?"

"He said Mickey would be there, but he lied. Mickey didn't know. I'm so stupid."

"No baby, you're not stupid." Sal brushed the hair from her damp face and rocked her gently. *Carroll, you rotten, dirty piece of shit.*

"I'm sorry I didn't listen. You said never to go there without Mickey, you told me to stay away from Mr. Albert and I didn't listen."

His stomach hollowed at the words, a gaping emptiness gnawed at his insides. How did he not see this? He should never have permitted her to get close to that boy. If she'd stayed away, Carroll would never have gotten near her. He'd failed to protect the only thing that ever mattered. How did he make this up to Amy? "Don't you ever apologize for what he did, baby. Not ever."

Sal rocked his daughter and stared unseeing at the empty bar. For sixteen years he'd stayed silent and pretended he didn't see or hear about the things Albert had done. For sixteen years he'd allowed that man to manipulate him. All of it for Amy's sake. Now, his silence had destroyed the only good thing in his life. He tried to protect her and failed.

Sal squeezed his arms, hugging her closer to him and mur-muring reassurance. His throat burned with unshed tears and he wondered how he'd get past this, how Amy would ever be okay again.

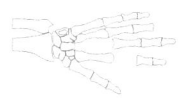

CHAPTER 26

"Hey, Mick?"

Sal. Shit. Mickey shifted the phone and glanced at his stepmother. She smoothed the page of her book and pulled a leg beneath her, nestling further into the soft brown lazy boy. The sunlight from the window behind her shone over her hair, creating a sort of halo. Right.

He turned toward the wall. "Yeah, can I call you back?"

"Cell phone, understand?" Sal asked.

"Yep."

He set the phone on the base.

"Who was that?" Julia asked.

"Just Amy." Shit. He sucked at lying and she knew it.

"Really? Your dad knocks her up and you still want to be with her?"

A dull roar began in his ears. "How did you—"

"I'm not stupid, honey. I know what goes on in my house. If you love that girl, get the hell out of here. As far as you can go."

She'd tell on him. Probably trying to set him up. "What about you?"

"Me?"

"Why don't you leave too?"

"I can't. Not while your father's still alive."

Ryan's hand rested on Audrey's back, trailing now and again lower, over her ass before he'd lean over and whisper something in her ear. Fuck, it was enough to make a man vomit. Carroll glared at them from the dairy section of the grocery store. Long forgotten his original reason for coming in, he wandered the aisles, picking up this and that and turning away when he thought they might catch him peeping.

At first, he wondered if this performance was for his benefit, but as he trailed after them he realized they were oblivious to anything beyond their little love bubble. Disgusting. And weak.

Carroll turned. He'd seen enough. Pushing through the front door of the supermarket and into the damp air outside, he fished the phone from his pocket, punched in a number and drew it to his ear.

"Yeah," Fred's mouth sounded full.

"I think I've figured out the solution to our problem." A door slammed next to him and Carroll turned to the brooding stare of Calvin Chambers. Fuck, that ass-packer had a disturbing look about him. Carroll would lay bets Chambers salivated at the thought of pounding him a time or two. Not the pounding Carroll would prefer either.

"Morning," Calvin muttered, pocketing his keys.

"Hold on, I have a job for you." Carroll smiled. Fucking queer. He turned back to Fred. "Meet me at my house in an hour."

"Shit, Carroll I'm buried in paperwork here. A murder don't go away on its own you know."

Carroll let a breath whistle through his clenched teeth. To his right, Calvin shifted, his boots crunching in the snow. "First, you're on a phone, dipshit. Second, the paperwork is the least of our concerns. Two hours. That's it. Be there."

"Done."

Carroll shut the phone and turned to Calvin. "How's Kim

doing?"

"Fine."

"And your wife?"

Calvin's cheeks filled with color. He shrugged. "All right, I suppose."

"Samantha? How's she doing? She got that weight issue under control?"

Calvin's bushy brow shot up and his dark eyes narrowed. Carroll wondered for a moment if he'd pushed his luck but banished the thought. He had him by the balls. Fuck, he could force the little bitch to her knees right in front of him and Calvin wouldn't do a thing.

"She's okay. I... uh, I didn't know about any weight problem."

"Well, it's unimportant, she's a kid. I'm sure she won't wind up like Anita. Anyway, you and I need to talk. I'm going to rid us of the Cassidy problem. You'd like that, wouldn't you?"

"Sure. What do you need me to do?"

⮌ ⮎

"Hey Aud?"

"She's gone out," Justin called from the den.

Ryan sighed. Justin had taken over his computer, but given the tragedy that had struck the kid's life over the past weeks, he didn't have the heart to force him to do anything but what made him happy. His newfound fascination with the Internet made him ecstatic.

"Did you have anything to eat?" he yelled. Audrey said something about reminding the boy he needed food.

"Yep," he hollered back.

Ryan grabbed his wallet from the dresser and left his room. Should he believe him? The kid considered a Snickers bar and a Coke a meal, and Audrey swore growing boys needed actual food. Ryan didn't have time to make anything though, so he'd let it slide for now. He'd act just as surprised and disappointed as Audrey later, if she figured out Justin hadn't eaten.

The house was dark. The only light at the bottom of the

stairs came from the den. Ryan walked down the hallway to stop at the open door. Justin leaned back in the comfortable chair, a controller in his hand. He looked up when Ryan cleared his throat.

"I have to go out again," Ryan said.

"How many people are you going to beg before you realize they won't budge?"

"Someone will. I just have to catch them at the right moment."

"Right." Justin's fingers moved with lightning speed over the control pad.

Ryan marveled at how kids could do that but couldn't understand the simple process of picking up a sock. "Audrey and I have keys, so don't answer the door. Hear me?"

"Yeah, don't answer the door, ignore the phone and don't go outside. Don't unlock the door for any reason, even if I think it's harmless. Definitely don't open it to Carroll or Fred no matter what they say. In fact, it's best if I pretend that no one's here and if they break in, I should hide somewhere like a frightened little girl."

Ryan smiled as Justin recited the warning he and Audrey gave him each time they left him alone in the house. He hoped the kid took it more seriously than he sounded. "Good. As long as we're clear. I'll be back in a couple of hours. If I'm not—"

"If you're not then I e-mail the guy in your address book and tell him to come get me and bring the cops. Got it. Can I play my game now, *Dad*?"

"Okay, smartass. Sorry for giving a shit."

Ryan moved away. Justin's soft laughter followed. He didn't know what they'd do with Justin. For his sake, he hoped that Audrey's plan of adopting him would satisfy children's services. Though Carroll was named on his birth certificate, Ryan planned on leaving Albertsville only when he was locked up in a cell and unable to assert his rights to anything.

As he walked to his car, Ryan breathed in the cool air. It had warmed considerably, and they'd had no snow in a few days. The roads were passable, Audrey had a delivery at the store the day before and the driver said that the roads were sloppy but manageable.

He had to convince someone to drive down them before the next storm hit. Or before Carroll did something drastic. So far he'd visited nearly every resident, under the guise of his run for town council, and while a couple hesitated and told him they really would like to, none would talk about Merle. Not one.

Ryan opened his door and sank into the driver's seat, cursing the cowards. Sal wouldn't even talk to him. Only once did he reply "I'll talk to you when the time is right. Just let things be for now."

Audrey later overheard Carroll ranting into his cell phone near the Taj-Ma-Albert that Mickey had vanished. Sal must have sent Amy away and Mickey left with her. Good for him, except one would expect he'd do more than that, like cut the fucker's nuts out.

The man had nothing to lose and still he stayed quiet. These people baffled him. Ryan shifted into reverse and backed up until he could turn down the lane that led to the road.

He slowed at the end of the driveway, his thoughts a jumbled mess when a face filled his window. He screamed.

"Sorry," Kim mouthed.

Ryan drew one hand to his chest, sure that his heart would just give up on him any moment, and rolled down the window.

Kim backed away, darting a glance in both directions.

"You nearly made me shit my pants." Ryan said.

"Sorry, I saw the lights coming down the drive and backed out to let you out. I wanted to catch you before you drove off."

"You were coming to see me?"

Kim nodded, his gaze darting again up the empty road. Fidgeting with his keys he shifted from one foot to the other before he turned back to Ryan. "I've been reconsidering things lately. I can barely look at myself in the mirror anymore I'm so ashamed at what my life's come to. If we could—can you really help us?"

"You can do that yourself, but I'll do what I can."

"No, not enough. I'll talk and I think I can get some of them to talk too, some that are sick to death of this bullshit. Merle, he was the nicest, most upstanding guy any of us ever knew. Aside from your father, he was the only one who ever treated me like I was human, not some kind of science experiment gone wrong. Most of them can't stomach what happened. Farley's already been around, told Calvin what he saw and what he'd tell the cops if you called them."

"I figured they'd shut everyone up. What does Calvin say about everything? I bet he has more dirt on Carroll than most."

Kim shifted again. "Can I get in the car? Let's drive up the road a bit and come back. Then we aren't as conspicuous."

He reached down to unlock the passenger door. Kim jogged around and climbed in. Ryan shifted into drive, slowly moved down the road, and waited.

"It's like this: Calvin and I are lovers. We have been for a while now. We love each other, and that's a problem. It's been the only reason I've done what I've done. I just can't let Carroll hurt him. Calvin has a family, kids and he doesn't want them affected by our relationship. He's still having trouble admitting that loving me is just as normal as loving a woman. Carroll knows how tormented and ashamed Calvin is and uses it. He's had Calvin do unspeakable things because of the pictures he has of us together."

"What kinds of things?"

"Murder. I—it was just once, but still, it'll put him away for life."

Ryan bit his lip. He suspected, but he didn't want to believe anyone other than Fred was in that deep. Shit. Calvin wouldn't talk. Even without the pictures of him and Kim, the evidence against him that Carroll would have for those murders would see him locked up forever. "So, what am I supposed to do?"

"When your dad was killed, it wasn't because just because

Carroll hated him. I mean, he'd hated Chad for years and never done anything about it. Chad found something at the mill. I don't know what it was, but Carroll got wind of it. They trapped him, led him to believe they had no idea, gave him the right clues to find exactly what he'd been looking for. He called some reporter, and the reporter called the Reeve, Carroll's father, for comment. That's how they knew."

"Okay."

"Cal refused to discuss the Baker's and the guys that took them hostage. He said it's better left alone. I bet Chad found proof that Carroll's family been lying all this time. He was going to blow the lid on all of it. The mine, the crops, the murders—see where I'm going?"

"Last time I checked, Calvin hated me. I'm sure he's not feeling much friendlier now. So does Farley. So, how to you propose I get into the mill to look?"

"It's shut down for the winter, no one's around. I go in once a week to service the machines and shit like that. If you go in, just let me know when it is and I'll make sure to stay away, but I'll leave the gate key somewhere."

"This stinks… it stinks real bad. Why does it always come back to me making the first move? Do you people have any guts?"

"If you force their hand, they'll back you up. I know it. They just have to see that what they're hiding is hurting them. Then, when the deed is done, you handle the cleanup. It's the only way."

Ryan reached the end of the dirt road and cranked the wheel around, spinning the car in a circle as he drove back toward where Kim's truck was parked next to his driveway.

"The cleanup? What is that? Never mind. I don't want to know. Every damn time I talk to someone here, I hit a wall. No matter what I promise, they make excuses. Sorry, but I am not putting my ass on the line for anyone who can't help themselves."

"I'll back you up, so will Audrey. Sal is in too. Cal said Carroll is foreclosing on the bar, so I bet it's something to do with Carroll and Sal's kid. I wouldn't be surprised if the cops don't show up here anyway. But listen, we don't need the cops. You understand? If we get enough of them to see that, we got Carroll and Fred by the balls."

Ryan digested this as he came to a stop. Kim put his hand on the door, but made no move to get out. He wanted to say no. He should refuse and forget this whole damn town. But he couldn't. If just a few of them followed through and they could find those bones... if Millicent's body happened to be there. Shit, maybe Merle's was there too. If anyone had told him he'd be searching this godforsaken place for bodies when he'd left Calgary, he'd have checked them into a mental hospital.

"Okay, I'll check out the mill, but you better not be fucking with me. I've made calls, left some information with important people."

"I want this to end as much as you do. I'm sick of hiding. So, you'll do it?"

"Yeah, but you know, it would be simpler for you to look. You do run the place."

Kim opened the door and turned. "I have looked. I can't find a damn thing."

"That's perfect. Needle in a haystack."

"Good thing you come from a line of farmers."

Ryan chuckled. "When's a good time for you?"

"Tomorrow."

"Why so soon?"

"I want to do the right thing before I have time to reconsider."

"And you think you could convince Cal to help us? What are you thinking of doing?"

"It's high time Carroll Albert tasted a little of his own medicine, don't you think?"

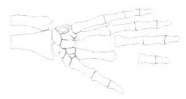

CHAPTER 27

"So? What's this all about?" Farley sat on the edge of a rotting sawhorse, long fingers tapping a dirty pant leg.

When she called and asked them to meet her at the mill, Julia expected more resistance from Farley. He just asked what time and hung up after a mumbled assent. Could he really be swayed? She turned to Sal.

He nodded, offering her a smile.

Mickey and Amy left only hours before and she imagined Carroll meeting them somewhere on the dark highway before they made it to safety. Ryan had him so tightly wound, that he'd overreacted and things had spiraled so far out of control that someone had to take the reins.

"Hello?" Farley's voice had an edge to it.

"I'll explain as soon as Cal arrives. You did tell him not to mention this to anyone, didn't you?"

"Think I'm a moron? Carroll's gonna be right pissed he finds out you met behind his back. He don't like any planning done without him."

"I know. But this plan can't involve him."

Farley nodded. Footsteps on the stairs sent her heart pounding. Please be Cal. She held a breath until the doorway darkened and Calvin's large frame entered the room. "Can you lock that behind you?"

He frowned, but did as she asked.

She gazed at the men around her; Farley, Kim, Calvin, Tim, and Sal. A small part of her wished Merle were there, but nothing could be done about it. He should never have made such a stink. That didn't end well when dealing with her husband.

"Now will you tell us?" Farley asked.

Julia looked to Sal.

He stood. "Thanks for coming out. This is a big step for all of us. I know it's odd that we'd meet here in the mill, especially without Carroll, but we have a problem that he'll just make worse.

"Tomorrow Ryan plans to search this place and he may find what the Albert family has worked hard to hide. When he does, Carroll will pull out all the stops. He does that, we're all in danger. We need to do something and fast."

"Like what?" Calvin crossed his arms over his chest and leaned against the door.

"Well, that's what we're here to decide. We've come to a crossroad, boys." Tim leaned forward in the old office chair. "Things have gone beyond what we're used to dealing with. Mr. Cassidy has pushed the envelope farther than anyone, even his father, and now we stand to lose more than just money. We've already lost much more than that. Merle, Millie... how many more?"

"Are you saying what I think you're saying?" Farley stood and shoved dirty hands into his pockets.

Julia took a breath "Yes, we are."

Tim waved a hand toward her, urging her to continue.

"We've been following orders. None of us has thought for ourselves in so long, I imagined we'd forgotten how. Until this morning. Carroll is one man. He can't possibly control everything. It's time we stepped up and stopped letting him make all the decisions. We need to take care of our problem, as a town."

The men remained silent, exchanging looks around the

darkened room. Kim nodded, then Calvin and slowly they all agreed.

She smiled. "Good, let's end this."

Audrey banged her head on the table, groaning. "We're never going to figure this out by tonight. Why didn't you tell him next week, or the week after that?"

"Because I don't want to give him too much time to change his mind. I don't want Carroll to get antsy either. He thinks I know something."

"Kim's going to tell Calvin and then he'll tell Carroll."

"Good, I hope he does. Then I call Justin, and Justin makes a phone call and bang. They're all fucked."

The sounds of whatever game Justin played in the den filtered through the wall. The morning had dawned cloudy, but the afternoon sun fought through thick grey clouds now and then, brightening the room. Ryan thought it was a good sign.

"We have two clues to figure out. It can't be that hard. Once we get there, I'm sure it will all make sense."

"And if it doesn't?"

"Then we're fucked."

"Goddamn it Kim, how stupid are you?" Calvin ran a trembling hand through his already messed hair. "Do you realize what you've done? He's searching the mill because of you. If you'd kept your damn mouth shut, this cloak and dagger bullshit wouldn't be necessary. What happens if he finds those bodies and we don't get to him in time?"

"I don't know why you're so mad. What's he gonna do to you? He's after Carroll."

"There are things I've done, things you have no clue about. Carroll goes down, I go down."

Kim stared, his cheeks filling with color. Calvin wanted to strangle him. He wanted to punch his confused face until blood distorted his fine features. He wanted to hold him and never let go. What the hell was he thinking?

"The police won't be involved. I told you that."

"I don't trust them. Carroll's too good at this shit. Someone is gonna leak this plan you've concocted and we're all going down. What if Cassidy decides he's too Christian or something for what you've cooked up?"

"He won't."

"I can't risk it. I'll do serious time if a word of what I've done gets to the right ears. Damn it, why would you talk to him before running it by me?"

"You said you were involved in one murder. I figured you told me the truth. What else have you done, Cal?"

"Don't tell me you thought Carroll would let Chad be the end of it? Remember the Connelly's?"

Kim's face paled.

Yeah, you stupid fuck. "They didn't make it past the mine."

"Where are they?"

"Only Carroll knows. If Ryan tries to fuck us over, you can be damn sure the bodies will turn up. I'm not going down for it. I can't believe you'd do something so stupid."

"Why, Cal? What possessed you to—?"

"Money. A shitload of money. Well, at first anyway. Then it was to keep you safe. He said he'd... never mind. It doesn't matter. The point is now there's no way out. Not while Carroll's still breathing. I have to tell him what they're doing."

Kim didn't speak. Calvin watched helplessly as his heart walked away from him, not turning to look back even once.

"Fuck him," Calvin said, though his heart tightened. If only Carroll didn't exist. If only... "Kim, wait."

The night sky had cleared, leaving a full moon to light a path around the gates to the mill. Ryan felt around the rusted "No Trespassing" sign, searching for the key Kim promised would be there.

"He lied." Audrey crossed her arms over her chest. She wore a camouflage coat and black pants. Ryan had eyed the coat when she met him at her door but said nothing.

"No, I don't believe it. Maybe it fell." Ryan ran his hand behind the sign and something dropped to the snow on the other side of the gate. "Shit."

"Yeah, it does us a lot of good over there."

"Listen, Negative Nancy, it's not over yet. We just have to reach it."

Her snort didn't improve his mood. Christ, she'd volunteered to come. He told her at least a dozen times he could do it himself. But no, Audrey knew the mill, could find a place to hide if necessary and she had no faith in his ability to take care of himself. Ryan tried to squeeze a gloved hand through the small opening in the gate, but he could barely fit the tips of his fingers in the hole.

"I'm going to climb over and toss you the keys."

"Are you nuts? That thing is at least twelve feet high. What if you fall?"

"It'll hurt." Ryan stepped onto the gate, testing it first to make sure it would hold his weight. He struggled up, inch by inch, the narrow gaps barely big enough for the toe of his boots.

Audrey paced below, mumbling softly.

He reached the top, and looped his leg over.

"Someone's coming." Audrey bolted, and disappeared into the darkness to the left of the gate.

He stared to the snow-covered path they'd walked up a short time before. The car was parked in a ditch a ways back. They should have parked it somewhere else. Damn it. If it wasn't for bad luck….

The lights loomed larger as they moved closer. He scrambled over the top of the gate. No time to climb. The lights moved over the snow just a few feet from him. A vehicle rumbled softly, disturbing the silence.

"Fuck it," Ryan jumped, landing in a bone-jarring heap on the snow-covered ground. He tested his legs, and satisfied the bones remained whole he scrambled toward the darkness that concealed Audrey.

The vehicle, a black truck, stopped at the gate and parked just over their tracks in the snow. Ryan retreated into the shadows, his gaze on the imprint his body had made in the snow.

Calvin Chambers exited the truck. He stood for a moment, eyeing the bushes next to the fence, and then approached the gate and gave it a tug. Placing his hands on the fence, he surveyed the snow on the other side.

The key. Where was the key? Ryan couldn't see it.

Turning in Ryan's direction, Calvin walked along the fence line. He stepped into the shadows. *Shit, this is it.*

Ryan closed his eyes. *Please, just keep going.* He held his breath, willing his body to stop shaking. He opened his eyes, and swore the other man looked right at him.

Tapping the fence, Calvin turned and strode back to the truck.

The engine fired up and the truck backed down the narrow road. Jesus, that was close.

"Ryan?" Audrey whispered.

"Let's go. I'll find you the key."

"Fuck that. Let's just go. This was a horrible idea."

"No. We're here, he's checked the gate and he's gone. He won't come back."

"I've got a really bad feeling about this."

"I've got my phone. I'll call Justin if we need help."

"What if help comes too late?"

Ryan didn't want to think about anything but success. The alternative sent him to shaking once more.

CHAPTER 28

Justin switched the screen off and leaned back in the chair. Dr. Reid had sent Ryan an e-mail. Why wouldn't he just call? He reread the man's message, his head spinning with excitement.

I've written many a fictional tale in my career. I think I'm ready to write a final chapter. I want our problem to go away completely. Not put away for a while; gone forever. But I need your help.

Justin hoped his words meant what he thought they did. Shit, he would never have bet on Dr. Reid turning on Carroll. That was big shit. He picked up the phone. Ryan would want to know this.

No. He'd wait until Ryan and Audrey got back, then they could decide whether to contact the guy or not. Justin set the phone next to the keyboard and stretched.

Larry bawled somewhere outside. Justin turned to the window and searched for the familiar silhouette. A shadow did move in the distance, but it didn't look like Larry. It passed the moonlit corner of the barn. Tall and skinny, it ran on two legs.

Justin reached for the phone, knocking it behind the desk in his haste. "No, no, no."

He dropped to the floor, reaching beneath the desk. His hand caught air, the floor, a baseboard. No phone. Footsteps clomped on the deck, heavy and fast footsteps. No, he would not cry. He was not a baby and he would not panic. Ryan told him what to do and he'd do it. He didn't know anything. He'd play dumb like they rehearsed, and he wouldn't break.

His hand found the phone and he almost cried in relief. Big man he was turning out to be. Glass tinkled in the hallway. Shit, the window. Just minutes to—

"Calling someone?" Farley asked.

Justin stared up at the man. Farley grinned. The shadows cast by the small lamp turned his face skeletal, ghostly. "N— no, I dropped it and Ryan hates when I let it run down. It's the only one he has."

"Really? That's too bad." Farley walked to the window and bent to the phone jack above the baseboard. Justin's heart plummeted as he ripped the entire thing from the wall.

"Why'd you do that?"

"Can't have you warning your buddy just yet."

"I wouldn't."

"Bullshit. Where is he?"

"I don't know."

Farley lifted an arm and Justin flinched. His nose exploded a moment later than he expected. Fire burned across his eyes and down his cheek. He gasped, fighting for breath but the pain sent stars to his eyes.

Farley gripped Justin's hair, forcing his face up. "Don't lie to me. Where is he? At the mill? The mine?"

"I said I don't know." Justin covered his face, the warmth of his blood pooling against his hand sent a wave of nausea through his stomach.

"Carroll knows. Won't be long now and Cassidy will be joining your mama. Won't that be nice? She'll have company."

"You won't get there in time."

Farley's booted foot caught Justin's ass. Jesus, he really was a miserable shit. Goddamn, it was hard to breath.

"Get upstairs. I don't want to look at you till Carroll gets here. Count your lucky stars that you're one of his." Farley yanked Justin to his feet by the hair. Justin stumbled out of the office and down the hall.

Stall, he had to stall him. "Where do you want me to go?"

"Upstairs."

Justin fell forward, tripping down the hallway and up the stairs. He slowed once, but Farley hurried him on with a boot to his backside. If he made it out of this, Justin hoped he got just one shot at the prick.

Farley shoved him through the first door, Ryan's room, and flipped on the light. He glanced around, spied the phone next to the bed and turned. "The only phone, eh? Lying little shit."

Farley took the phone from the base and walked out, slamming the door behind him.

Justin stared at the empty base, and then lowered his gaze to the darkness beneath the bed.

Their flashlights provided a pathetically dim beam and little more. Ryan explored the workroom. Large saws, and a frightening machine with a gaping mouth to which a conveyor fed some sort of wood through, sent a shiver of apprehension through him.

"So, any thoughts?" he asked.

"Let's get out of here," Audrey said.

"Only when I've either found this hiding place or Carroll catches us, and not a moment before."

"Great," Audrey pushed past him, heading toward the monster machine. "There's the old section back here. They said the floors were unsafe about ten years back and Carroll closed it off, but I bet we can walk across the beams if we're careful."

"What's under it?"

"Nothing. They used to bring the logs in under here somewhere, but there was a huge mudslide when I was a kid. The debris blocked off the entrance. They stopped using it because Farley said the risk of another slide was too high. The section you saw outside, with the new steel roof and all that? That's where the log trucks drop it now, then it's fed on a conveyor and milled according to what's needed."

"What do they do with those shavings?" Ryan imagined cleaning the itchy bits of wood from every crack and crevice for a long time. They left the lights off, and the piles of sawdust at the front of the building had tripped him up when they entered.

"They sell it to locals. We use it for bedding in the barns and the cedar shavings are great for flower beds."

"How nice, I guess. Looks pretty old school in here." Ryan shone his light on the exposed beams in the high ceilings and over the machinery. To his eyes, everything in the room, save the beast in the corner, looked rusted and very dated.

"If it works, they won't replace it. Carroll would never approve. Besides, they don't rely on the mill too much anyway. They make firewood, lumber for construction, and that's really it. Basically, it makes a good cover for whatever else Carroll has going and provides a believable source of income for families here." Audrey stopped, running her hand over a wall covered in paper.

Ryan joined her.

"There should be a door somewhere. I haven't been here in forever, but a door led to the back room. They used to have all kinds of stuff in there when Jarrod Albert was alive. For a while, they made furniture here. I'd swear it."

"Walls aren't solid." Ryan said. He pulled down a couple of pages, the tacks clattered on the floor at his feet. Works schedules, safety rules, and a list of phone numbers. Just like any other work place. He felt along the beams, but nothing appeared strange, or loose. Maybe Audrey was mistaken.

"It's here. I know it. They might have covered it up or sealed it shut."

"It wasn't used, so why not?"

Ryan stood back, turning the light to the corner and raising it up and down the wall. Nothing. Maybe the clue wasn't talking about this. Maybe his grandparents were completely bonkers. Not surprising in this town.

"Wait, there's a crack here," Audrey knelt in front of him and pushed against the wall. It moved back to reveal a small gap.

"Anybody home?" Calvin's voice, muffled by the outer rooms was clearly recognizable.

Ryan's gaze locked with Audrey's.

"Come out, come out, wherever you are."

"Fuck, push again." Ryan shoved above her but the wall shifted barely an inch.

"We need to hide," Audrey's voice broke.

No, don't panic now. "Push, hard."

They threw their bodies against the wall once, twice, and it gave another several inches.

"You think I'm stupid, Cassidy? I could smell your fear when you hid in those bushes. I knew you were there. Fucking stupid as your daddy." Laughter echoed through the thin walls.

"Is that Fred?" Ryan whispered. Audrey's nod was barely noticeable. "Can you fit through there?"

Audrey stood and with effort, disappeared through the gap. Ryan followed her. His body refused to move about halfway in and panic bubbled into his throat. *Shit.* Audrey grabbed at his coat, tugging and then pushing. A frantic sob escaped her lips.

Ryan wiggled, turning his body and inching through slightly. Audrey's fear seeped into his bones. She had to calm down or he'd lose it. "Relax, they're still at the front. We've got time. I can't even hear their feet yet. They're fucking with us."

Audrey pulled on his arm and Ryan turned his hips. Like magic, he slipped through the narrow opening. The ripping of his coat echoed in the darkness.

Audrey was already at the wall, pushing it back into place.

Ryan stepped beside her and shoved. The wall moved slowly but more easily than it had from the other side.

"Turn off your light." He flicked his own off.

Audrey did the same, her back against the wall as she side-stepped away from the opening. "There's still a gap. It's not closed," she whispered.

"I know. Let's try to get down to the lower level. If they notice the gap, they might not expect us to go down there. They might think we've been and gone." Ryan looked around the darkened space, lit only by a small cracked window: a sliver of moonlight and little else. If desperate, they'd break the window and run. It couldn't be so high that the fall would kill them.

"How the hell do we get down?"

The gap lit up.

"Shhh."

"Where do you think they're hiding?" Calvin's voice sounded close, too close.

"Only so many places. Think they went up to the offices?" Fred's voice was distant, but still too close for Ryan's comfort.

"I'll wait here and search, you go upstairs. Carroll's due any minute. He'll know where to look if we don't find them by then."

"You think they found the—"

"Chad thought they were here. I'm betting his little bastard knows everything he knew and then some. He gets to take the secret to his grave, just like Daddy. You hear me, Cassidy? You'll never leave here alive."

Justin sat against the bed, his gaze on the door. He felt around behind him until his hand hit the laptop. Just as Ryan promised. Would it work? He dragged it out, and set the small black rectangle on his lap. The cords dangled from the side. He slid along the floor and plugged the power cord into the wall outlet. The jack hid behind the nightstand. Should he pull it out and risk alerting Farley?

He didn't have time to worry. He pulled on the nightstand and the cord slid, whispering across the smooth wood floor. He yanked the charger, plugged the laptop's phone cord into the jack and opened the computer. The power light flashed. *Come on, faster.*

"Yeah, he's in the bedroom," Farley said.

Shit, shit, shit. Justin slid the open laptop under the bed and moved to cover it with his body. The voice had sounded close, but he heard no one else. If Farley was on the phone, he wouldn't be able to connect. Ryan said the connection had to be high speed to do that. Tears stung Justin's eyes once more. No, he would not cry like a fucking pussy. He was a man. Men dealt with shit. They did not cry about it.

The door swung open and Justin's stomach fisted into knots. Carroll stood smiling down at him. "Hello, son. I hear you've been up to some mischief."

"No, sir."

"No? Don't lie to a liar, boy. I know you've been plotting with Cassidy."

"No, I haven't. I don't have anywhere to stay. With Mom and Merle gone, I've got no one. Audrey said I could stay with her. But she's staying here so… " Justin let the words trail. Men didn't ramble either.

In the room, Carroll ran a finger along the large mirrored dresser that filled the far wall. He paused, gazing out the darkened window for a moment and then turned his full attention to Justin. "I'm going to let some things slide, because you've had to adjust to a lot lately. You're young, so Cassidy seems pretty damn impressive I'm sure. I want you to tell me where he is and what he's planned and we can start fresh."

"I don't know anything. I swear."

Carroll pushed from the window and strode across the room. Justin scrambled back, but the bed blocked him. Carroll knelt, so that their noses almost touched. "You want to live through this?"

"Yes sir."

"Tell me."

"I wasn't lying to you. I don't really know what they were going to do. Him and Audrey, they wanted to find those bones. I told them it wouldn't make any difference. They're just bones and no one can do anything about them now anyway."

Carroll stood. Justin closed his eyes briefly and then looked toward the door. Farley leaned against the frame, examining a dirty finger. Fuck, if they'd just leave. Justin dared to glance down. The laptop cord curled around the nightstand. *Please, if there's a God up there, do not let him look too closely.*

"The problem is, Justin, if they find those bones and the news gets wind of what happened here, everyone is fucked. Those fugitives had family. That family is probably trash just like their ancestors. You know what trash does, boy?"

"No sir."

"Trash feeds off of the rest of us fine, upstanding, hard-working citizens. They'll get wind of how wealthy we are here, and they'll start to thinking about how they might get a piece of that wealth. Lawsuits would follow and while they might not win, we'll spend a large part of our wealth, money we fucking earned, to defend ourselves. That's not to mention what will happen if anything else is discovered because of nosy outsiders coming around."

"But you're not guilty. How can they sue you?"

Carroll shook his head.

Justin wished he'd learn to shut his mouth. Damn, he needed to get Carroll out of the room.

"If the authorities get wind of certain… businesses, this town is sunk. Do you understand? Done. Destroyed. Finished. We'll have nothing left."

"Oh,"

"Yeah, "oh." So, that's all they said? Find the bodies and what?"

"Tell the news, I guess. Honest, I don't know any more than that," Justin lied.

Carroll snapped his fingers, and Farley stood from the doorframe. "Keep him in here for now. I'll deal with him once Cassidy's been taken care of. And take that computer away from him. The internet is a poor influence for a young mind.

Jesus, the screen! How could he have forgotten the screen? Lit like a goddamn Christmas tree under the bed. Stupid. Now it was over. Ryan had no hope if he couldn't get help.

"You got it." Farley stepped back as Carroll exited the room.

Justin held his breath, his gaze following Farley's.

Farley walked to the bed, knelt next to Justin and pulled the laptop toward him. "You won't be needing this when we're through with you."

RENÉE MILLER

CHAPTER 29

His knees ached. Ryan crawled next to Audrey, testing the boards beneath him. "There's nothing wrong with this damn floor."

"I see that now," she whispered.

"I don't think there's anything under here."

"I don't care. I just want somewhere to hide."

Shouts erupted from beyond the wall.

They froze.

"He can't be far." Carroll's voice and the click-click of his boots across the wood floor neared the wall.

Ryan's throat closed up. *Fuck.*

"Well, what have we here?"

"Shit, I forgot the wall." Calvin stomped to the wall as well.

Ryan's hope died a miserable death; leaving a black hole in his heart. They were done. The wall shifted and light spilled into the long narrow room. Ryan stood. He held out his hand. Audrey's trembling fingers lacing through his did little to boost his confidence.

"I'm sorry," he whispered.

She squeezed his hand.

"Mr. Cassidy, glad you made it," Carroll said.

"Expecting me?"

"I figured you'd make your way here. What do you think you'll find?"

"Buried treasure."

Calvin snorted and Carroll shot him a pointed glare. "Treasure?"

If they kept him talking, they bought time. Time to do what, he wasn't sure yet, but anything that delayed death would do. "Can I just commend you on your expert manipulation of every person in this town? Well done. You deserve a prize of some kind for your hard work. What do they give to someone who excels at breaking people down?"

"I'm not sure, but I bet it's shiny." Carroll smiled.

"You're going down."

"For what? I've done nothing wrong."

"Come on, let's be honest for once. It's not as though you're letting me walk out of here alive. So why not humor me? I know about Millicent. She didn't hang herself. I know about my father. My grandparents left me a letter that hinted at what happened to them as well. Then you consider the amount of disappearances around here, the whispers among the kids about what you did to Amy, and the family that disappeared. What do all of these people have in common?"

"Tell me, I'm dying to know."

"They crossed you. That's unacceptable isn't it? I know what you've done and I'll see you go to jail for it."

"Really? Will you really? I don't think you will. It's sad the way you're trying to turn your crimes on me."

"My crimes? Are you kidding me?"

"I know you and Millicent had an… altercation. She could be so difficult sometimes. I don't blame you for losing your temper. She tended to become possessive. I guess I could have warned you, but Millie needed a good fuck. I saw no harm in it. Her temper got the better of her when she heard about Audrey. What else could you do? But that's no reason to try to make me suffer. I won't tell anyone what you've done, even if Fred has gathered evidence. I can make it go away."

"You're insane. That's it. Certifiable. I had nothing to do

with Millicent's death. *You* strangled her and *you* hung her in my barn. She was leaving and no one is allowed to leave without your say so."

"Can I let you in on a secret?"

Ryan crossed his arms. The way Carroll smiled, how his eyes lit up in absolute glee, Ryan knew he'd never leave alive. He pushed Audrey toward the window.

She resisted and he turned to meet her gaze. She stared, and then nodded. The quiver in her lips mirrored his hopelessness.

He turned back to Albert. "Go on. I'm sure you're bursting to tell me."

"I know what you're up to. You won't ruin this town, not after I've worked so hard to build it. Actually, I have a few questions for you, Mr. Cassidy."

"I didn't kill Millicent."

"No? Okay, fair enough. Millie hung herself. I'll go with that. Who did you call before coming here?"

"Everyone. How's that? I'm not stupid either. I called the papers, the cops, everyone. You're a sick man, Albert. When they get here, you're fucked."

"He's not the one who's fucked," Fred stepped into the room. Calvin moved back and Ryan's gaze fell to Fred's raised arm, the barrel of his gun level with Ryan's chest.

Amazing that such a large man could enter a room so silently, like a fat, plaid ninja. Hysteria threatened to take over and a giggle bubbled to Ryan's throat. He looked from one to the other, out of cards to play. "All right, I give. You give me a phone, I'll call them off. I only called the paper."

"I want you to stop lying. That's first. Then I want you to die. Easy," Carroll said.

"No. You'd be making a huge mistake."

Carroll sighed and waved at Fred. Audrey gasped. Ryan's ears popped and he went down. No, his ears didn't pop. The gun, Fred fired the gun. Fire exploded through Ryan's leg and he bit back the scream of pain that filled his lungs. Son of a bitch, why his leg? Why not just end this? *Because they're psychopaths.*

"Stand up," Carroll instructed.

"What? So that jackass can shoot me again? Just get it over with, and then you can explain what happened to me to my friends when they get here."

"Stand up." Fred cocked the gun and leveled it at his head.

Ryan couldn't have stood if he wanted to.

"Please don't kill him."

"Aw, listen to little Audrey, fighting for her man," Calvin said.

Ryan glared at the big man.

Calvin winked.

What the hell?

"No, please don't do this." Audrey's voice rose. "He really did call someone, Carroll. He was only trying to get them to write about the Baker's, so the whole thing could be laid to rest. He's not out to ruin you."

"Audrey; dear, pretty, sweet, *lying* Audrey." Carroll strode around the room, moving closer.

Ryan put his head down. If he died, that fucker was coming with him.

"I'm not lying." Audrey backed away stumbling over Ryan's outstretched leg as she moved.

"But you are and I know it. You called no one. How do I know? I know Ryan wouldn't call in the cavalry without something to give them. Isn't that right, reporter boy? A good reporter gathers the story first."

"I'm not a good reporter."

"Ah, but you lie again. You won awards for your mad skills. You want the bodies? You're looking in the wrong place. If you hadn't been so stupid, you'd not only have found the bones, but you'd have found a few more bodies. Although… you might not recognize them now."

"Jesus, like Chad?" Calvin backed to the wall. Carroll turned and Ryan leapt forward. His leg screamed in protest but he gritted his teeth and lunged at Carroll.

Fred fired, shattering the window behind them.

Audrey's scream echoed in Ryan's head. He swung his arms

around Carroll's neck, bringing the Reeve's body in front of his own. *Shoot now, you crazy redneck.*

"Really?" Carroll laughed, but Ryan felt the tension in his body. He was scared.

"You okay, Audrey?" Ryan didn't move his gaze from Fred. The police chief followed his path with the gun. He wouldn't give him the chance to fire again.

"Yes, I'm okay. Please Ryan, this isn't going to work. Just tell them the truth."

A shadow passed through the light beyond the room they occupied. Farley? Damn it. He couldn't catch a break. "Where did you put the bodies?"

"In plain sight." Carroll pushed against Ryan, but he held tight to the man's neck. His leg throbbed. The cool air of the room chilled his blood-soaked skin.

"Where?"

"You that dumb?" Calvin asked. "They're at the fucking town hall. Shit, why didn't I see that before? The bones in the display? Right? I'm right, aren't I? The base is hollow. Fuck, that thing never made sense to me when you insisted that ugly piece of shit be put into the new building."

"Bravo, genius," Fred drawled. "Maybe now you can let him cram the bastards in there, eh? I've had my fill of dead people in my truck."

"Yes, and you'll both keep your damn mouth shut. When we're through with Mr. Cassidy, he can join his buddies."

Bile stung his throat. Sick son of a bitch.

"Shoot him, Fred."

"Can't get a clear shot."

"One, two—"

"No, I don't think so." Calvin interrupted, slipping his hand into his coat.

Carroll stiffened. "Pardon?"

A shadow filled the opening. Calvin winked again.

Ryan didn't dare hope that Kim could convince Calvin, but unless the man had totally lost his mind, it appeared he might be on their side. Ryan almost wept in relief, but he still had two problems; the gun in Fred's hand and the man in his arms.

"Cal?" the slight tremor in Carroll's voice was music to Ryan's ears.

"Put the gun down, Fred." Sal's voice came through the opening.

Audrey's body pressed against his back. He leaned into her, releasing the reeve. Carroll stumbled forward, and a gun fired one last time.

Ryan hit the floor.

Carroll cried out, clutching his neck before falling with a dull thud.

Audrey threw herself over Ryan's body. Her tears warmed his face. "Jesus, are you okay?"

"My leg hurts," he offered.

Another shot shook the walls of the old mill and Fred stumbled back. He stared at the widening swath of red on the front of his jacket, as though in a dream. Although it happened fast, to his eyes it took an eternity for Fred to hit his knees, dropping he gun.

Ryan's head felt light, but he tried to stand.

"Just stay put," Sal said. "We've got a few things to discuss. Tim's on his way. He'll look after your leg. Hey, Cal? Tell Farley his shot was perfect. He can come down from the tree."

Farley? No fucking way. Calvin took a phone from his pocket.

"Why didn't you guys tell me? Who else is in on this?"

Sal looked to Calvin. "Everyone."

"You ready?" Audrey brushed a lock of hair from his forehead and he pulled away. She treated him like a gunshot turned him into a two-year-old.

"Yes, but scared as hell." Ryan smiled. His leg pained like a son of a bitch, and the crutch Tim promised would help only made his armpit hurt too.

"You should have let Justin help you with the floor. It could have waited until you were better."

"I had to make sure they were gone, you know?"

Audrey looked away. She hadn't been pleased when Sal asked Ryan if he could take care of Fred and Carroll's bodies. Understanding their intention, Ryan agreed but told them he had to do it alone. That way no one in town had anything to hold over anyone else. Well, sort of.

"A floor has no bottom." she whispered.

Excited murmurs filled the council chambers. At the front of the room Farley paced, shredding his thumb in his teeth. Ryan sat in Carroll's chair. Indeed, it was comfortable. He didn't meet any of the curious eyes that stared back. God, he was insane to go along with this plan. Someone would know.

The big doors at the back of the room opened and Julia Albert entered, dressed in black. She met his gaze and smiled. "Thank you." She mouthed and took a seat near the wall, next to Mickey and Amy.

"Can we call this meeting to order?" Tim clapped his hands and the murmurs quieted. "Thank you. I'll turn the meeting over to the other members of council now."

Calvin cleared his throat. He pushed out his chair; the one Millicent had occupied only a short time ago, and stood. "We've called this meeting so that we could share some bad news and discuss Albertsville's future. Our reeve, Carroll Albert, and our police chief, Fred Smith, were heading home a couple of nights ago and encountered a moose in the road."

Whispers filtered through the crowd, a cough, and then quiet as Calvin held up a hand. "We're not entirely sure yet what happened, but it appears as though Carroll swerved to miss the animal and they ran into a tree. Both died before help arrived on the scene."

Calvin turned, his gaze meeting Ryan's.

So far so good.

"And?" Anita, Calvin's wife stood. "You called us here to tell us they're dead? Come on, Cal, we've all heard about the accident."

"I know. But we also have a problem. We are now minus a reeve and a police chief. The issue of Fred's position is easily solved, but the reeve is another matter."

Anita's dark gaze fell on Ryan. She stared, her face blank for a moment, before his choice of seating filtered into her brain. "You wouldn't dare."

"Excuse me?" Cal asked.

"That's okay," Ryan stood. "My motion to run for reeve still stands. The Council asked me to attend the meeting to remind you all of that and to request that anyone else interested in running put in their bid as well."

A nervous rumbling erupted through the room. Audrey smiled at him from her seat in the front row.

"Anyone object to Ryan Cassidy's nomination?" Farley asked.

No one spoke. Anita glanced around at her neighbors, her cheeks a fiery red. But she said nothing.

"If no one else wishes to run, and you're all in agreement with us that Ryan Cassidy would do a superb job as reeve, then all that's left is the paperwork," Calvin announced.

Silence. His leg throbbed. What if someone objected? Did he really care? He didn't have to be reeve, didn't really know what it entailed, but to ensure everything stopped he had to have some power.

"What happened to your leg?" Anita's voice.

Damn woman. "I fell…over a plow."

"Really?"

Sal chuckled. "Yeah, he got spooked by that old moose on his property the other night. Tripped over that rusty old plow, blade cut right into the tender spot on his thigh."

Anita crossed flabby arms over her ample chest.

Fuck, why couldn't she just go along with this? Just shut up, woman.

"Seems kind of convenient that we never had a problem with that moose till now. And all of a sudden he's caused a major accident and an injury."

"Want to see the stitches?" Ryan asked.

She chewed her lip and shrugged.

The room remained silent. He had to sit or he'd fall over. He sank back into the chair and sighed.

"Okay, everyone in favor of Ryan Cassidy assuming the position of reeve, raise your hand." Calvin raised his hand.

Every hand but Anita's went up.

"Congratulations, Reeve Cassidy," Calvin said.

"Thank you."

"I hope you can set this town to rights." Farley leaned over and clapped him on the shoulder.

"Me too."

Applause erupted around him. Ryan shook hands automatically, accepting pats on the back, but his gaze remained on one person.

Audrey smiled and blew a kiss.

Checkmate, Carroll.

THE END

COMING SOON

OTHER THRILLING NOVELS BY

RENÉE MILLER

RENÉE MILLER

Thanatos, god of death, has a flawless record...
until the birth of Caerus Thornton.

Is he falling for the woman he's spent
more than two decades trying to kill?

"It's okay, baby. I've got you. Watch the steps. Okay, just breathe. Good girl." The tall, thin man in the too-short khakis and frayed jacket practically carried his pregnant wife to the car. An impressive feat to an onlooker, considering the woman must outweigh him by at least fifty pounds.

Thanatos never enjoyed bringing death in these situations. Expectant parents were always the most emotional. As if they thought their happy little bubble made them impervious to Fate.

The man closed the passenger door of the rusted red Chevy and ran around to the driver's side. Dusk had just settled over the rundown neighborhood. The porch light over the small gravel driveway was too small to illuminate more than the rocks directly beneath it. The bare bulb only served to highlight the shabbiness of their rented two-bedroom home.

On the upside, the cramped rooms would feel just a bit bigger when this night was over, although Thanatos knew they wouldn't see that as a positive thing.

Flashing into the backseat, he observed their nervous excitement. The man could barely fit the key into the ignition. He laughed when it finally went in and she touched his arm, a tender smile on her face.

Thanatos cringed at their eager anticipation of the child that would never be. He could do it now, or wait until they arrived at the hospital. It didn't matter to him much either way, but sometimes his job went more smoothly if he arrived before the doctors could muddle things up.

The woman cried out as the baby fought to break free from her tiny prison. If he did it now, he'd save the woman a little physical pain, as well. The process of bringing a human life into the world seemed positively barbaric. With all of the technology humans had at their fingertips, it baffled him why they still allowed the arrival of new life to rip the mother apart, as though they believed pain made it more important, more meaningful. If only they knew the reality.

Squealing the tires as he left the driveway, the almost father took off at full speed, which wasn't all that fast for the old car.

Thanatos smiled as the man fought to keep his eyes on the road and not on his panting wife. So much emotion over something natural and commonplace. Each one thought their little bundle of joy was special and unique, even though they knew thousands more just like them entered into life every day.

They breezed through a red light, honking horns in hot pursuit, and Thanatos leaned forward, his hand poised over the woman's distended belly. The car lurched and her husband's arm shot out, blocking Thanatos's path. Their fingers touched and the man shivered.

Damn.

The man's face paled to a sickly grey. He clutched at his chest, panic filling his bloodshot blue eyes. This had never happened before.

"Charlie?" The woman's voice was breathless from the contractions.

"I don't—can't..." Charlie gasped.

And then he collapsed. Unplanned perhaps, but a casualty or two was not unusual. Occasionally the Fates felt the need to add to his workload without telling him. Thanatos sat back as the car left the road. The woman screamed, her dead husband oblivious to her distress, as they careened into the ditch. A sickening crunch preceded their stop, and she lay still for a moment.

Thanatos exited the car through the roof and observed the carnage before him. Once upon a time such things affected him, but not for very long. Erebos made it clear that gods had no use for emotion.

The humans couldn't see him, not until their time came, so he was free to roam the scene and make sure the heart he came for had stopped beating. He tried to make it as gentle as possible, but sometimes his sisters required more force and less finesse. No one questioned the Fates, not even Death.

The woman's door opened.

Not done yet.

A car sped through his body, screeching to a halt before the twisted red metal. A man leapt from the driver's side, cell phone to his ear.

Dusk rapidly turned into night, and he stared for a moment before running to the woman, who struggled to exit her vehicle.

"You okay?" He helped her to her feet.

"My husband," she glanced at the wreckage of their car, wincing as a contraction ripped through her abdomen. The child was a fighter apparently, like her mother.

"Help is on its way, ma'am. Let's get you out of here."

Thanatos folded his arms over his chest. The Good Samaritan coaxed her from the car and her dead husband, toward his own vehicle. Sirens screamed in the distance. Thanatos walked toward them, intent on finishing his job. As he approached, the Good Samaritan tripped, falling almost into his arms. Instinctively, Thanatos put out a hand, touching the man's head. A heartbeat later the man stumbled forward as he fell through Thanatos's intangible form.

For the love of...

Stumbling to the road, unable to gain his footing, the man did a nosedive onto the pavement. The sirens grew deafening as the emergency vehicles shrieked to the scene, the lead one screaming over the Good Samaritan's head. This had to be the worst day Thanatos had ever experienced.

"No!" The woman screamed again. Holding her belly, she hit her knees in the ditch. At least it was dark enough now that most of the gore was hidden from her view. The paramedics, quite agitated over what just happened, jumped from the ambulance. One ran to the squalling woman and the other shining a flashlight on the dead man under the tires.

Thanatos glared at the scene.

His sisters would have a fit.

Jackson Murphy will pay any price for freedom.

RENÉE MILLER

The Legend of
Jackson Murphy

But can he get away with it?

At one time Jack loved his wife. He couldn't pinpoint the exact moment when it ended, but he didn't love her anymore. It wasn't as though he woke up one day hating the way Jenny drooled on her pillow, or grinding his teeth when she shredded his favorite songs with her shrill nasal whine. It just faded away. Like rust on an old car, the loathing he felt for her ate away at the framework of their life together.

The past year had been the worst. Jack couldn't stand anything she said or did. Once upon a time, he tried but it was hopeless now. Love couldn't be forced—despite what those bible-thumping freaks up the street claimed.

He might have just left. Most men would rather die than live with a bitch like Jenny. But after serving a fifteen-year sentence in the institution of marriage, leaving wasn't so simple. Not with three kids and a successful business.

The kids weren't an issue. He didn't see them every day and courts nowadays made sure that one parent couldn't monopolize the children. He wouldn't battle for custody; Jack loathed the idea of paying her money for a job she'd nagged him to give her. Jenny should never have been a mother. She'd made his kids into ungrateful little snots. Even if he never saw them again he would have to pay through the nose. He'd lay bets on that.

That was the bottom line for Jackson Murphy. Money. More importantly: *his* money. He'd worked his ass off while she shopped, had babies, and joined the Parent-Teacher Association. He lunched with assholes, built up a reputation, and a healthy bank account by working eighteen-hour days while she watched the Late Show from the comfort of the king size bed *he* bought her. If he left, she'd take it all and then some. Jack couldn't stand the thought.

Call him greedy, he didn't care. He worked for what they had while she did nothing.

Seated in his custom-made kitchen, with its built-in stainless steel fridge and stove—and the many other high-priced appliances that Jenny never used—Jack pondered how to get out without getting fleeced in the process.

Jenny sat at the oak table she pestered him to buy—made by one of the finest artisans in France and shipped over at a huge expense—tapping a manicured nail on its chipped surface. His blood pressure rose as he counted the nicks that she and the kids had left in the once-beautiful piece of furniture.

She set something on the table. He looked away from her nails and a low growl stuck in his throat. Yet again, she'd ripped the paper apart to find the gossip column and left the rest in a mess.

What a waste of time. Yelling at her in his head, Jack picked up the wrinkled, torn pages, and tried to press them flat enough to read. Jenny could have at least put the fucking thing back together, but no, she just crumpled it in a heap in front of his empty coffee cup.

Jack swallowed a curse. She used to fill his cup every morning. It's not as though he asked a lot from her. Just serve the damn coffee. He paused in his mental tirade and lifted his gaze. Did she despise him as much as he despised her? Jenny seemed to enjoy doing things to annoy him. Was she trying to shove him out the door?

Pushing his chair across the floor, Jack stood and grabbed the empty cup. He made a big production of setting it on the counter and hefting the pot. He managed to fill half the cup with what she left before returning to the table.

If she did hate him, then how long did he have before she'd had enough? Probably not long. Jenny wasn't made of the same stuff he was, so she'd give up pretty fast. His chest burned as he imagined Jenny planning how she'd make him pay. Knowing her, she'd already been to a lawyer and waited for the ink to dry on her demands. And there he sat, just waiting for it like a moron.

"Are you working late tonight?"

Her question caught him by surprise. He blinked, pausing in the task of not reading his wrinkled paper. The light from the window over the sink created a halo over her head, bringing out the blond highlights she spent hundreds of dollars of his money to put in. Jack would never understand why anyone would want stripes on their head.

She raised an eyebrow.

He considered her question. Why did she want to know? She usually didn't care if he came home. Was she hoping he'd be gone? "I'm not sure," he lied. "Why? Do you have plans?"

Color bloomed in her cheeks.

Jack bit the inside of his cheek to hold his temper. Jenny could look a person straight in the eye and lie through her teeth. The only evidence lay in the slight blush that dotted each cheek, so faint that most people missed it. Not Jack. His wife was about to lie.

Lowering her gaze, eyes he'd once compared to dark chocolate—yes, he used to be an idiot—Jenny picked at the chipped enamel of her cup. "No, I was thinking of taking the kids out for dinner if you're going to be late. They don't get to go out much." She stared at the paper as though it might contain the secret to life. "If you'll be home, you can come with us."

"Where are you going?" He sipped his coffee and grimaced. For crying out loud, the woman couldn't make shit properly.

"Just to Frankie's."

Jack choked as he swallowed the bitter liquid. It burned his throat and seared up into his sinuses as he forced himself to swallow the scalding sludge. Just to Frankie's? She had to be kidding. "Jen, you aren't taking the kids to Frankie's. Christ, just a salad at that shithole costs more than my shoes."

"It's my money too. If I want to go to Italy to buy pizza, I will. Don't tell me what I can and can't do. If you're coming I'll make the reservation for five."

"You do know that pizza didn't originate in Italy. It's actually—"

"Jack!"

"Fine. You're right. We can go. I'm sure I'll be done around six or seven."

Jenny glared, coffee cup midway to her lying mouth. She didn't really want him to go with them. He knew it. The last thing Jack wanted to do was to share dinner with Jenny at that snobby overpriced spaghetti house, but he couldn't resist calling her bluff.

"You better show up then. They get pissed when you don't show for a reservation."

"If four out of five show, I'm sure they won't care."

"They *will* care and I might not get another reservation on short notice."

"We're just finishing up the Sampson job. That's all I've got on the table for today. If anything comes up I'll get Ray to take care of it."

Jack didn't like having anyone look after the business, but he'd do it to get under her skin. Getting on Jenny's last nerve was one of the only joys left in his life.

Ray could handle things for an hour or so. He was after all Jack's partner, and had invested nearly as much as Jack had financially. Ray had little knowledge of the construction business, materials, or bids, but was always whining about Jack's tendency to run everything. Why not let him do some work for a change? All he really did was handle the books. Ray was one of the best when it came to numbers. But it was because of Jack that Jay-Ray had become one of the busiest construction companies in Pickleton. It wasn't a big area, but being the best in any area was better than nothing. If anyone deserved half of Jack's money, it was Ray. Not that he'd ever get it, but it wouldn't hurt to make him earn his share now and then.

Jack stood, checking his watch. "I should go if I'm going to finish in time for dinner. See you around six."

He left before Jenny could haggle over the time. She couldn't get a reservation at Frankie's on such short notice. She probably already had one. Maybe she'd have to expand a reservation for two to accommodate all of them. Her red cheeks told a story she wasn't telling him, but what kind of story? Jack pondered as he pulled out of the drive if she could be running around under his nose. Nah, Jenny wouldn't cheat, it wasn't in her to lie and deceive on that level. Or was it?

Natalie doesn't believe in vampires,
until she meets sweet and handsome Gabriel.

Sometimes love is worth every bite

The girl crashed through the dense vegetation, desperate to escape. With no moon to light her way, she ran away from the road and deeper into the woods.

Risking a look back, she lost her footing. Not far behind, two green lights trailed. No man's eyes could light up like that. It couldn't be a man. As she stumbled through the trees and thick underbrush, she cursed. How could she have been so stupid? She should have bolted from the bar when he called her by name. *He knew my name.* Instead, she allowed herself to be carried away by his charm and good looks. Later, Shelley ignored the warning bells ringing in her head and left the bar with him.

They went back to his house, if this was his home. Shelly didn't know where she was or how long they had driven to get there.

Inside Shelly's small car, she lost track of everything except him. He wore no cologne, but his scent was overwhelming. She inhaled his sweet musk, her head reeling. Soon they pulled into a winding driveway where he helped her out of the car. She followed him inside.

It was unlike her to lose herself like this. Now she ran for her life.

"Shelly," he called.

Even now, terrified as she was, Shelly fought an insane urge to surrender. She didn't know why she should want to and shook the feeling off.

"Don't be silly, Shelly," he sounded closer with every word. "You cannot escape me out here. There is no reason to run. I won't hurt you."

Liar! Not after what had happened at that mausoleum he called a house. *Silly Shelly my foot!*

He had pulled her close and nuzzled her ear—whispering to her in a language she didn't understand as he trailed his tongue down her neck tasting her skin. Then, when she expected a kiss, the bastard bit her. Her neck still throbbed where he had sunk his teeth. He pulled away, blood on his lips, but worse than that, his eyes shone with a pale green light. Shelly ran as fast as she could out the nearest door only to find herself surrounded by strange woods.

"I didn't want it to be this way, Shelly. If you stop, it will go much easier for you. I'm afraid there are worse things than me out here."

At his words, Shelly missed a step again. What could possibly be worse? She doubted anything could be worse than returning to him.

"I can smell your blood and so will they," he warned right behind her.

She spun and stumbled backward, her heart skipping a beat. A few feet ahead, he floated in midair, his arms held out.

Her mind reeled. He wasn't human, he couldn't be. *Then what?* If he was a man, the creep must have slipped something into her drink. Either way he was bad news. People didn't hover. "Who are *they*?" Shelly stalled as she backed away.

"The others. You didn't think I lived in that big old house alone did you?"

Her heart raced and a sob escaped her lips as she tried to move away from him. His blond hair was no longer tied back, it floated in a white-gold halo around his body.

"Please let me go," she begged. "I won't tell anyone what happened. I don't even know where I am. Please, I promise."

He shook his head, disappointment in his eyes. "Why does it always comes to this?" he murmured. "You humans are all the same. Such cowards. You *do* know my name, Shelly." He reached out to brush a strand of red hair from her face.

Shelly shook her head and retreated until the rough bark of a tree dug in her back. She tried to step around it to put something between them, spinning around in fright as he moved with her, his feet light on the ground like a dancer's.

"Oh God," she cried.

Behind her stood another man, shorter than and not nearly as attractive as her pursuer. With a swift movement, he grabbed her arms and held her close. He grinned at her upturned face to display long canine-like teeth, his eyes blazing with orange light rather than green.

Her legs trembled. Lightheaded, Shelly thought she may faint. *Maybe it will be better to be unconscious for your own murder.* No, they would likely wait for her to wake up before beginning her torture. She turned back to the blond man; her best bet would be to appeal to him. "I don't remember your name," she lied. "I was so drunk, really. Please I swear. I won't say a word to anyone."

"She smells heavenly," the man holding her growled with a thick accent she couldn't place. "You are sharing aren't you Boss?"

"I wasn't going to," he said, and stepped forward to toy with a red curl. "But I seem to have lost my appetite having chased her so far. Actually, I don't desire her at all now."

Shelly looked between the two men. She wasn't sure which one frightened her more, the one who held her close and licked the wound on her neck at even briefer intervals, or the cold and imposing blond who stared down at them. "I just want to go home," she sobbed, her knees buckling. "Please let me go home."

The blond man moved so that his body touched hers. Her skin tingled. Nice. She looked up and wondered why she suddenly wasn't frightened. His eyes were beautiful; she couldn't look away from their glow. Staring into them she felt light, as though she would simply float away or dive into their green waters.

"Your hair is like fire," he whispered. "I so wanted to make you one of us, Shelly. I wanted to bring you into our family. This would have been your home forever. You would have wanted for nothing." He touched her cheek.

She turned her face into his hand. Maybe he wouldn't hurt her after all. Maybe she could get out of this alive if she played along. He wasn't ugly, far from it. A little strange, perhaps, but if she humored him until morning, she might stand a chance to run away. She looked up and gave him a shaky smile.

"It's too bad," he sighed. "You were nearly perfect, but I'm afraid nearly isn't enough for me."

He walked away and the blackness rustled around her.

Orange lights glowed from the gloom. "Please Aedon," she called. "Please, don't leave me here."

He turned at the sound of her voice and smiled. His strange teeth shone in the darkness. "I see you've remembered my name," he said, and disappeared.

"Aedon," she screamed as more shapes materialized from the night to surround her.

"She's bloomin pretty," one growled in a thick brogue. "Let's take 'er back and play a bit."

"No. We can't do that," the man who held her said. "The boss wants us to do her out here and leave her for the wolves."

"Bloody hell. We canna have any fun anymore. Since he made that blasted bleedin' heart one of us it's been nothing but caution an' cowardice."

Shelly listened to them argue and searched for a nonexistent chance to escape. There were at least six of them. She was doomed and her spirits plummeted in despair.

"Would you fools stop your bitching and get on with it?" a woman's voice cut in.

Shelly turned to a tiny, dark-haired woman standing to her right. She was beautiful, her skin like ivory. Her luminous eyes didn't glow and hope stirred once more in Shelley's chest. "Please help me," she whispered. "Please don't let them hurt me."

The woman leaned closer and brushed Shelly's cheek with one long fingernail. Shelly searched her face for a sign of mercy but her hopes plunged when the woman smiled and bared the same long teeth as the others. Shelly recoiled against the brute pinning her but the woman entwined her fingers in her hair and forced her to be still by yanking it roughly.

"Oh, they won't hurt you a bit, love." The woman moved closer to brush her lips across Shelly's. She should have been disgusted; women were not her thing. Instead, her belly fluttered in unmistakable arousal.

"I think we should let it be ladies first tonight, lads," a voice from the darkness drew a flurry of laughter.

"You'd have been better off with us lass," the man who

held her whispered into her ear. "Olivia isn't known for her tenderness." He let her go and moved away.

Shelly stood rooted to the spot, uncertain. Shouldn't she try to run? She couldn't just let them kill her.

"Running would be very stupid," Olivia warned, as if reading her thoughts. "I hoped you would be a companion, as he had promised. It's a shame our Aedon is so fussy. I would have enjoyed playing with you. You *are* very lovely."

Olivia pulled Shelly against her and tugged on her hair forcing her head to the side. "I see he's already started for me," she whispered and kissed the wound on Shelly's neck. "Do you know how close you came to heaven?"

"I'm sorry," Shelly sobbed, but didn't try to move away. "Tell him I'll do whatever he wants. I just want to go home."

Olivia's nails dug into tender flesh, returning Shelly to reality. She tried to turn away but the tiny woman jerked her back with a rough tug on her hair.

"Oh no, sweet Shelly," she whispered as her eyes lit with the orange light. "You will never go home again."

Dirty Truth. A grain of truth so dirtied by lies that it becomes fiction.

RENÉE MILLER

Dirty Truths

Fate gives Kristina Riley what she wants most, but keeping it may be a dirty job.

Joe McNeil sank onto the stool, his face shadowed, haunted.

"Rough night?" Wade set a Coors in front of his friend. "Just let me lock up and I'll join you."

"Thanks. Shit, I forgot you closed early on Wednesdays. I'll finish this and get out of your hair. I just needed somewhere to calm down."

Wade slid the bolt across the door and strode back to the bar. Joe's leg vibrated against the stool as he took a long swig of his beer.

Kristina. It had to be. Nothing else could get Joe worked up like this. She could get Wade pretty worked up too, but for different reasons.

He lifted a glass from the rack and scooped some ice into it. Grabbing the bottle of Jack Daniels off the shelf he walked around the bar to join Joe. "Kristina?"

Joe nodded and finished his beer. Wade filled his glass and slid the remaining whiskey to his friend. "Probably not the best idea. I could kill that little fucker."

"Who?"

"Who do you think?"

Wade didn't speak. Daniel Riley. Useless piece of shit. He waited. Joe would share what he wanted to share and no more. It was his way and Wade wouldn't push.

"When we got there, Kristina said she was carrying the baby and fell on the stairs." Joe's voice broke. He cleared his throat and rolled his shoulders. "I told her she better stop lying to me. No one breaks their ribs and gets a shiner from falling on the stairs."

"He hit her?" Rage burned in the bottom of Wade's gut.

"Christ, when isn't he hitting her? This time, he punched her, kicked her, bit her…fuck. Then he hit the baby. Might have been his worst mistake."

"The baby?" A red haze distorted Wade's vision.

"She had a small bruise on her cheek, but she's okay. You should see Kristina. Wait." Joe dug into his jacket and pulled out his cell. He pressed a couple of buttons and passed it to

Wade. "There. See for yourself."

Hands trembling, Wade looked at the images. The eyes, once a bright blue so full of life it made a man ache just to look into them, held a hopelessness that broke his heart. He skipped through the pictures, unable to look at them for longer than a moment, stopping at an image of Kristina's abdomen. The right side covered by an angry purple bruise, swollen and scraped in spots. "Did you call the cops?"

"She did. After we made her."

"You know, I could take care of this. Call it a favor. Just between me and you. No one would hear from him again." He would pay Joe for the privilege of killing Riley with his bare hands.

"No."

"How many times are you going to just let this shit go? He's going to kill her and your granddaughter."

"You know what Kristina's like. Just let her do this on her own. I think she's finally had enough. If we get involved, she'll know and she'd never forgive me."

"Joe—"

"No, Wade. I mean it. Leave it be. Please." Joe glanced up, his eyes pleading.

Christ. "Fine. But if you ever change your mind, you know where to find me."

"I do."

"He hurts her again, I don't make any promises."

"Me either."

ABOUT THE AUTHOR

Renee Miller is a freelance writer living in Tweed, Ontario. Small town life is busy, but she's managed to sandwich a book or two between the demands of housewifery and hiding from the neighbors.

Reneemiller@bell.net
www.twitter.com/ReneeMJ
www.facebook.com/pages/Renee-Miller/548882035137022

Website: www.OnFictionWriting.com
Blog: www.authorreneemiller.com

www.ingramcontent.com/pod-product-compliance
Lightning Source LLC
Chambersburg PA
CBHW071255170626
46809CB00001B/234